How to Earn Your Keep

Katie,
Such a pleasure
to discuss this
sty with you –
thank you
for the kind
invitation,
Deann
Berrin

Also by Deahn Berrini

Millkweed: A Novel

Deahn Berrini

How to Earn Your Keep

Four Square Press
Boston, Massachusetts

Four Square Press
85 Devonshire Street
Boston, MA 02215
www.foursquarepress.com

Cover art: “The Mask” by Anne Johnstone
www.johnstoneanne.com

Library of Congress Control Number: 2012948413
ISBN 978-0-9851689-3-3

How to Earn Your Keep

One

Kit Lavoie zipped herself into her black skirt like she was wrapping herself in a shroud. The loose, high waist, the shiny, synthetic material, the matronly hem that fell just below her knees, these were daily reminders of how, at twenty-one years old, her life had veered off course. She should be a college student, in her senior year, free to wear flip flops and dye her hair pink. Instead, Kit worked as a secretary for an attorney, an ambulance chaser who liked to joke he was "one severed limb away from early retirement." She woke early and worried about car insurance.

How had Kit come to this? She could blame the angry ex-boyfriend with a penchant for throwing large objects through glass windows.

She could blame her conveyor belt father who paid attention to what was in front of him, but once life had carried him forward didn't bother looking back at the family he'd left behind.

She could blame her mother for being born with a stage light so blinding that she noticed only herself in its glare.

But, of course, Kit's current situation was mostly her own fault. The mistakes that had brought her to this morning lined up like bright red, ignored warning flags, clearer at a distance.

With a sigh, Kit sat down on her bed to put on a pair of heels. Evidence of her most recent error rested on her dresser—a letter from Sea-to-Sea Lenders announcing that the monthly mortgage payment for their three-bedroom ranch home had gone up again. Short of cash when their father's child support stopped after Kit left school and her brother didn't go on to college, Kit couldn't believe her luck when she had come across an ad for a variable mortgage that would significantly lower the monthly payment. Convincing her mother to sign on had been easy.

Kit, however, had gravely misunderstood just how "variable" a variable mortgage could be; she hadn't figured on the payments rising so soon and so steeply. So far the household—she, Larry, and Ruby—could squeak by, but with a scary-thin margin.

She stood up and took a deep breath. Kit hated a crybaby. Don't, don't you do this, she admonished herself: if I'm defeated in my head, I'm defeated for real.

With that small pep talk, she grabbed her work sweater and walked quickly down the narrow hallway toward the kitchen. Through some quirk of construction, their small ranch was placed backwards on the lot—the front door in the living room faced the back, and the back door in the kitchen faced the front of the lot and the road. Kit like to think that the builder had envisioned a vast backyard pool and patio area to be added on later. The alternative was to admit to living in a dwelling so hastily constructed that no one had noticed, or cared about, the mistake.

Passing through this kitchen at the front of the house, Kit found her brother wearing a dramatic dressing gown—bright yellow silk with an elaborate green dragon breathing elongated bursts of orange fire. The gown intimated exoticism, luxury, and danger as it slid over his naked white calves covered in wisps of red-blond hair. Larry Lavoie carried it off, too; the loose material didn't hang on him sadly, but shimmered in precise, narrow waves as he moved.

Kit stopped and had to smile, "Shopping in Chinatown."

Larry turned to his sister, spatula held high.

Their mother, Ruby, cooed from her seat at the table. "Isn't it beautiful. I want one too."

Larry shrugged. "It's one of a kind."

"It's gorgeous," said Kit.

As Larry attended to his bubbling pancakes, he executed a quick half turn to regard the swirl of color. "It's almost enough to make you want to learn Chinese."

Kit put on her coat and picked up her bag from the counter.

"Oh," said Ruby, "you're not having breakfast?"

"Some of us have to work." She tucked her *Vogue* into a side pocket. "You don't have much time either," she said to

Larry.

"Shipments in late this morning," he mumbled.

Kit turned to her brother sharply. She tensed as an onslaught of images of white papers with red "OVERDUE" stamps flew through her imagination.

"Larry…"

"Oh, Kit. Take that look off your face. You'll get wrinkles," Ruby scolded.

Kit said nothing, even though her mother hadn't held a job since the Reagan Administration, and had stopped paying the bills years ago.

Two

At the Law Offices of Rioux & Rioux, the fall chill was winning its battle with the ancient heating system. Kit, alone in the office, got ready for her day by taking five minutes to scan her *Vogue.*

Rubbing her arms for warmth, she lingered over a rich coffee knee-length shearling coat with leather buttons before she stowed the magazine back in her bag and hung her own navy blue wool, sporting wide lapels now dropping out of style, in the closet.

Her morning agenda began with phone calls.

Kit had barely completed two semesters, but she had listed Boston College on her job application for the position of administrative assistant for Rioux & Rioux. Her small deception had met a kindred spirit in her new boss. In the two years she'd been working at Rioux & Rioux, Jack had given her only one slight raise, and he was not above borrowing four dollars for lunch and then neglecting to pay it back. Kit still hadn't decided whether Jack was miserly—he seemed to wear the same three suits and his car was several years old and domestic—or whether he just didn't make that much money.

Kit did discover that there was no second Mr. Rioux, only the one Jack Rioux, erstwhile criminal defense attorney, now in a more general practice. Somewhere Jack had acquired the notion that two names lent his practice a certain gravitas; the extra Rioux also provided a convenient absent partner for unwanted phone calls from wronged girlfriends and bill collectors.

As Kit was courteous and collected on the phone, Jack often had her make calls to fish for random information. Kit enjoyed the uncertainty of these encounters, but she also relished building the trap ahead of time, planning strategies to put callers at ease and extract information.

Her first call this morning would be to a woman planning to sue one of their clients for injuries allegedly incurred in a car accident. While dialing, Kit breathed deeply, and reminded herself to sound casual. The line rang and rang. Kit imagined the injured plaintiff hobbling across her living room, step by tiny step. Finally, someone picked up.

"Good morning. Is Mrs. Sandra Carson at home?" Kit asked brightly.

"Yes…"

The voice was hesitant, and suspicious, so Kit moved quickly to put her at ease, with pen poised to take down every word. "Mrs. Carson, a friend gave me your name."

"Oh" she replied, her voice opening a bit, and Kit knew she had bought some more time.

"Yes, I'm calling to schedule a free rug and sofa cleaning with Quicktime Carpet Company. When would be a convenient time for us to come by?" Jack suspected the woman of lying, of exaggerating her injuries, so he wanted Kit to find out how active she was, whether she admitted to working. Kit had chosen the carpet-cleaning story because her mother was forever letting people come by to clean rugs and furniture, and also because by booking a cleaning, she could learn a lot about a person's schedule.

"How about Tuesday morning?"

"No, I watch my nephew in the mornings."

Kit sensed a little tension in her voice. "Your nephew, how sweet. Is the little guy a handful?"

"He's just two, so he keeps me busy."

"How kind of you to help out."

"Oh, I get paid for it, believe me."

The lady clearly would have gone in this vein for a while, but Kit changed tacks before Mrs. Carson had a chance to realize that she'd told her anything. "Wednesday evening?"

"That's my bowling night. I never miss that."

Kit considered asking whether she enjoyed a beer or two at the lanes. Quite a good trick, a woman supposedly in a neck brace and barely able to walk, driving home with a few drinks in her. It would be easy enough to wait by the bowling alley and then video her as she left the parking lot.

"Thursday evening?"

"Nope, bingo."

Her basic schedule thus laid down, Kit then managed to schedule an appointment, somewhat in the future so that when no one showed up, time would have blurred Mrs. Carson's memory of the phone call and her suspicions wouldn't be raised. Jack would be pleased with her morning's work. None of the conversation was admissible in court—ethics forbade attorneys talking to opposing parties—but still, Jack would find a way to use the information to his advantage.

The first time she had made one of these calls, she'd bragged to her best friend, Angela Minnizone, about how much information she'd managed to gather. But Angela, who hadn't ventured beyond a commuter school and wanted to be an accountant, hadn't seen it that way. "Couldn't you get arrested for shit like that?" she had asked.

After she hung up the phone, Kit felt a sense of accomplishment coupled with a need to smoke. This then mingled with guilt as she had promised her brother she would quit what he called her "nicotine habit."

Her boss would be out of the office until after noon. Jack was in court to argue a preliminary motion for one of his many Driving Under the Influence clients. These clients, all stopped by the police for one reason or another and then charged with driving drunk were one of his specialties. Most often desperate, Jack demanded and received a considerable retainer, often in cash. To earn these high fees, he had developed an elaborate rubric in which every step in the police-client interaction was an opportunity to throw the case out. As it stood, there was no requirement in Massachusetts to take a breathalyzer test, and Jack, with his long run of making the argument that a client wasn't really drunk, had invented a thousand reasons why his clients continued to swerve across yellow lines or neglected to put their headlights on at midnight.

Kit left the office, went into the hall, and paused at the door of Attorney Aaron Levinson's Office, listening for signs of occupancy. Mr. Levinson, who dealt mostly in real estate, paid Kit on the side to run small errands for him at the Registry of Deeds, located just down the street. Unlike Jack Rioux, Mr. Levinson, an older man who had children the same age as Kit, took the time to explain how each task he assigned fit into a larger pattern, either for a particular case or as part of a larger legal philosophy. Free with his money as well as his time, he often paid her with whatever large bills he had around the office, curtly refusing any offer of change. This money Kit kept in an envelope that she hid in an old pair of boots in the back of her closet at home. She considered this stash as a sort of emergency fund, like a rope ladder out a window, for use in case of fire. Hearing nothing from Mr. Levinson, she continued outside.

A clear, bright, and chillyfall morning met Kit. She agreed with her brother that cigarettes were a filthy habit, so she compensated by not smoking in front of her boss or any of his clients. Perched on the granite pedestal at the end of the stairs outside the kitchen, a spot that caught a stretch of morning sun that ran down the street between the rows of buildings, she closed her eyes to the warmth. A few deep drags later and close to satisfied, she felt a gust of wind cut through her and shivered. Maybe she and Angela should just move to Florida, like they had talked about a thousand times, mostly after Trey had come to her dorm that last time. After that disaster Kit had stalled and not registered for classes the following semester, and then her scholarship lapsed.

She had taken up with him senior year in high school, and he had been fun, a change. He had started his own business, seemed more mature, more responsible than other boys her age. The trouble really started when she went to college, and Trey wouldn't let go. He visited her again and again over the course of her year at BC, each time arriving drunker and louder than the time before, until toward the end, he was banned from campus. This hadn't stopped him from showing up anyway. Her roommates ceased being anything but barely civil after he called them every name in his narrow-minded and ignorant vocabulary, and they ratted her out to the Dean's Office, resulting in a very uncomfortable meeting and a note on her record. Upset and scared every time she heard his booming voice announcing himself down the hall, she had begged him not to visit her at school, still she went with him when he came, screwed him time after time in the back seat of his truck. Toward the end, she screwed him to get him to go away. Mostly, to shut him up.

Kit opened her eyes to the clear azure sky. To remember all this made her heart race, but she couldn't stop turning the events around in her mind over and over, hoping for the insight that would put them to rest, hoping for the absolution that would allow her to forget.

That last time Trey came, during finals week, she hadn't

obliged, had given him the slip at a local convenience store. He'd followed her back, found her in the common room, and thrown a chair through a plate glass window and ripped off her top by the time the police arrived--the real police, someone had called the real police, not just campus security. She'd stood there in her black lace bra and jeans, shivering by the open window as Trey, handcuffed and later charged with a host of crimes--all charges dropped eventually--called her every vile name, again, she had ever heard and never hoped to hear again.

After Trey had been taken away, the police treated her with an unjudgmental courtesy. What had been the worst were the crowd of undergraduates, staring, horrified and revolted at the display. What's wrong with you? she'd wanted to shout. Hasn't anything ever been messy in your good little lives? Are you all so perfect? Drinking yourself into oblivion so that you couldn't remember who it was you slept with the night before was all right as long as you confessed your sins on Sunday, but rage and desperation were beyond the circumstances of acceptability? She wanted to leave with the cops, one of whom had fetched a sweater for her. No other girl, all of them merely feet away from their own closets in their own dorm rooms, had thought to do the same. It was those faces, those dispassionate and staring faces, she could never return to.

Kit flipped the cigarette to the ground. Knock it off, she reminded herself, you always get down in the fall about the school thing.

Her coat was barely off when the door opened, and in walked a slightly overweight girl with feathered blond hair and an older woman in a modest brown plaid skirt—she knew these people—Linda Appleton and her mother.

Linda's sister, Janelle, and Janelle's fiancé had been killed by an elderly driver on a slick, leaf-sodden road a few weeks before their scheduled December wedding, now almost a year ago. Kit hadn't seen Mrs. Appleton or Linda since the wake and the funeral, and, judging by their bedraggled appearance, the time in between hadn't been kind to either of them. To further complicate matters, lately Kit's brother had been spending a lot of time with Linda, which made no sense whatsoever. What were the Appletons doing here? Linda and Larry's friendship, if you could call it that, had not extended itself to the families.

Kit met the Appletons with an awkward smile.

"Let me get you some coffee," said Kit in an attempt to anchor them until Jack's return. "Linda, Mrs. Appleton, have a seat." She pulled over two wooden captain's chairs from where they rested against the wall. Each chair had stamped on its back a faded coat of arms, a gold and red design evocative of the seal of Harvard University, a school Jack had never attended. Before they could refuse, Kit headed to the kitchen.

The Law Offices of Rioux & Rioux were tucked into the second floor of an old Salem ship captain's home, converted to business use near the turn of the century. Rioux & Rioux shared narrow stairs, elaborate molding, uneven heat, and a communal kitchen with two other small law offices. Grolin & Stedges, which comprised two attorneys and two secretaries, one of whom was convinced the house was haunted, occupied all of the first floor that wasn't the kitchen, and the Law Offices of Aaron Levinson, Esq., took the remainder of the second.

In the kitchen downstairs, Kit grabbed two clean mugs from the shelf, unsure why her heart was beating so fast. She turned with a start and nearly dropped them both.

Mrs. Bergen, who worked for Mr. Grolin, stood four inches from her. "Don't forget the cream and sugar," she whispered. "Here," she gestured, "use a tray. Although," and her voice dropped further, "you really only need one cup. The other one won't drink it." A quick chill fluttered through Kit. Mrs. Bergen habitually made creepy remarks, but she was also uncannily right. "It would be rude, though, wouldn't it, to only bring one?"

Kit returned with the coffee a few minutes later. She was unaccountably pleased when Linda put some sugar and milk in one and handed it to her mother. Mrs. Appleton was a slim woman, thin bones in her hands, with dark hair and a fine-featured face. Janelle, the sister who had died, had looked like that, too, refined and little. Linda was different—larger, louder, blond. She favored the father, who had disappeared years ago, when the sisters were little.

"We just were driving to Salem, and I remembered you worked for a lawyer so we thought we'd drop in," explained Linda. She looked around. "Where's your boss?"

Kit glanced at the clock, close to noon. Jack still had not returned from his preliminary motion; either he was at the rear of the line at the docket, or he'd gone off to other adventures. "He has an appointment at twelve-thirty," she explained. "He'll be back for that."

"We should have called," sighed Mrs. Appleton, and she smiled at Kit.

The smile caught Kit off guard. Piano lessons, she remembered, that's what Mrs. Appleton did for a living.

"Mr. Rioux will have time for you," assured Kit.

"What will it cost us?" asked Linda.

"It depends," said Kit as evenly as possible. Linda had not touched her own mug of coffee, just as Mrs. Bergen had predicted. Why were they here? Was the car insurance company holding out on them? Kit didn't think so, because everyone knew it was the other driver's fault. She had been all over the road; there were witnesses.

When Jack barged in, his mustache almost twitched with glee at the sight of Mrs. Appleton in her neat brown clothing. Short and a little stout, with a wide upturned nose over the dark mustache, he had a beguiling, loquacious manner that had mesmerized Kit more than once. "Good afternoon," he crooned in his most soothing tones. "Coffee? Excellent work Katharine."

Kit repressed a scowl. No one called her Katharine. But she played her part. "Mrs. Appleton, Linda, this is Attorney Jack Rioux."

He beamed.

"They've come for a consultation, and looking at your schedule, I suggest you take them right in now, before your next appointment," Kit suggested, although this would make him late for his twelve-thirty. The twelve-thirty couldn't complain; a minor criminal matter, he was a court-appointed case, the fees Jack billed paid by the state, and odds were he had nowhere else to go.

As Jack followed the Appletons into his office, Kit noticed him watch Linda's shifting weight, wrapped tight in her jeans. In the two years she had worked for him, Jack had had a steady string of mismatched girlfriends; if the Appletons became clients, however, he would leave Linda alone. As Jack liked to remind her, at Rioux & Rioux, cash was king.

When the twelve-thirty appeared, thin and nervous with darting eyes, cleaned up in loose work pants and a faded cloth jacket, Kit told him he would have to wait. And she didn't fetch him any coffee.

At lunch, on a busy sidewalk, Kit ducked behind a parked truck to avoid Angela's brother, Chris Minnizone, the only person she had dated since her return from college. In his work clothes and lugging a huge pipe from the back of a flatbed into a building being renovated, he waited several seconds before entering the building, metal pipe balanced on his shoulder, for a troika of men in suits to pass by on the sidewalk. She had a clear look at his face, patient, concentrated, his knees bent just a little to accommodate the weight of the pipe. Trey had been like that too, handsome, competent, older than his years—working more than anyone else his age, talking about trucks and drivers and customers in a way that led her to believe he'd succeed.

That was before he had turned his ability to organize on her, when he began to sense she wouldn't give him what he wanted.

Kit told herself that she walked past Chris only after he had entered the building for a virtuous reason, that she hadn't wanted to throw him off balance by startling him, that it all happened too quickly for her to say hello. All lies, she admitted a few steps later but, in no mood to dwell on the uncomfortable, she made herself take firm, decisive steps in order to mimic a person in charge of her own future.

Back in the office, Jack ignored her for the rest of the afternoon as he often did. Moody, his genial bonhomie swung frequently toward sullen silence. On several occasions, he'd allowed himself to toss a law book or two, which fell with an alarming thump on the other side of their adjoining wall, somewhere behind Kit's head.

Sometime just before five o'clock the golden late fall sun slipped behind the courthouse across the street and abandoned the office to shadows. Kit clicked on a desk light and sorted her papers to leave. Jack burst out of his office and seated himself in the chair in front of her desk, one she had pulled up earlier for the Appletons and had not yet replaced against the wall. He crossed his leg over his knee, revealing a thin black sock, and stared at Kit.

He must have nowhere to go, she thought, and now he is going to waste my time. But she was pleased, too, as she sometimes unaccountably was by his attention. She looked up. "Yes?"

He squinted at her for dramatic emphasis, an old trial trick he played for the jury at certain junctures, just before a closing argument maybe, or before a particularly defensive witness. Trick or not, it was effective.

"What is it?" she repeated.

"How well do you know those people?"

"The Appletons?"

"It's a terrible story." And he meant it.

"Linda was ahead of me in school," she told him and then hesitated. As little as she knew the Appletons, she was conscious of an element of betrayal in giving Jack too much information about a world, her world, he knew nothing about and had not earned his way into. But wasn't this what business, what money, was all about, people with information, with tips, trading it with other people? Isn't that the world she wanted to hoist herself into?

"Her mother gives piano lessons and Janelle, the..." He nodded and she continued, "Janelle was musical like her mother."

"And?"

"She's sort of… close… with my brother."

Jack's eyebrows lifted straight up into his high forehead. "Your brother dated the dead sister?"

The thought of her brother, good looking as he admittedly was, dating anyone made Kit want to laugh. "No, my brother…" She searched for words.

Jack shook his head impatiently. "This is what I'm after—what would make them come in here, almost a year after the accident, just before the statute of limitations runs out, and ask me to take on this case?"

Kit thought about Mrs. Appleton's reluctance, almost her apology at finding the office too busy to receive them, in contrast with Linda's insistence and concern with the cost. She shrugged. "Are you sure they're an even team?"

"That's typical in these kinds of plaintiff suits. Some people don't have the will for it. Which one is it?"

Couldn't you see, she wanted to say; it was so obvious to her that Linda was behind the whole scheme, whatever that scheme might be. "Linda was the one who wanted to be here."

Jack sat up straight. "Really?" He stared at Kit and leaned forward.

"Mrs. Appleton was reluctant. She's not a loud kind of person."

Jack continued to stare, and Kit began to feel less sure of herself.

He sat back. "Of course," he said, "this might not go anywhere. It depends on what kind of fight she'll put up."

"Who will put up?" Kit asked, confused. "The older driver or Linda or Mrs. Appleton?"

Jack stood up, stretched his arms in the air. "What kind of lawyers she hires, how much money she really has. Although if one can't take the heat, the other still has standing." He rubbed his hands together. "Thank you, my dear. You might as well go home," he said even though it was now well past five. "We're all done here."

Kit took her bag from the bottom drawer and her navy coat from the rack in the closet. She thought about the beautiful brown leather one, lined in sheepskin with leather buttons, shown in *Vogue*. Maybe some lesser label would knock off the style for a price she could afford. She'd been wearing the same winter coat since early high school yet, desperate as she was to fling the old rag away, she didn't want to settle for cheap and functional; she wanted to feel glad to have the sleeves glide up her arms as she slipped it on.

The hallway was dimly lit by a small wall fixture. Mr. Levinson had gone home early, as he often did. She walked slowly down the narrow back steps to the darkened kitchen. The cups she had washed out earlier sat in the drying rack. Mrs. Bergen often brought in her extra Halloween candy, and Kit was hungry, but the bowl was empty. She continued into the front hall. The light was still on behind the frosted glass door of Grolin & Stedges; most likely Mr. Stedges was staying late again. But out popped Mrs. Bergen. Her high gray hair glowed with the backlight of the hall sconce behind her head.

"Burning the midnight oil?" she asked as they left the building. Her laugh was high and tinkly.

"It's not even five-thirty, Mrs. Bergen."

"Is Mr. Rioux still upstairs?" Mrs. Bergen insisted on addressing all the lawyers using only their surnames.

Kit nodded.

"Well, yes, of course he is." Mrs. Bergen's countenance darkened. "You do understand, Kit, that the choice made will not be a good one."

Kit hesitated, but she knew better than to question one of Mrs. Bergen's pronouncements. Often she was unable to explain them herself. Only in Salem, she thought. "Sure, Mrs. Bergen," she answered.

Mrs. Bergen patted Kit's arm as they parted on the corner. "Good night, dear."

On Kit's way to her car, she passed the spot where, at lunchtime, she had noticed Chris Minnizone holding the pipe. She recalled Mrs. Bergen's words—the choice made will not be a good one. That caveat, she thought as she unlocked the door and started the car, felt as if it could apply to almost everything she'd done for as long as she could remember.

Three

Larry Lavoie walked into the tiny bar of the Poirier Motel.

Mike Poirier, a thin man with a precise, graying mustache, greeted him. He placed a bottle in front of Larry. "No smile today?"

Even though he was underage, Mike had regularly served Larry since he had wandered in late one night after a particularly difficult stretch during his senior year in high school. His grandmother had died the previous spring, Kit had left for college that fall, and Larry had found himself, for the first time, really alone, and charged with cooking for his mother.

Mike hadn't said much that evening, just given him the beer he'd asked for and the ham sandwich he hadn't. They had talked some since, but mostly Mike was one of those adults who made Larry feel comfortable, one of those adults who, if they saw anything different about him, didn't let on or acted like it didn't matter.

"I got let go again," Larry confessed.

Mike waved his hand broadly. "Forget it, Larry. It's not your fault. The economy's tough."

Larry nodded, unconvinced, as Mike retreated to wait on other customers.

The TV showed the news, insistent, titillating, and Larry worked hard not to listen. Stories others half-heard while chomping through their hamburgers could worm their way into Larry's imagination and upset him. Some detail would haunt him for days—the child's flowered sneaker abandoned on the sidewalk, the heart tattoo on the neck of the person burned out of her apartment.

Tonight, Larry ostensibly waited for his friend Linda, but she was late and he knew she wouldn't show. They had first gotten together last spring, at a party where he had found himself in a back bedroom with Linda trying to ride on top of him, her large breasts spilling out of her sleeveless, low-scooped shirt like urgent, trapped animals.

It was not until middle school that Larry fully comprehended his sexual propulsions. At thirteen, like his peers, he carried his burgeoning physicality like a ticking bomb duct-taped onto his kidnapped body. The knowledge that when it finally blew previous life as he knew it would disappear, coupled with the natural fear of the inevitable explosion, left him and his fellow seventh graders crippled in reason, hostage to impulse.

For Larry, though, a funny difference occurred. When pressed up against girls in a slow dance or a spin-the-bottle session, desire chilled. With this sangfroid he cultivated a certain calculation. When Larry put his tongue in an ear or swooped his fingers below a waist during a swing in the music, like a scientist, he stepped back and noted the effects of his actions, while his bumbling classmates couldn't manage to cross the gym floor to where the girls stood, giggling, apprehensive, cruel.

With nary an outlier, all the girls felt his difference, felt the lack of real heat. Results then diverged clearly into two separate camps—those that played and those that didn't. A certain group of twelve- and thirteen-year-old girls allowed Larry access because he wanted nothing from them, took no advantage, and the contact conferred a certain social currency. Another, more mature group, felt his repulsion and were equally repulsed by the encounter.

This physical coldness toward the fairer sex, Larry finally understood, was irrevocable. On the bright side, he longed passionately for certain boys, and while not an easy way to grow up, he also understood enough of the wider world to know that while he might have to wait a little longer, he would be eventually be rewarded.

With Linda, though, he reverted back to his middle school days, for the untethered loneliness he'd felt since leaving school had been difficult as well.

And Linda's urges had little to do with him. Linda was sad—her sister and the sister's fiancé killed by an elderly driver weeks before their wedding, and more than anything else, her pathos had kept his interest. Then in a funny twist, it was his empathetic feelings that sent her running hard in the opposite direction, as if Linda had picked up on his kindness and was repelled. He had tried to take her to Boston, to the old brick buildings, to the shops, to Chinatown, but she had been impatient, bored. This afternoon on the phone, she had been more distracted than usual when he'd told her he'd lost his job, and he sensed that whatever had propelled her into their friendship was finally overcome by inertia.

He drank the last of his beer and wondered about what to do next, trusting that something had to be just around the corner. At whatever job Larry had he was always the last guy hired, the most expendable, the one with the least invested. He'd slid around community college for a few semesters, but remained unable to find the point to school. Most months he managed his share of the bills, but Kit was so efficient, so dependable that he knew he could skip some paychecks too, and come to no harm. His mother got the alimony, but without Kit the whole unit would disintegrate, death by insolvency, the pieces unable to fend for themselves.

The bar door creaked open, and as The Poirier Motel bar catered to a mix of regulars and motel guest, Larry turned to glance at the entrance. Half a dozen men of various ages, most wearing tight jeans and riding boots, headed in, accompanied by a musty, animal smell. A man with a small build, about his age, light brown hair falling onto his shoulders stepped onto the carpet. The man raised his head and looked straight at Larry, as if pulled in by Larry's attention--his gaze fell on Larry like a charge. Larry turned quickly back in confusion to his beer.

The group ordered drinks and made a congenial semicircle between the bar and a nearby booth. When someone hailed the bartender in the snaky r's and long vowels of foreign English, Larry couldn't resist listening in, hoping to get another glance at the one with the hair swooping down the side of his face. They turned out to be part of a group of traveling groomsmen and horse trainers from the last of the season's polo matches, and their talk turned to unusual names that he soon discovered were the names of horses. During a lull in the conversation, the guy with the hair sat down on the stool next to Larry. For a second Larry was a wreck of nerves as to what to do, but then the other man held out a hand and gave up a guarded smile, which put Larry at ease.

"William—Billy Potter," he said, as he introduced himself in a perfectly ordinary way. Had Larry imagined the glance? Pulled in by his new acquaintance's reserved charm, it wasn't long before Larry sat amidst the general bonhomie of the larger group. And, after several more beers, he found it easier to stop returning to the memory of that first spark and merely enjoy the company of his new friend and his amusing companions.

Billy didn't leave his side, however. At one point during the evening, Larry looked over and caught Mike Poirier, drying the glasses hot out of the dishwasher with a soft cloth, watching him. A quick burst of the familiar panic surged through him—caught—but before he could cover his impulses with the usual shrugs and demurrals, Larry could have sworn that Mike smiled at him, perhaps even nodded imperceptibly before looking away.

Four

Orange leaves fought against a deepening blue sky, while their fallen brown cousins swirled in the dirt of the stable yard. Billy Potter had hinted at a possible job for Larry with his wealthy and elderly boss, a horse lover with Yankee blood going back to the Mayflower, but as it turned out, on this day Curtis Wainwright Rutherford was in Delaware, visiting relatives.

Before they entered the barn, Billy pulled a silver flask from the back pocket of his loose jeans and leaned it against the barn wall. "The girls don't like it when I drink," he whispered, and gestured to Larry to follow.

The wooden interior smelled of hay and manure. The girls, two mares and a gelding with tape wrapped on his leg, had been watered, fed, and bedded down, and stood quietly in the darkened barn. Billy spoke to the horses in turn, Lady Cakes, Blue, Riding High, each coming to him to receive a caress. Billy took a large brown head in his hand and ran the flat of his palm firmly down the wide neck. Lady Cakes bowed her head and closed her eyes. Larry stood awkwardly in the narrow corridor between the stalls; caught off-guard by the intimate moment, he looked at the ceiling, at the rafters softened by cobwebs.

Outside, dusk had gone to black in the rapid pace of a New England fall twilight. Larry shivered in his jean jacket. "So you like horses?"

"You're a funny one," laughed Billy, and offered him the flask. "Here," he said. "Take the edge off."

Larry swallowed, some kind of whiskey, maybe scotch, he wasn't sure, but the drink was smooth and warmed his stomach.

"Good stuff, huh? It's Mr. Rutherford's." Billy took back the bottle. "Come on, let's finish the tour. The estate's been in the family for generations." The grounds included the barn, a large paddock, and pine and oak woods that ran towards the salt marshes and the ocean; a large mansion sat on a curved, stoney drive. They climbed the short hill to the house and entered through a side porch enclosed with large glass windows. The slate floor was empty of furniture save for what was covered in a heavy tarp and pushed against the back of the room for the winter. Billy took off his barn boots, and so Larry removed his construction boots, purchased last spring to protect his feet from falling cargo at the loading dock at his last job. French doors led them into another high-ceilinged room, appointed with matching furniture set off at angles.

In the oversized kitchen, done in yellow and black, Billy pulled serving platters from the double fridge. "There's so much food because Mr. Rutherford had quite the bash before he left. Here," he handed Larry a few dishes and pointed, "bring them into the dining room and I'll grab the rest."

Larry peered at the cold meats and vegetables, carefully garnished and cut into precise patterns Larry recognized as not home-cooked as he walked backwards through the heavy swinging door to a room dominated by a long, narrow, gleaming wooden table. He placed the platters on the table.

"Jesus!" rebuked Billy, who followed right behind. "Don't they teach you anything in the public schools? You don't put platters on the wood!"

"Maybe it would be easier if we ate in the kitchen," said Larry.

Billy balanced the plates and utensils he'd been carrying against his hip and reached into a broad drawer in the wooden sideboard. He pulled out some thick placemats and scattered them deftly over the table. "Why? This is a whole lot nicer."

Larry watched the familiarity with which Billy placed candlesticks, candles, and a bottle of scotch on the table.

“How many people live here?” he asked.

Billy paused as he set out the silverware, heavy and weighted at the handles with intricate scrolls. “Mr. C.W. Rutherford is the only one who lives here,” he announced as he gestured with his hand for Larry to have a seat. Larry adjusted the heavy chair in front of the table.

"Mr. Rutherford and I have an arrangement. Of course I care for the horses. And then, I guess you could call me a house sitter," Billy continued in a quieter tone. He placed a red wiggling mound on Larry's plate. "Try the jellied beets."

The pile sat bright red and melted at the edges. Larry lifted the cold, shaking mass to his lips. At first, the cold made it hard to enjoy, that and the odd texture. He clearly tasted beets, but other flavors came through too, and to discover what those flavors were, he took another bite.

"Mmm, good," he offered.

"I first came here to the estate for the horses. My uncle facilitated the introduction. My family had horses when I was young, but we lost them along with everything else when my father lost his money. I never got over them. You know how they are, once they're in your blood."

Larry nodded, but today was the closest he'd ever been to a horse. All he could say with certainty was that now he'd recognize the peculiar odor of them, if he had his eyes closed and was asked in some kind of test.

"Mr. Rutherford keeps the stable for the polo, and I care for them. Blue—he was the one with the bandage on his foreleg," Billy looked up from his plate.

Larry nodded again. Clearly what the horses did merited conversation to Billy. He wondered if this extended to other animals as well, and remembered his grandmother in her last years who, when asked what was new, reported in detail what her cat had been up to, as in she brought me a young blue jay yesterday, and laid it right down on the back step, and I told her, Queenie, not the birds, don't bring me any more birds, although the birds aren't as bloody as the mice, I'd still prefer to see a dead rat on my stair than a thing with feathers.

"Blue got a nasty knock a few matches back and hasn't been the same since. C.W. wanted to put him down, but I…"

"Put him down?"

"Well, they're shot if they break a leg, because it can't heal properly, you know…"

"I didn't know that," said Larry. "How's he doing now?"

"The doctor's been here and the leg is fine," he continued, somewhat defensively, as if Larry had disagreed. "Some horses are born nervy. Others will get so spooked over a thing and no amount of convincing will make them comfortable again."

Larry had never considered that horses had personalities. He looked at the ceiling, painted a light blue and hung with a delicate chandelier of glass.

Billy poured another drink. The bottle was half empty now; Larry didn't remember whether it had been full when they had started. "C.W.'s losing patience with Blue. If it wasn't for me… Sometimes I think he's looking for an excuse to get rid of him."

Larry shivered. The reflection of the candle repeated a dozen times in the now black windowpanes behind Billy's head, and the large room had gone from chilly to cold.

Billy reached out and quickly rubbed Larry's arm. "You're cold again. Too bad there wasn't any hot soup left." He stood up. As he cleared dishes from the table in the low light, his hands grasped the plates firmly, and he was perfectly at home, just as he had been in the barn with the horses. You couldn't say if his hair was more brown or blond, but Larry couldn't stop staring at how it hung down around his face in inviting waves. "Come on," he said as he maneuvered around the chair through the swinging door to the kitchen, "Let's clean this up and continue the tour."

They wandered into the dark and underheated house. Billy flicked on a switch and announced, "Library." Vast bookcases hung around a cabal of thick armchairs.

On the wall hung a painting of a sharp-nosed man with thin lips and a yellow cravat. He looked like the kind of person who would shoot a horse. "Is that Mr. Rutherford?"

Billy laughed. "He's the one who earned the old money. Something to do with machines that make shoes. Although Mr. Rutherford makes a lot on his own, that's for sure. He's into high finance." He flicked off the switch, and lingered a split second with Larry in the half-shadow of light thrown in from the hall before going out the door. Once again Billy put his hand on Larry's arm. It was just long enough, Larry understood, to give Larry a choice. He could finish the tour, or he could go home.

As Billy coaxed him forward, he knew the enormous house, built with old money and mysterious wills, the fierce honeyed liquor, and the shaky red food in the fridge were all bait, laid neatly in a row toward, well, toward exactly what? His sister, Kit, had some fancy friends, but Larry had never wanted any part of that private school scene—that lot all talked way too much, all the time, about absolutely nothing. But Billy—Larry followed every word with attention.

Billy turned the lights on in the next room. "Salon."

Reds and greens played off each other, sending his gaze toward two couches covered in an intricate pattern that reminded Larry of something he'd just seen in Chinatown, but that was nowhere near as detailed or vibrant as the material in front of him. He walked toward it, fingers outstretched. Billy caught up with him and grabbed his hands.

"Be careful around silk," he said gently.

Larry put his hands in the pockets of his jeans and smiled, self-conscious.

"Look, Larry," he pointed to the couch. "You noticed it when you walked in, it's an antique. Look at the design, the boats, and the gold woven into the trunks of the trees, and the orange lines in those bird wings."

He listened because by now he would listen to anything Billy said, but he also listened because he had always loved all things Chinese, from Bruce Lee movies to chicken chow mein, and because Billy seemed like a reliable guide. He saw more precisely how this material was better quality than what he'd seen in Chinatown, how there were more colors in the feathers of the birds, how the boat had been carefully outlined in black threads. He wondered how his new silk bathrobe would feel while lounging on this couch.

"Old money buys old furniture?"

Billy laughed. "Now you get the picture." They sat on two gold lacquered chairs that faced the couch and finished the bottle of scotch. From an intricately carved cabinet, Billy produced another bottle, sherry this time, and two small tumblers, cut glass and heavy.

By the time they got to the bedroom, Larry had to lean against the wall in between every few steps forward. Billy pushed him lightly onto the bed, where he lay on the thick red bedspread and watched the vaulted ceiling spin above him. Billy knelt in front of the stone hearth, and soon a small fire sprang from the grate and warmed the room. He moved back to the bed, pulled the velvet pillows up behind his back and sat against the dark, wooden headboard, and turned out the lights.

When Larry felt Billy's hands move down his chest, onto his thighs, and work at his buckle, he grasped Billy's shoulders and pulled him up, found his lips; Billy murmured, "not so shy anymore." The voice, the heat of his chest, Larry felt such a sense of ease, a sense of something that was both random and arrived at out of luck, as well as something earned and understood.

It was dark, the fire dead. Billy stood, dressed, by the bed and prodded him awake. "Come on," he whispered, "you gotta get going. Mr. Rutherford doesn't like dirty sheets." Larry sat up and Billy handed him his clothes. "You can use the bathroom downstairs. Just let yourself out. Come back tomorrow afternoon, and I'm sure you'll get a job."

Larry fumbled, groggy and freezing, through the cavernous house. Jesus, he said to himself, as he waited a long time for the hot water to come out of the tap. He smiled as he walked through the darkened rooms, to the night outside, which was pitch dark and bracing, the stars bright and sharp in the dry fall air.

Five

"You bastard!" Larry woke with a start to his mother's voice. Thwarted in her ambitions to become an actress, she played an interactive role while viewing TV. Larry opened his eyes.

"How could you!" she shrieked a second or two later. Sleep finished, his feet felt for the floor.

Ruby sat in the living room, in her flower harem pajamas, her anger directed at Asa Buchanan from *One Life to Live*, which meant that Larry had slept later than he meant to. This soap was one of his favorites, and featured a character who had two personalities, one evil, Nicki, and one good, Vicki. With a simple shift in hair style and an on-again, off-again drinking habit, Nicki and Vicki had managed to fool the town of Llanview for many years. Larry sat down next to his mother.

Ruby shrieked again, and in one surprisingly athletic move, she turned, stood, and chucked her cup of morning coffee at him.

Larry jumped up. "What the ..." he stopped himself. Fortunately, the morning long gone, the coffee was cold.

"Why aren't you at work?" Her hair, pushed up to one

side from sleeping, framed her face at a comic angle. "I thought you were a rapist!"

"And you used coffee to defend yourself?"

"Instincts, I used my instincts. Don't try to change the subject."

"I got let go." The cold coffee sucked his T-shirt onto his chest and brought goose bumps.

"Let go? Kit's not going to like that." Ruby sat back down.

"It wasn't my fault. There were some cousins they brought over who needed jobs." He pried the shirt away from his skin. "I got a lead on another job, though."

Asa Buchanan's soon-to-be new wife came onto the screen. Ruby almost spit in disgust. Larry decided it was time to take a shower.

"What's the job?" she called to him as headed toward the back of the house.

Larry hesitated because he doubted that there really was a job, that Billy had made the whole thing up just to, well, whatever, but he banked on his mother's lack of attention to detail and poor memory. "C. Wainwright Rutherford's place."

"Isn't that a stationary store?"

"No, Mom."

She turned her attention from the TV home-wrecker to her son. "It better not be anything illegal."

"No, Mom."

"I mean it. Kit can keep us going for a bit."

"Cold coffee and a lecture?"

She readjusted the wide legs of her pajama pants. "You need some of your sister's drive."

"And what does she need that I have?"

Ruby laughed. "Leave me alone, and let me watch my show."

A few hours later, Kit slammed her faux Chanel bag onto the counter. "What do you mean, it wasn't your fault?"

Larry had not managed his situation well. The day had gotten away from him, and Kit returned from work at six o'clock, early enough to catch him watching *Candlepins Bowling* while Ruby was at the grocery store fetching a missing item for dinner.

Kit hadn't even wasted her time to ask why he was fired. Now she trolled through her purse for her lighter, never a good sign.

Larry stood to defend himself. "The Speranouses had these cousins just off the boat."

"It's always something, cousins off a boat, false accusations..."

A lot has happened since I lost that stupid job at the banana distributer, Larry wanted to tell her, but he wasn't about to share with Kit the details of what had happened at the Rutherford estate.

"I bet you didn't save a penny for the bills! Did you? How much did that fancy Chinese robe cost you?" Kit continued.

As the image of the swirling colors of his robe mingled with the fancy couch at the Rutherford house, Larry turned away from Kit and headed toward the kitchen.

Sensing vulnerability, she followed closely, unlit cigarette in hand. "What?" she asked. "What's wrong?"

He opened the refrigerator door and scanned for onions and peppers. He'd told his mother he'd have the sauce cooking by the time she got home with the spaghetti. Kit couldn't boil water, and this thought rallied him. "Kit, you know the Greeks aren't going to hire me over their own relatives. This really wasn't my fault."

"Didn't they hire Ricky at the same time they hired you? Did the Speranouses let him go too?"

Larry shuddered at the thought of Ricky, Ricky who never shut up, not for one second. He remembered seeing Ricky's time card a few weeks ago, and noticing his extra hours. "Come on man," Ricky had said. "Got nothing else to do."

"No," Larry admitted, "they didn't let him go." He waited for the pounce.

It didn't come. She exhaled in a quick burst, leaned back against the counter, and put the cigarette to her lips to light.

He pulled it out of her mouth and held it over her head. She swatted him, "Give it, give it back!"

"Not in the kitchen! How can I cook if you two stink up the kitchen with your cigarettes!"

"OK, just give it back." Again she hit him on the arm.

"It's a vile habit. You should quit."

"I can't, I'll get fat," she said, but moved to the doorway.

He returned the cigarette. She put it in her mouth but

didn't light it. "You can't change the subject."

"I'll get another job."

"You've got to have a plan. You've got to earn your keep or we'll all be on the sidewalk."

His sister had chastised him on this very topic more than once before. She worked harder than anyone he knew, especially in the years since she'd left college, and he felt guilty when he took advantage of her. But the crazy fierce way she went at things—that would never be him, and he was not sure it made her any more satisfied either.

Ruby breezed into the kitchen and plunked down the grocery bag. "What, didn't he tell you?" She had exchanged her harem pants for sweats, and thrown her ex-husband's jacket over her pajama top. "He got a job, what was it," she turned to Larry, who bent over the cutting board, "was it at a Hallmark store?"

"You have a job at WriteRight?" demanded Kit. "You can only work there if you're over sixty-five."

Larry continued to chop onions, and counted on his mother's poor recall. He regretted ever mentioning C.W. Rutherford. Any way you told the story, it twisted around: I met him in a bar; we had dinner leftovers at the old man's house without the old man; I think they're all queer; that doesn't bother me because I am too. At this last thought, he almost sliced his finger while chopping the onions.

"He doesn't want to say, it must be illegal," said Ruby.

He put the knife down before he drew any blood and checked out the spaghetti his mom had bought, supermarket brand. I can't taste the difference, she'd protested when he'd suggested she buy the name brand. How could you when your taste buds are gone from smoking, he'd answered. "It's not illegal. What makes you think it's something illegal?"

"If it's not illegal, then why are you acting so funny?" chided Ruby.

Kit stood her unlit cigarette end up on the counter, tapped it back and forth between her pointer fingers. "Because he doesn't have a job."

"I do. Almost. It's at the Rutherford place, working with horses!"

"Horses!" Ruby laughed so hard she started to cough, the smoker's cough that Larry hated. You're going to sound like Mom someday, he wanted to tell Kit, like you have gravel in your throat. And, no matter what you say, no one finds that sexy.

Kit eyed him, but Larry avoided her gaze by searching for a larger pot. He reluctantly remembered that he was supposed to have met Billy this afternoon to be introduced to Mr. Rutherford. But he could go there tomorrow. Tomorrow was sure to be just as good.

The next day, Ruby was gone when Larry sat down to enjoy *One Life to Live.* Just as he'd settled onto the couch, though, the phone rang. It was Kit.

"You watching that show?"

Larry reached up and pulled back the curtains from the large living room window. The sun was bright and had already reached the back of the house. "Nope."

"I thought you said you had another job."

He wanted to finish the show and he would need to take a shower. "I have another meeting with the guy," he stalled.

"When?"

"An hour or so," he guessed aloud.

"I want to hear all about it when I get home." She hung up.

"Damn," he said to the dial tone. He wasn't going to be able to weasel out of this one.

Billy had told him to come back the next day, in the afternoon, that Mr. Rutherford would be at home all week. Although aware that arriving a day late, with barely any daylight left appeared lazy, Larry also knew that sloth was an easy sin in which to hide. While he was eager to see Billy again, part of him was also terrified. What happened next? And even more unnerving, what did he want to happen?

As Larry retraced the drive he'd made two days earlier, he wondered too about the world he'd wandered into. Apparently the money to create it all went back to the angry man with the yellow cravat hanging in the library, and the money he'd made from, what was it, shoes? Connecting an old shoe factory to this estate with the horses and the vast marshes made as much real sense as a Disney movie. Maybe the horse polo lifestyle was just a front for something more sinister and more lucrative since it was clear Mr. Rutherford made his own money as well. Larry pictured, though, the way Billy had held that horse's head so gently, and how he'd spoken to the animals as if no one else were listening. Whatever else he was into, he wasn't faking that.

The road curved through the huge old trees, colored in reds and golds for the season, and set against the browning marsh and cool blue sky. A steady swirling wind shifted the dying vegetation so that the scene sparkled and moved. Within a month, most of it would be blown away to make room for winter.

With C.W. Rutherford in mind, Larry parked only halfway up the drive, nearer to the barn than to the house, and walked toward the paddock. Two brown horses trotted across the field. He called out, but the wind gathered his voice with the dry leaves and sticks and swirled it about the yard. Tempted as he was to turn around and head back to the car, he didn't want Billy to come out the barn and see him walking away. He headed toward the open barn door.

"Hey, Larry, you made it." Billy's voice was cheerful as he led the black horse between the stalls. Most of Larry's anxiety about what would happen when he saw Billy again leached away into the warm barn and Billy's easy presence. He stepped back outside to make way for Billy, the horse, and a third person in tight riding pants and high boots who was holding a crop. "Mr. Rutherford, here's that guy I told you about."

C.W. Rutherford wasn't all that old after all. Sure, he was a bit lined around his mouth and his hair faded, but Larry had imagined a man who resembled his wealthy ancestor, and Mr. Rutherford was small and tightly muscled, with carefully groomed blond hair and a smile that didn't curve up at the ends. He put out his hand and bent it where the fingers meet the palm, in a light shake, as if waiting to be kissed. "The pleasure is mine, I'm sure," he said, looking over Larry's head. "Now, if you would just take Blue's lead and walk him around a bit, you'd be doing us a tremendous favor."

Wet air and snot blew fiercely through the horse's nostrils as he kicked at the dirt with a leg wrapped in some kind of Ace bandage. Billy handed the reins to Larry, and Larry felt intensely aware of Blue's huge, aggravated presence and his own fear. Trying to remember and imitate how Billy treated the horses, he took the flat of his hand and gave the side of Blue's belly a few firm pats. The horse was warm in the chilly air, and smelled musty. Blue shook his head, and his mane whipped against Larry's hand. "OK, Blue," he cooed. "Let's take a little walk, what do you say." He stepped forward. The horse followed. "All right," Larry said, more in relief than to the horse.

Billy called out, "Just circle the yard. We want to watch his gait."

At the sound of Billy's voice, Larry's heartbeat raced, and Blue startled and turned back to the barn. "No, Blue," Billy called. "Just take your walk." The horse seemed to listen to Billy, for he obeyed and continued along.

Larry tried to insinuate himself with the horse. "Come on, I'm not going to turn you into glue," he whispered to Blue. More confident now, they circled the yard. The tour would have been a perfect demonstration, if the cackle of a high-flying crow hadn't spooked the animal. As the caw sounded, Blue raised his forelegs up in the air and emitted a high-pitched whinny of pure terror that communicated straight to Larry—no filter, just pure emotion. He dropped the reins, and Blue skittered along the yard. It took Billy a moment or two, but he somehow got to the side of the horse, grabbed the reins, and talked him down.

Mr. Rutherford stood, rhythmically slapping the end of the riding crop into his palm as Billy subdued the horse and led him into the paddock.

"Look..." Billy started, but Mr. Rutherford held up his crop and Billy stopped talking.

He turned to Larry. "You don't know horses, do you?"

"No sir, not really."

“He’s running out of chances,” said Mr. Rutherford to Billy.

Billy started to speak, but Mr. Rutherford held up the crop once more. "He,” he motioned the crop toward Larry, “can help you down here, and replace Davis when he leaves for the season." He looked at Larry, blue eyes squinting in the sun. "I'm sure he'll do," he said. He turned and walked back to the house.

Larry watched the sun turn Billy’s hair different shades as it lifted in the breeze. He considered the rush of emotion Blue had shared. "That was freaky," he said.

Billy nodded. "The horses know what you're thinking."

The crazy horse, the stern man with the little whip, Larry hesitated. "I don't know if I can do this."

"He’s not a bad horse. He just needs a little more time to recover.”

“Well,” said Larry, searching for a reason not to take the job. “What about…”

“Sure, there's lots to learn," Billy interrupted, and then touched Larry’s hand. "But I already know you're a quick study."

Larry watched as Billy flipped the hair out of face with a quick, horse-like toss of his head. The word “no” disappeared from his mind, and he nodded his assent.

Six

While reviewing the folder of information Mrs. Appleton had handed over to Jack, Kit came across a clipping of the accident taken from the local paper. She unfolded the article, and lingered over the photo of Janelle. Her face sweet and unformed, she looked to just be graduating high school, although she had been a year or two out of college when she died, and not too much older than Kit was now.

The driver's name was Vivian Faye Pierce. According to the insurance papers, the two companies had come to an agreement fairly quickly as to fault; eye witnesses and a police report expedited that process, but given Massachusetts' highly regulated car insurance system, the payout was also regulated, and therefore limited. Mrs. Pierce was not charged with any crime, such as vehicular homicide or manslaughter. Although Jack Rioux was not popular in the District Attorney's office, he was well known, and after a few well-placed phone calls, he ascertained that this was due to Mrs. Pierce's advanced aged, seventy-six at the time of the accident, and the inclement weather—the heavy, icy rains and the dark.

From the point of view of Rioux & Rioux, the accident could not become a case unless Mrs. Pierce had enough wealth to make the effort worthwhile. Most drivers do not get sued, do not become civil defendants for the simple reason that most drivers are not rich, or even moderately wealthy enough to justify the time of the attorneys. When a simple phone book search revealed an Edward Pierce owned a house on Argilla—the road to the beach and a prestigious location known for its large lots and views to the marsh and the water—Jack decided to pursue the investigation farther.

"Do a Registry search on the Pierce property," Jack had barked. "And," he added, before he shut his office door to take a phone call from his most recent girlfriend, some kind of performer, "while it's light out, take a drive up there and check things out."

On a whim, Kit dialed the number listed for Edward Pierce. After twenty rings, her personal limit, she hung up. Then she went across the street to the Registry of Deeds.

Something about the oversized granite building fronted by a line of columns three stories high, which held the records of all the land in the county, gave Kit an immense sense of security. Inside, every bit of land in Massachusetts was divided up and accounted for, each with its series of owners and their attendant personal dramas neatly packaged within legal boundaries. Kit cared less about the greed, spotty luck, or desire that drove these transfers of property than the comfort that all the answers were here, if only you knew how to find them. Farms divided up among family members and then sold off, mortgages taken out and interrupted by death, parcels with owners going back to the sixteen hundreds: it was all proven and made legal within these bound books of documents.

The Registry Directory referred the Argilla Road address to a book and page quite a few years back. When Kit pulled this book out of the shelves, the page revealed a death certificate filed eighteen years before for an Edward Fitch Pierce, of pneumonia, at age sixty-eight, with the property devolved to Vivian Faye Pierce, his widow. As the documents receded in time, both the language and the script—changed from computer font, to typewriter, and then to ink—were harder to decipher. Eleven years before the Edward Fitch Pierce death certificate, there was a something about a trust, and another death certificate, this time for a Whitman Fitch Pierce, age twenty, gunshot wound.

Kit lost track of what it all meant. So she carefully Xeroxed all the pages, with book and page references back to 1838, when the property seemed to have first come into the Pierce family, placed them in chronological order, and brought them back across the street.

Kit wondered if it ever occurred to Jack that the reason she could do Registry searches in the first place was because of his neighbor, Attorney Aaron Levinson. Mr. Levinson was the one who had taught her, early on, to Xerox everything she found and not to rely on memory or notes, to make a list of what she had, and then to keep the papers in the same order in which she had found them. He had even accompanied her on a few trips across the street to the Registry of Deeds to make sure she understood the nuances of the task.

Mr. Levinson's office sat at the end of the under-lit corridor. His door was thick, and unless you could spot light from underneath, it was difficult to tell if he was in, and impossible to know whether you were bothering him until you'd already intruded.

Kit knocked, and waited until she heard a faint, "Come in."

Aaron Levinson was a large, bald-headed man, with a quiet, steady gaze that made Kit careful. Every suit he wore had a vest to match, and although he often draped the jacket over the back of a chair when not with clients, he did not unbutton the vest nor loosen the tie. On days with bad weather, he didn't keep his boots on for convenience or warmth, but rather changed promptly into neatly polished shoes. In his presence, Kit had the sense that every word she spoke hit a target. That type of communicative efficiency, she had concluded, was rare. So many people didn't listen. Either they were lost in their own thoughts, like Mrs. Bergen talking to her spirits downstairs, or they did not find you important enough to really focus on, like her own boss. Or the person they thought you were scrambled their perceptions. Trey had not listened to her, and then he had become furious when she was not what he had imagined she had been, really furious.

Kit smiled as she stepped into Mr. Levinson's office, a

long, undivided room, brightened with a daylong stream of light let in by a row of high windows overlooking the parking lot.

"I hope I'm not bothering you."

Seated at a round table, manila folder opened in front of him and another pile to his side, he nodded. "Not a bother, Kit, what do you have there? Another Registry mystery?"

"I'm confused by some of the documents." She set the papers down and pulled out her list of copied pages. "The property's been in the same family since 1838. So, that's easy. But a lot of the documents are hard to figure out, there's some kind of trust, and there's this death certificate from 1967. I'm not sure why it's even here. And look, this guy, Whitman Fitch Pierce, died from a gunshot wound at a really young age, twenty or something."

Mr. Levinson frowned. "Let me see that."

Kit handed over the document.

"This is issued by the U.S. Army, Kit."

Kit looked more closely at the paper, and then compared it with the most recent death certificate, issued nineteen years later. She should have looked more carefully at the documents before running to Mr. Levinson with questions.

"What was going on in June 1967, Kit?"

"War." She hoped she didn't have to explain further because she was fuzzy on the details.

"The Vietnam War. This boy died in combat. It's here because, see here, he was the sole beneficiary of the trust, the land trust that held that property. A lot of wealthy people don't hold family properties individually, or they skip generations, especially with land that's been in the family for so long."

"So why didn't they set up another trust with new beneficiaries?"

"There could be many reasons, Kit."

She glanced at the other end of his office toward the book case, to the photos of his children, a young girl and two teenage boys, before refocusing her attention. Kit knew she needed to be careful not to discuss confidential case details with Mr. Levinson because that was privileged information. She knew also that Jack Rioux's motivations were rarely about anything but money, which did not often put her in a flattering light. Still, her goal was to evaluate the worth of the property. "So the son dies, and the father dies nineteen years later. And now, the widow owns the property, but it's hard to know the value because it really hasn't been sold in more than a hundred and fifty years. But," she added, "there are lots of acres."

"Twenty-eight acres of land is a lot, but you don't know how much of that land is marsh, and therefore unbuildable, and therefore…"

"Less valuable."

Now he smiled. "Buildable land is valuable land."

"Thanks, Mr. Levinson." She knew that he helped her with the Registry searches she made for Jack because it made her more valuable when she did her searches for him. But he also helped her because he was a nice guy and they got along. The way he always managed to match the facts to the existing rules felt as solid to Kit as the Registry building itself.

"Hey," she said. "Mrs. Bergen's been bringing in some really good leftover Halloween candy."

Mr. Levinson laughed. "Is it cursed?"

"Probably, but there are some of those marshmallow bites you like."

He patted his round stomach. "Well, I know I shouldn't, but some of those with a nice cup of black coffee would really hit the spot."

"No sooner said than done." She wished, not for the first time, that she worked for Mr. Levinson instead of Jack. At the very least, with him she never had to worry about whether she was doing something illegal, or just plain sneaky.

The morning Kit chose to investigate the property was sunless, in a white-sky, November kind of way that made her notice that the leaves had finally left the trees. The houses situated at the beginning of the road, those nearer the state highway, were all neatly numbered, and if not close together, at least separated by small stands of bush, and clearly visible from the street. As the road wound deeper into the marsh, the larger properties were hidden in the leafless forest, revealed only by slender drives and mostly numberless mailboxes. On her first pass down Argilla, Kit drove all the way to the beach without finding the Pierce home. On her way back, between ninety-seven and one fifty-six, Kit found a small drive on the even side of the road. She took it.

The drive, once paved, was deeply rutted. Branches of wintering bushes batted her car, a second-hand Ford with a custom paint job courtesy of a buddy of Trey's. Proceeding slowly to lessen the damage to her weakened shocks, she rehearsed a few explanations that might explain her presence. At this time of the morning, the old lady would probably still be in bed, if her own mother was any indication of how much people with nothing to do slept. Or maybe, just having a cup of coffee, Mrs. Pierce might spot the car. Who knew if she was even home—she could be traveling in Italy to attend operas, for isn't that the type of thing the rich did after running over people parked at the side of the road?

The tangled driveway led to a large gray colonial in sloping disrepair, the yard overgrown even in its late fall stage of shrunken plants and brown grasses. Rhododendrons grew up nearly to the second floor, and dusty windows revealed nothing of habitation inside. The front steps were laced over with a still-green, weedy vine that lapped the bottom of a heavy wooden door clearly not opened in decades. Kit turned off the engine. Clearly no one lived here. Maybe Mrs. Pierce had died; but no, if she were deceased, this property would be someone else's and that transition would have been duly recorded in the Registry.

Kit stepped out of her heated car into a gray cold unwarmed by any hint of sun. The ground was hard with last night's frost, and she felt tough little mounds of frozen dirt through her high-heeled boots, the seasonal shock of the earth not yielding. Too thin for the weather, the boots gave her inches, and prevented her from lapsing into the fashion dumpiness encouraged by months of chilly weather, items such as thick-soled boots, mannish overcoats, and bulky sweaters in reindeer patterns. As the front windows were too overgrown with bushes to allow any view in, Kit stalked the house in search of a window with a clear view, or a door that looked used.

Once she turned the corner toward the back of the house, the wind whipping in over the broad marsh was bracing. Her cloth coat, nylon blouse, and pants did little to cut the chill, but the view was liberating in its wide expanse of browns and grays: only a small stand of oaks to the left before the steady downward slant toward the marshes, which were highlighted with the dull blue line of the river as it headed to the ocean; and across the banks, the scattered shores of a small, marshy island. The biting wind only added to the sense of desolation and exhilaration of the scene, and Kit trod down a narrow but clear path through the brush and past the trees toward the water.

In her exertion, her body warmed, but her exposed skin was still chilled, so she dipped her chin into her coat collar and switched between stuffing her hands in her pockets for warmth and holding them out to her sides for balance. Just beyond the stand of trees, her sight to the marsh was straight and clear and there, a hundred yards in front of her as the path led to the marsh proper, was a figure.

Kit stopped short.

A rogue green scarf carried up in the breeze drew her

eyes to someone bending over the marsh, head bobbing up and down like a large bird, the remaining drab and formless clothing blending in almost completely with the surroundings.

Kit's first impulse was to flee, but if she was noticed, her flight would be easily followed up the leafless trail back to the house, and she would be a common trespasser, a charge she knew was like all crimes, a crime whether you knew it or not.

She then had the uneasy realization that this could be Mrs. Pierce, as there wasn't a boat or a car or another house anywhere in sight. Pushing aside as well the unreasonable feeling that this stranger had interrupted her own reverie at the view and the morning, Kit tried to gather her thoughts into a story that would explain her presence.

Unwilling to throw her voice into the morning and shout out a hello, she pushed her hands into her pockets and marched on toward the unsuspecting figure ahead. As she progressed, the path became more definably maintained. Someone had taken the time to cut back the wayward brush, to beat down the grasses. As she got closer to the figure now, the dirt gave way to a frozen, porous surface of shorn reeds. Kit hesitated, unwilling to risk getting her feet wet. The person, now clearly a woman, was thirty yards away. Some kind of clippers in hand, she was bending and cutting away the browned and dying marsh in haphazard rhythm.

She looked up at Kit. Kit waved. The woman stared at her for a few beats, and then returned to her work.

Kit took a tentative step onto the marsh. Her footing held. She knew from living in this landscape for most of her life that these marshes filled and emptied with the tide, and that a layer of ice rarely held unless it was a particularly cold spell in the deep of winter. The woman ahead wore sensible thick rubber boots, and Kit worried about ruining her own. As it was, they were now scratched and dirty.

At ten feet away, Kit stopped again. "Mrs. Pierce?" she called.

The woman stopped cutting and looked at Kit. Twisted braids of white hair lay beneath her brown woolen cap, and her green scarf continued to trail up in the wind. Her rough tan coat looked like an old, dirty version of the nice raincoats men wore over their suits. Beneath that, Kit could make out at least another sweater or two. Her hands were gloved in thick, dirty gardening gloves; her face was red with cold, and clear mucus dripped from the end of her nose. Her eyes, watery and red rimmed, were a startling deep blue.

“Mrs. Pierce?" Kit repeated.

"You're not the girl with the groceries?"

The question contained a vague accusation. Kit was torn between feigning knowledge in order to open up the conversation or distancing herself from the topic so she could make an easier break. She was conscious of having stumbled upon a landscape as frozen and unknowable as the marsh upon which she stood. "No, no I'm not," she answered.

Mrs. Pierce, if it even was Mrs. Pierce, looked Kit in the

eye. "I need my groceries."

Kit was startled into trying to at least sort out the situation. "What days does the girl come with the groceries, Mrs. Pierce?"

"I don't have my car anymore," the woman answered. She turned back to snipping. Kit glanced back and noted the long, narrow path to the water Mrs. Pierce had carefully maintained. The sky was still overcast, but a little to the east, the clouds looked thinner and brighter.

"So, that's your house up there?"

"Oh yes."

"And this is your land?"

"Of course."

"Do you have any other properties?"

"Oh yes."

Kit itched for her pen and notebook. Part of her investigating technique was in her transcription of every word so that her concentration was not wasted on trying to remember anything, but was entirely focused on the conversation at hand. "Where would those other properties be?"

"My husband has a place in town."

Kit was aware of the intense cold of the morning, and how little her coat protected her. She could be remarried, there was no reason why not, but the sinking realization that Mrs. Pierce, and it was Mrs. Pierce, it had to be, was more than a little confused was unavoidable.

A strong updraft caught Mrs. Pierce's green scarf and it sailed behind her head like a small kite. "My son's a good boy," she said. "He visits whenever I want him to."

Maybe there was another son, Kit thought wildly, one not included on any of the registry papers.

"And your son," Kit hesitated, but then she recalled the name from the death certificate and took the plunge, she could always blame the wind for confusing the sounds, "Whitman, does he come to see you?"

"Oh yes, of course."

Kit remembered her own grandmother, who had cared for her and her brother Larry for many years in place of their overwhelmed mother. As she had gotten older, she expressed herself more and more in certain repetitive phrases, phrases that encompassed a wide range of details into one observation. "Well, I'll be," she'd say, to convey the randomness that accompanies all experience. Kit watched Mrs. Pierce's scarf wander around her head as she started back to the grasses with her clippers.

She abruptly stopped and turned around; the eyes that caught Kit's were lucid. "Are you here to help?"

A flush went through Kit that registered as uncomfortable heat. She pictured Jack, how he had guided her through her initial investigations with his driven insistence that she cull every detail while giving away nothing.

Kit thought of Mrs. Appleton as she handed over the tired manila folder that held the newspaper clipping; "Fatal Crash" read the headline, and then, "No Charges Brought" in smaller type. She pictured Linda Appleton at the wake, awkward and mute in the receiving line, unsteady in her heeled shoes.

Maybe somewhere a warning would register and Mrs. Pierce would rally herself against the danger she would soon be in when Jack filed the lawsuit and her house was the only asset.

Kit looked toward the strip of blue that was the river, how the sun lightened the sky to the point of color as it poked its way through the clouds.

"No," she answered. "No, I'm not here to help."

Even with the heat blasting high from the dash, Kit could not stop the shivers. Something about that marsh breeze blew right through to inside. Agitated by the cold perhaps, her thoughts began to stir up like a cyclone, spinning faster and faster, as if Mrs. Pierce's aggravated state were contagious. The private storm of her own household bills—the mortgage, the oil, the electric, the phone, the car insurance—joined in as Kit recalculated the amounts over and over, as if the numbers might magically become manageable. She cursed her brother; Larry had been working nearly a month now and she had yet to see any of it. The electric bill, already two cycles overdue, would have to be paid soon. The company couldn't easily turn it off, but her credit would be shreds.

By the time Kit reached her office at Rioux & Rioux, she could not settle in. In winter, its northeast location kept her office chilly until well after noon. Keeping her coat, Kit first retreated downstairs to the kitchen, where large back windows let in the morning sun. The coffee pot was warm too, but Kit did not want coffee. What she really wanted was a cigarette. The sunshine was an illusion, however, for the minute she opened the back door, a brisk wind reminded her that this time of year, it gave all clear light and no heat. The desire for a smoke was stronger, though, and she huddled between the house and the cement sidewall of the back steps to avoid the breeze. Her fingers were shaking, almost too stiff to spin the metal wheel on her lighter. The nicotine, though, settled her down enough to return upstairs to the empty office.

Just settled at her desk, Kit hadn't taken off her coat when Jack burst through the door and raced toward his office. "Pimfield file!" he shouted, "The Pimfield file, now!"

Kit stood quickly. The name Pimfield didn't sound familiar, so no big money or serious crime must be involved. Jack was due at Criminal Court this morning, only four blocks down the street; he must have left the courtroom and raced here from there, looking for a criminal file. A book thumped on the floor from his office, and Jack swore. "What am I paying you for?" he shouted wildly. "Find the goddamned file!"

Kit scanned her desk while she thought. Criminal file, should have taken it last night, didn't, why? "Is that the only one you're missing?"

"Yes!"

Kit nodded, walked the four feet to the file cabinet next to the coat closet, and found the file neatly tucked between "Percy" and "Oliver." Jack must have forgotten to pull it, which meant he must have forgotten to review it, which meant no one would notice much if he just continued the case until a later date. Those guys in prison can't complain about much, after all.

"Found it!" she called out.

He raced by to grab the file.

"Call me next time," Kit yelled after him, but she figured the line at the pay phone was probably too long; at this time of the morning there was often a line of lawyers calling into their offices to let secretaries know where on the docket their cases fell, and so how much waiting around was in store for that morning. Kit had shadowed Jack to the court house on enough occasions to know that criminal law, for one, involved a lot of waiting around punctuated by quick bursts of activity. A ripe occupation for heart attacks, she mused.

Although Kit had scheduled dozens of small tasks for herself this morning, not one jumped out as interesting or important enough to tackle first. Her mind wandered to the windy marshes of the Pierce back yard, so she began to put together a file: a blue tab for a civil case; a typed information card about the client; the papers gathered neatly together with pockets and metal clips, with space left free for future court filings and documents. Kit tried to decipher what few notes Jack had taken at the initial meeting with Linda and Mrs. Appleton, aware that what she learned she could not share. Jack Rioux had warned her about the attorney-client privilege when he hired her. She had wanted to laugh at the phrase, having never heard it before, but Jack was not smiling when he'd said it. He merely stared at her over his thick mustache, lowered his dark eyebrows, and leaned forward just enough so that all will to snicker was gone. What I do here can't have legs, he had explained. Information is my merchandise and every time you open your mouth, you are giving away my merchandise.

As much as Kit knew about the family and the accident, that the night had been rainy, that the couple had stopped for an unknown reason by the side of the road, that Mrs. Pierce's car had hit them both together, she did not understand what led Linda Appleton to look for money out of the old lady, almost a year after the deaths. Was it reruns of Perry Mason? Did Larry have anything to do with it? Her brother had always wanted to be a millionaire.

Kit wrote a few notes of her own on the morning meeting. After recording the date, time, and place, her pen stopped. What exactly had she learned? Grounds were extensive, she wrote, and beautiful, she added, with views to the water. Exact value unknown at this point. Mrs. Pierce—Kit hesitated to record the odd layers the old lady had worn, and that she had asked Kit if she was bringing groceries. What could she conclude from this? That she was barely there was probably the closest to the truth, but that sounded odd, unnecessarily poetic. She wrote that Mrs. Pierce no longer drove a car, a detail she knew would make sense to Jack. This isn't a diary, she reminded herself.

Kit considered other strategies. Angela's mother, Mrs. Minnizone, worked part-time at the savings and loan in town and, if Mrs. Pierce had an account there, Mrs. Minnizone, in exchange for a juicy story, was never above looking up and sharing the account balances of strangers. Kit just had to decide how much information was enough to get Mrs. Minnizone's curiosity going.

She put her pen down and picked up the phone. Kit loved to hear Mrs. Minnizone's normally loud voice modulated down to a demure, "Union Savings, may I help you?" It must kill her to hold herself in, Kit figured, because she had seen her many times come home to the Minnizone kitchen in a cacophonous fury of comments, accusations, and stories.

"I need a quick peek, Mrs. M," Kit got right to the point. "Pierce, Vivian, in town."

"Geez, isn't that the one who ran..."

Kit rolled her eyes in frustration. God, this woman remembered everything. Since Mrs. Minnizone took pleasure in being part of the larger machinations of the business and legal worlds, Kit chose her words to that effect. "I'm calling from the law office, Mrs. M., and am not at liberty to speak about that matter at the present time."

"Gotcha honey, I'm right on it."

"Thanks Mrs. M."

By noon, Jack was still absent, and Kit couldn't face the lunchtime kitchen, which always included Mrs. Avery, Mrs. Bergen's partner in crime at Grolin & Stedges, who was sure to talk about the casserole she'd made for dinner the night before for her dyspeptic husband. Kit slipped outside, and the burst of sunshine was followed quickly by a gust of early November wind. Cursing, she pulled her coat tighter around her, and dreamed of the shearling leather beauty. Maybe she could find some variation at the Filene's in Peabody, she would have time after work to check. With her restricted budget, she hadn't bought any new fall clothes, but Larry was sure to come through with something soon. She passed by the old building being renovated where she had spotted Chris Minnizone last week lugging in pipes. She quickly pushed their brief liaison out of her mind. He had barely graduated high school and gone straight into some voc-tech program; with him, she could see, she'd be wearing inadequate coats for the rest of her life.

As she turned the corner, another gust blew through her. She hadn't really rejected him for lack of money in the future; she had planned to earn that herself. Clearly, she had just used him to get out from under Trey. Someone educated, though, would be a much better match. The wind blew, and she shuddered suddenly at the thought that college boys thought of her in the same way she looked at Chris Minnizone, someone who might always take them in, but someone too dull to take them anywhere at all. She shook this away. No, she, Kit Lavoie, was going places, going places in a good coat.

Kit fought the rush hour traffic to cross town toward Filene's. This large department store anchored a corridor of smaller stores as well as a Carmelite shrine that sat on a windswept hill the next town over. In the fine-coats selection, Kit found what she was looking for, almost an exact match to the untrained eye. The color was not as subtle, the stitching wider apart, the buttons less distinctive, but it was still a beautiful coat—sheerling lamb and brushed leather. There were two in her size. She tried one on and it fit perfectly. As the saleslady approached, Kit turned the tag on the sleeve to check the price. A fifth of the price of the *Vogue* coat, it was still expensive. When she calculated what the monthly hit would be if she put it on layaway, with reluctance, she took the coat off, and the saleslady veered in another direction. Until she saw some cash from her brother, this coat was off-limits.

The coat back on the rack, Kit couldn't resist reaching out and fingering the lamb's wool that peeked out from the cuffs, so soft and plush. Then it struck her: Linda Appleton, had she ever seen that girl in anything but jeans? Jeans and a parka in the winter? She, Kit Lavoie, might be someone who would sue someone just for the money because she could find a thousand ways to spend it, but Linda Appleton and her mother in her decades-old suits? She could not imagine them sitting down and deciding that maybe it would be nicer to have a little more cash. Kit let the sleeve drop from between her fingers. Whatever it was that drove the Appletons to Jack's office, it was more complicated than money, of that she was suddenly sure.

Seven

Larry began his workdays at the Rutherford estate near dawn. Billy insisted on a rigorous routine guided solely by the needs of the "ladies." To start, Larry cleaned the stalls after Lady Cakes and Riding High, the two mares, and Blue, the unpredictable gelding with the bandaged leg, had left the barn. He scooped each stall empty and lay down fresh hay. Some days he hosed down the barn.

Despite his initial reluctance to take the job, the work suited Larry; he patiently used the sharp edge of the shovel to pick clean the angle between the wall and the floor, and he found something comforting in shoveling the urine-and-manure–filled hay into a wheelbarrow and carting it away. When the warm straw met the cold dawn air in the compost pile by the edge of the trees, it steamed with a satisfying hiss, although sometimes the ammonia stench of a sodden clump of hay could take his breath away.

Cleaning stalls, with its daily repetitions based on basic bodily needs, was really not so different from cooking, he mused. The cook's work gets eaten and is gone in a lot less time than it takes to prepare, so if the cook wasn't somehow content in the chopping and the stirring, he had better find himself another job. Larry had never looked at a pile of green beans and worried about having to pick the ends off all of them. He had just set to it, one after another, in a sort of rhythm. It was the planning required in getting beans to the sink in the first place and then the void of completion, the what to do after the beans were done, that had always tripped him up. Here at the Rutherford grounds, though, his tasks were both basic yet necessary; there were few distractions and hardly ever any other people, and he had managed during his first weeks to be on time every day.

Each morning, Mr. Rutherford's green Mercedes passed in and out of sight down the drive through the leafless trees, like a jeweled scarab beetle shining in the sun, and was gone. From what Billy had told him, his new boss made a lot of money buying other people's businesses, and worked long hours.

On this morning in late November, the ground was too close to frozen to do any serious work on the fences, but Billy asked Larry to check on some loose slats along the far edge of the paddock. Larry loaded some nails into his jacket pocket and hooked the large hammer through a loop on his jeans, jammed his hands into the warm front pockets of his pants, and trudged through frozen tufts of dirt and dead grass. Despite the cold wind blowing steady off the water, Larry liked the winter landscape. Mr. Rutherford's land was one of a half dozen old estates off of the beach road, gracious homes situated on a strip of forested land that twisted through a large marsh. For Larry, it was the wetlands on both sides and the ocean beyond that gave this spot its peculiar sense of expanse, of being at the edge of the world; the constant breeze added to the paradoxical impression that all happened elsewhere, but all that mattered ended up here.

The horses, blanketed and communal, stood together fifty feet away. Larry knelt to inspect the weather-beaten boards. A few had loose or missing nails. He pulled one drooping slat up, held it steady, set a nail, and pounded. Before the echo of the hammer had died away, a wild whinnying followed: Blue reared high up on his back hind legs, front hooves battling the air. The horse then turned a few tight circles before racing toward Larry. When Blue got within a few yards, Larry saw clearly the impossibly wide nostrils and the crazed look in his huge eyes before he reared abruptly and headed in the other direction. Something in the look Blue gave Larry, desperate and unreachable, reminded him of Linda's face, in that first night she was atop him in the back bedroom of the party. This upset Larry so much that the hammer dropped from his hand to the ground, and he missed exactly how Billy had come into the paddock to calm the horse.

"Blue, settle!" Billy called to him in a commanding tone as he raced toward the horse, a rolled blanket in hand. When he reached Blue, the animal still pranced in an agitated manner. Billy came at him from the side in one quick motion, took hold of the halter, and covered his head and eyes with the blanket. This stopped Blue from tossing violently from side to side, and he stood, panting heavily. Billy slowly moved the horse out of the paddock and into the yard. There, the two walked in wide circles as Billy laid his hand upon the brown, sweaty neck and whispered into his flattened ear until the horse stopped shivering. Larry noticed that Blue's gait was uneven, that he wasn't putting all his weight on the bandaged front leg.

Lady Cakes and Riding High stood sentry nearby. One neighed, her voice rising and falling in, to Larry, a foreign but oddly affecting sound. A few minutes later, she neighed again. When Blue whinnied back, Billy returned him to the paddock, where Blue ran to the other horses, and the three stood in the sun.

"What did you do?" Billy's self-possession, usually turned to Larry in a warm invitation, now unnerved him.

Larry looked at the sky, the sun on its low winter arc. "I was fixing the fence?"

He pointed to the hammer. "With that?"

Larry nodded. He didn't think he'd done anything wrong.

Billy swore.

Larry thought of Linda, of her open mouth, her flared nostrils, her eyes that were seeing nothing in front of her. "I'm sorry. I didn't mean to send the horse out on a bender."

Billy shook his head, short and quick.

"I mean it was freaky. It kind of reminded me of my girlfriend." Larry stopped. He could not believe he had just said that. It wasn't even close to the truth.

But apparently Billy's attention was only on Blue.

"Anything can set him off."

"How did it happen?"

"On-field collision. Blue got away easy. They had to shoot the other horse."

Larry considered what kind of understanding Blue might have of those events.

Linda had called him just the night before, just when he had thought he would never hear from her again. Noise in the background, lots of music and talking, he hardly heard a word she said. She had woken him up from a sound sleep, so when she called it had felt like three in the morning but it was most likely not too far after midnight. Thanks for calling, he had said over and over again, but her response was lost in the din. After some kind of crash, Larry thought that maybe she'd dropped the phone, there were a few minutes of noise and then her line had gone dead.

Billy looked away. Mr. Davis, the caretaker, a weather-beaten guy of indeterminate age and few words, began to walk toward them from about fifty yards away. "I forgot to tell you, Mr. Davis wants you to put up a new barn roof."

"Sure."

"So Blue reminds you of your girlfriend?" Billy laughed, and his hair blew around his face in the wind.

“It isn’t what it sounds like,” he answered quickly. But then Larry thought of Blue's gimpy gait. "I guess you could say she got spooked too, maybe.”

Billy nodded.

“Couldn’t you have gotten hurt, getting so close to him when he was all agitated like that?”

Billy shrugged. “It comes with the territory.”

Mr. Davis shouted. Although he was less than ten yards away, his first words were lost in the wind. "A menace," Larry thought he heard him say, and worried briefly that Mr. Davis was referring to him.

Billy glanced at the approaching figure, and walked away quickly to the barn.

Mr. Davis pulled up next to Larry and spat on the ground. He grimaced, revealing a set of yellow and overlong teeth. "He can sugarcoat it all he wants but that horse is out of control."

Larry didn’t respond. He was out of his element, without a proper understanding of what was and wasn't acceptable behavior in a horse. He did say a little wish, however, that Blue's gait would improve.

When the sun dipped so low that he feared the shadows would cause him to misstep, Larry knocked off pulling battered shingles from the barn roof. Since it was just three o’clock, he made a great show of picking up the ripped shingles scattered on the ground below, in case Mr. Davis questioned his quitting time.

But, so far, almost three weeks into his new job, no one had gotten on his case about anything. There was no casual, but, to Larry, strained, bantering to partake in, no guarded answers to the usual questions. He punched no time clock, but merely showed up, did what needed to be done, and went home. Somewhere in the middle of the day, he and Billy, and sometimes Mr. Davis, scavenged lunch from the Rutherford kitchen. They didn't eat at the long table under the formal chandelier; they took their meals in a small side room, at a wooden table painted a soft, durable yellow, with matching benches built into the wall.

The early hours pushed Larry's schedule forward, so that when he arrived home by three thirty or four o'clock, he was often ready to cook dinner. Either his mom had gotten out to the grocery store to pick up the items on Larry's list, or she had not. If she hadn't, he sometimes made her go out because he was too tired or too dirty to show up in a grocery store, but sometimes he went out. He didn't mind trolling the quiet aisles of the A&P with mothers and their squalling children. Turning over packets of meat or sniffing oranges and melons distracted him in a pleasant way, as did reading the suggestions on the sides of the spice bottles.

He found, though, he could not shake off the memory of Linda's late-night phone call. They had never really broken up, but then they had never really been together. Since she had stood him up at the motel bar, he just hadn't called her. By the time he had picked up the last fallen shingle, this situation, which he hadn't fully considered before, made him uneasy, and he determined he had to talk to her.

Larry considered how best to find her. She had once been enrolled in the local commuter college, but since her sister's accident, she'd held a shifting series of part-time jobs with irregular hours and of indefinite duration. He remembered an early shift at Donutland, but she must have quit that by now because Linda had never been at her best in the early mornings. She had also had the late shift at the Cumberland Farms convenience store, as well as done stints bundling and delivering the weekly newspaper. At one point, she had talked about working for a veterinarian, but Larry wasn't sure what became of that. Now, three thirty in the afternoon, he had no idea where she would be. He could stop by her house, but he was dirty from work and would probably run into her mother, who was always at home and so sad looking that he dreaded being alone with her for fear of what she might say.

He compromised by driving by the Appletons on his way home. Not too far out of the way of his normal route, the very old colonial where Linda lived with her mother stood near the center of town, considered a more desirable location than the subdivision of small houses the Lavoies called home. Built sometime in the seventeen hundreds, it lacked the traditional charms of an older home, and retained most of the inconveniences. The rooms were small, the ceiling low, and the floors sloped. It creaked in the wind and was always freezing.

He didn't slow down, but he could see Linda's beat-up old Dart parked in the driveway. With her mother's car nowhere in sight, Larry considered turning around and dropping in. But shingle tar stained his wrists and his clothes, and he smelled like sweat and horses. Linda wasn't exactly what he would call fussy, but this was no way to make an entrance. His only viable plan was to rush home and shower and hope she was still alone when he returned.

With this in mind, he stepped on the gas.

An hour later, he was back. Now that the sun was down, the temperature had dropped accordingly. Although not the wisest choice for the weather, Larry had put on one of his favorite shirts, a silk blend with swirls of blues and grays, and then left his coat unbuttoned so that the pattern was visible. He parked in front of the house, making sure not to block the driveway. A light illuminated a top floor window, and one or two shone dimly from the small windows on the bottom floor. With no outside lamps, the yard was in shadows as he made his way to the side door both Linda and her mother used, and knocked.

As he stood waiting, he questioned what exactly he was doing, why he had showered and put on a nicer shirt. He hadn't eaten since lunch, and he was suddenly aware that he was hungry, that hunger was screaming from every overworked and underfed cell in his body. This made him cold, and he shivered in his thin shirt and pulled his jacket toward him. He knocked again and waited. Impatient, he put his hand to the doorknob and turned. The knob turned, and before he knew it, Larry had stepped into the small anteroom to Linda's kitchen where she and her mother kept their boots, umbrellas, coats, and snow shovel.

A little shocked by his sudden entry into the house, but glad to be out of the chill, he called out Linda's name to cover his tracks, as if he walked into her house every day of the week, as if his presence would be welcome and accepted without comment. "Hello, it's me, Larry," he added, and pulled the door shut behind him.

He took a tentative step closer to the kitchen. A rush of water running through pipes stopped him; embarrassed, he considered stepping back outside. Instead, he amplified his calls so that Linda would hear him as she stepped into the hall out of the bathroom, but a few more minutes passed and still there was no answer.

In the kitchen, there was no sign of a meal being prepared, no lingering smells of cooking. Perhaps no one was home, the rushing water merely some kind of refill to the heating system. Low ceilinged, dim, and cluttered, the room was lit only by a weak bulb over the stove. Unopened mail and unread papers on the small kitchen table, the chairs casually askew, this stopped him: he recognized himself as an intruder. He returned to the anteroom, had his hand on the knob when he heard footsteps on the stairs, wooden and creaky. Quickly stepping outside, he now hoped that Linda was nowhere near the house, had for some reason taken her mother's car out, and Mrs. Appleton would appear, confused and maybe awoken from a nap, or in some similar condition from which he could easily escape.

Just then Linda appeared in the anteroom and peered through the window, a white specter of blond hair beyond the cold condensation crawling up the glass.

This sight unnerved him and he opened the door. Her hair was wild, unkempt, at odd angles from her head, spilling over the too-large red plaid bathrobe she clutched at her neck. Her skin was ghostly pale, and she wore no shoes, just heavy gray socks that made her calves look thick.

"What the hell?" she swore, a sentiment that mirrored Larry's reaction exactly. "But the cold feels good," she added, and fanned with the edges of her tatty bathrobe. Larry wondered briefly how such a mannish, oversized, intimate garment made its way to the Appleton house, consisting in its happiest years of only a mother and two girls. Linda padded back into the kitchen and collapsed into one of the chairs set near the table, a shaky metal match to the three others, all covered seats cracked and baring their stuffing.

"Catching up on your sleep?" Larry ventured.

"Nope. I just feel like crap."

"The flu maybe?"

"Who knows."

He walked over to her and put a hand to her forehead. No heat, but her skin felt dry. "When's the last time you drank anything?"

"When I could keep it down."

"Today. What did you drink today?"

"You a doctor now? In that pimpy shirt? I don't know. I can't keep anything down."

"Tea?"

Linda quickly put her hand to mouth and gagged.

"You gotta pick something or you'll really be sick. Soup?" Larry pulled open a loose cabinet door next to the sink and rummaged through the detritus of what might have been a baking shelf.

"Watch out for the mousetraps," Linda warned.

Larry pulled his hand back to his chest. "Geez!"

"For the mice," she added.

"The what?"

"They came in with the cold, we could hear them scampering around, and I put down some traps."

He switched cabinets, rooted around gingerly before he found some bouillon cubes. In the refrigerator, he discovered two carrots, drying but still workable, and in five minutes he had a soup simmering on the stove.

Linda watched him listlessly, her head bent over on her folded arm.

He cleared a spot on the table and lay down a bowl. Linda lifted a spoon of broth to her nose, sniffed, and then ventured a small taste. She quickly finished the bowl, and ate one more before the soup ran out. "What's with the outfit?" she asked.

Tempted to ask her the same question, he held his tongue, figuring she was sick, and riling her up wasn't fair.

"I don't know. Where's your mother?"

She snorted, opened her robe a bit to reveal generous portions of her chest. "What? You came here to get some?"

Even with her matted hair and ooze of sickness, there was something rakish about her.

“Come on, Linda. Why do you have to talk like that?"

"Like what?"

He was beginning to regret reviving her.

"Like I’m only here to hump you, for one thing."

"I don't know."

Her answer surprised him. He looked at her. She really did look awful.

"What are you doing here?" she asked again.

"Because you called me?"

Her hands dropped between her knees; she gave him a hard stare. "That was good soup, thanks." She put her hands on her knees and stood. "I need a shower. You can stay," she added.

Although he was hungry, he followed her up the crooked, narrow stairs to the second floor. A thin, beaten rug lay on the landing. Larry had never been upstairs in Linda's house before, so when she disappeared into the bathroom, he was unsure which of the three remaining doors led to her bedroom.

The ivory paint, plain brown doorknobs, and quiet hall gave no clues, so he opened the door at the end of the hall. This room was dark, and the drawn shades let in no ambient light from outside. He opened the door wider to let in light from the hall, felt along the wall for a switch. But he could tell even in the dark that the room was spare, neat almost, with a wide bed and uncluttered dresser, clearly Mrs. Appleton's room, not Linda's. He closed the door gently, although the shower was on and Linda could not hear him. Mrs. Appleton's room eliminated, he opened the next door with confidence—a glimpse of a pink curtain confirmed his hunch, and when again no light switch was on the wall, he walked toward the bed to fumble at the small lamp set on a bedside table. Once the light was on, he knew he had made a terrible mistake. A pink flowered patchwork bedspread stretched neat across the bed, a small pink dog nestled on the pillow, an empty desk, a few trophies shaped like pianos—this was Janelle's room. A sharp chill went through him as he took in her presence and then moved as quickly as he could to turn out the light and shut the door behind him on this tomb resting between her mother and her sister. How could he have forgotten Janelle?

The shower shut off. The next room had a light shining under the door; how had he not noticed that before? Once he stepped in, he was chastened that he had even considered the other orderly rooms could have possibly belonged to Linda. Faded yellow wallpaper with twists of green indicated an original decorative intent, but its occupant had strayed so far from that domestic impulse that even the yellow curtains were half pulled off their rod. With the only chair hidden under a mound of clothes and papers, he headed for her bed, where the clutter was more easily pushed aside so he could sit on a piece of the bedding. Scattered mugs and cups littered the surface of her dresser and bedside table, and the small yellow lamp poking up from the clutter was a mirror of the pink one in her sister's room next door. As he was kicking away some clothes on the floor to clear a spot for his feet, Linda reappeared, pink from the shower and wrapped in a light blue towel. With luck, Larry hoped, the ratty bathrobe had made its way into a trash can. With her hair flat on her head revealing the features of her face, her wide brown eyes approached kind. She sat down on a lump of clothing on the bed, next to him, and he toyed with the hair that fell down her back. "You're all wet," he said. "You're going to catch pneumonia."

She took the towel from where she had tucked in one end near her armpit, unwound the material, sat up briefly to free the rest of it, and handed it to him. "Here," she answered, "you can dry me off."

Her skin damp and vulnerable, Larry gently patted her shoulders. After ten seconds, she tugged impatiently at his jacket, "Come on," she wheedled, "take something off."

She flipped around and sat in his lap, her legs straddled to either side. He tried to push her gently off of him. "Aren't you supposed to be sick?" he complained. She pushed him backwards on the messy bed and pulled at his pants. He maneuvered around some half-eaten toast and sighed. All you could do with Linda was to let her run her course. His attention wandered.

"What's going on," Linda wheedled.

He closed his eyes and recalled Billy's back, reflecting an orange glow from the fireplace.

"That's more like it," she said, and climbed on top of him.

This Linda thing has got to stop, vowed Larry. When she had had enough, Larry wrapped her in her random collection of sheets and blankets. He gathered up what cups and bowls he found around the room and, before he left, he kissed the top of her still-damp head. She swatted at him, like his caress was a mosquito irritating her in her sleep.

Before he left the house, he washed those dishes and whatever else was lying about and left them to dry in the rack. Looking around at the darkened kitchen and its emptied shelves, Larry wished there was some way he could have cooked something for Mrs. Appleton too without having to talk to her or explain what it was exactly that he was doing there.

Eight

As the autumn dark galloped in, a round yellow moon shone on the familiar array of Minnizone cars spread over the front yard—Chris's rebuilt Ford truck, Angela's repainted Pacer, and Mr. M's mint-green Chevy.

Kit hesitated at the curb, her car idling.

She and Angela had been close ever since they had been thrown together in a middle school social studies class and given the task of creating a Puritan village. The Minnizone home had been a warm and friendly place in which to create their diorama of toothpicks and clay, and Kit had quickly been adopted into their family routines, in which meals appeared like clockwork on the kitchen table, and the TV was turned off at ten on school nights.

It had been Kit's grandmother, though, who had been the driving force behind both the girls being the first in their families to go to college. And while Kit had initially landed the bigger prize of a scholarship to a more prestigious school, it was Angela, studying accounting and due to graduate the following spring from the local commuter college, who was going to be the one to get an actual degree. Yet if either Angela or any other Minnizone thought any less of Kit for this failure, Kit never felt it.

Tonight, Angela was insistent that they go out, insistent that she meet "someone." For Angela, who never went in much for casual dating, to make such an announcement was an event. Kit, though, couldn't shake feeling weary. Maybe, she told herself, she was just worried about getting the electric bill caught up before the onset of the winter heating cycle.

Kit yawned, and stepped out of the car. The back porch light popped on. Dried stalks and stems lay in neat piles at the side of the yard, the gardens now brown and square and bare for the winter. Mrs. Minnizone's head appeared at the window, the curtain drawn back. Kit braced the chilly night and went up the side steps.

Mrs. M. opened the side door into the kitchen in hushed hurry. A petite, bustling woman, she pulled Kit inside and, before she shut the door, glanced around the yard as if to check if Kit were followed. "Nine thousand three hundred sixty-four dollars and twenty-seven cents. That's it," she said in a low voice.

"Are you sure?" asked Kit, quietly. "There was only one account?"

Mrs. M. tugged her cardigan sweater across her chest and briefly patted her curly, graying hair. "Not too much for a rich lady, heh?"

Kit had to agree.

She leaned in closer to Kit. "It's probably all in Switzerland," she stage whispered.

Kit tried to picture the figure on the marshes managing complex bank accounts, and couldn't.

“So, tell me.”

Kit begged off, "I don't know too much, Mrs. M."

"Pah," she exhaled sharply. "Of course you do. Your brother's dating the sister, isn't he?"

For simplicity's sake, Kit ignored Mrs. M's purposeful ignorance of her brother's romantic inclinations.

Mrs. M. put her hand on her chest. "It was terrible, terrible what happened to that girl. I pray for the mother every night. Why shouldn't she get a little money to help her along her way?"

Chris came into the kitchen. Kit noted the scruffy beginnings of a beard.

Mrs. M. caught Kit's glance. "Will you look at him? He looks like a lumberjack with all that hair on his face."

Chris shrugged.

Kit smiled. "I kinda like it."

"It's Julia's influence," said Mrs. M. with a sly look at Kit.

With this casual introduction, Kit felt an unreasonable betrayal seep into her.

Chris briefly returned the scrutiny before he stepped to the refrigerator and opened the door, back to both women. What did you expect, Kit cursed herself, that Chris Minnizone would spend twenty years in monastic seclusion after a few encounters with the marvelous Kit Lavoie?

Chris lifted a quart of milk to his mouth and chugged.

"Hey!" protested Mrs. M.

In his haste, some dribbled out of his lips, crawled down

his new beard, under his chin, and onto his neck.

Kit couldn't help herself. "Is that Julia's influence too?"

Chris burped.

"What an articulate comeback."

Chris smiled with satisfaction. "Kit, Kit, I always said you were a sweet-tempered girl."

"Knock it off," said Mrs. M, as if she had nothing to do with this imbroglio.

Angela stepped into the kitchen and, from her quick look toward her mother and brother, Kit knew the conspiracy was complete. No one had wanted to tell her about this Julia. To express any frustration at this realization would only confirm their initial fears, so Kit relied on a familiar strategy: she pretended not to care.

"Hey, Angie." She turned toward Angela and opened her coat. "Look at this new bra I got at Filene's."

Angela's expression quickly became awe. "How did you do that? They look huge!"

As Chris and Mrs. M. shifted imperceptibly toward Angela, Kit kept her back to them. She leaned forward and shifted her shoulders to demonstrate. "Look, they hardly move. It's this special wiring. Feel it."

"It's so stiff," said Angela. "Isn't it uncomfortable?"

"Don't you even think about it, young lady!"

Kit smiled back at Mrs. M. "Come on and take a look, I'm wearing a sweater over it."

Chris returned the milk to the fridge. "Angela doesn't need stuff like that anymore, anyway."

Bingo, thought Kit. Angela did find someone. "The store

clerk told me that brides are buying these off the shelves," Kit said lightly.

Mrs. M. couldn't resist. She hurried over and pried her fingers down the front of Kit's sweater and into the wiring. "Look, Angel," she said. "You could wear one of those off the shoulder numbers with this bra."

"Do you think I could, Kit?"

Angela was pixie thin, and Kit doubted her small shoulders would carry the look, but her friend's expectant look molded her answer. "With a little bit of sleeve, maybe" said Kit. "It would be nice to meet the groom, though."

"Angela was afraid you'd gnaw his head off," remarked Chris.

"Come on and take a look yourself," Kit snapped. "Maybe Julia would like one."

Mrs. M. gave Kit a light swat across the head. "Don't be a bad girl."

"Why not?" She closed her coat demurely. "It's more fun."

"I didn't plan for you not to meet him, there just never was a good time," Angela said once they were alone in the car. She pulled a cigarette from her bag. "Want one?"

"Nah. Larry wants me to quit."

Angela laughed. "Too messy?" She lit hers and leaned back against the padded denim seat covers Kit had bought on sale last spring.

Kit turned on the heat and a blast of cold hit their faces.

She banged at the dashboard with her palm.

"Too bad Trey's friend wasn't a mechanic instead of a detailer." Angela threw the name out casually, as if they hadn't spent years discussing Kit's messy breakup.

Kit made herself smile. "Come on, you have to admit that sky blue's the perfect color for a Ford."

"I wanted to tell you right away about Matt. I just got too far into it," Angela continued. "And I knew you'd wonder why I kept him hidden, and question me about it, and I don't know what else."

Kit fiddled with the defroster and the blower.

"Wait another mile, Kit. It's really not so bad." Angela's hands gripped her elbows and her legs were tightly crossed.

"Liar," said Kit. "You're freezing." Then, "You probably just kept him to yourself until you were sure."

"You just always have something to say, Kit, about everything. Sometimes it can be, I don't know, kind of intimidating, I guess."

"That's what Trey told me. That I always have to open my trap."

The car was warming up. Angela shifted in her seat toward Kit. "Come on, Kit, that's not what I meant."

Kit fought the impulse to ask about this Julia person Mrs. M. had mentioned in the same sentence as Chris. She knew that Angela secretly wished she would end up with her brother, so she would wait for that information, until Angela told her everything without realizing how much Kit wanted to know. "I know it's not that you're afraid that I'd steal him away, what with my track record."

Angela looked out the side window. "You can be a little scary to guys, I guess."

Kit had not expected that response. How could saying what she was thinking be scary to anyone? She didn't have any power, any money, any control. Why did people listen to her if they didn't like what she said? "Trey didn't have any trouble pushing me around."

"Sure he did. That's why he treated you so bad."

The car warmer now, Kit pulled impatiently at the top buttons of her coat. By that logic, Trey only yelled at her, threatened her, threw her around because she was hard to handle, and deserved it. Kit couldn't believe that's what Angela meant. Angela hated Trey, hated him with the passion of a best friend. But Kit had considered more than once that she piqued the worst in him. Why would an outwardly normal guy just flip on her if she hadn't done something to provoke him?

"I know I shoulda told you about Matt."

"OK, so tell me now."

"We OK?"

"OK." Kit rubbed Angela's leg. "You getting warmer over there?"

"Kit, he's nice. I don't want what you want, I just want a family, and I don't need exciting."

Kit resisted pointing out that the comparison made no sense—Angela was only trying to make her feel better. Kit didn't know what she wanted anyway. She only recognized what she didn't like, a limitation she couldn't seem to find her way out of.

The Green Street Pub in Salem, equidistant between Angela's state college and Rioux & Rioux, operated in a forgotten block, with a small-parts machine shop and a couple of unrented storefronts for neighbors. A weathered wood interior hinted at a barn, but the lowered ceilings and a lingering scent of beer quickly dispelled any bucolic notions. Dinner was served to those able to afford steak tips or the fiery barbeque chicken, and these diners lingered in their seats while the band set up. By the time Kit and Angela arrived, the bar tables were already taken in a crush of bodies. The heat was so intense in contrast to the cold evening that they both immediately took off their coats. Kit instantly attracted attention in an uncomfortable way. She could feel eyes glance off her face and drop to her chest.

"You need a seat, ladies?"

It's just a bra, you idiot, Kit wanted to answer, but Angela grabbed her arm, hard. "Help me look for Matt." She searched the room with a glazed expression Kit had not seen since high school when Angela had developed a serious crush on the boys' soccer coach, a charming Brazilian.

"Check, check," the band's sound person punctured the din. "Check, check."

Kit glanced toward the tiny spot the band had cleared for themselves between the bar and the corridor to the bathrooms. A thin man with shaggy black hair placed a microphone atop a metal stand, burning cigarette at the corner of his mouth. She briefly wondered whether he considered the Green Street merely a stop on the way to rock 'n roll glory. Something, though, about the way he paused to run his hands through his hair before he sank the butt under his shoe made Kit think he'd set up once too many times for the ritual to hold any illusions.

"What about that guy?" Kit pointed to the sound man, but Angela was steps ahead of her, leaning over to place a kiss on a closely shorn man seated at a small table near the back. Angela's hair hid his face, so Kit couldn't catch how he received her affection.

"Kit, this is Matt."

Kit looked at this Matt. Thick and large boned, Matt wasn't fat, but Kit was sure that someday he would be. Since Trey, she had distrusted men with any weight on them.

"Hi," he said, and nodded. Kit noticed that his eyelashes were yellow. She wondered if dark Angela might have blond children.

Angela smiled unaccountably. She gestured toward Matt's companion. "Kit, this is Derrick."

With a calm imperviousness that bordered on the stolid, Derrick nodded in her direction, and returned to his beer. Well, thought Kit, at least they haven't arranged some sort of blind double date.

"Have you been here long?" Angela asked as she sat.

They shook their heads.

Kit looked to the small stage. Perhaps the music would begin soon.

Derrick sipped his beer.

"So, Angela," asked Kit, reluctant to trap herself in the

empty seat next to Derrick, "you want to come get some sea breezes?"

"What the hell's a sea breeze?" chortled Derrick.

"Girl drink," said Matt.

"I'll just stay here," said Angela. She patted Matt's arm.

"You don't want a drink?" he asked her.

"I guess I'll have a beer."

"She'll have a beer," said Matt.

"You don't mind?" asked Angela.

"Not as long as I get my tip," said Kit.

She wound her way through the maze of tables to the end of the bar where the waitresses placed their orders, and there was less of a crowd. She held up her hand. "Sea breeze," she called out. "And a Rolling Rock." A large guy on his way to the men's room jostled her from behind. A few feet away, the guitarist strummed heavily, and the band took off in a wailing roar of sound so loud it felt like it was inside her head.

Drinks in hand, on the route back to Angela, Kit noticed that the sound check man was also the drummer.

Kit loved music for the way it took her out of herself—sometimes listening was like being alone on a boat on a rolling ocean, invigorating and exciting--but in her exhaustion, all she heard was a wall of sound. It was too loud to talk. Kit mouthed, "Want some?" when Angela eyed her drink, but Angela shook her head no, and raised her beer bottle.

She began to sympathize with silent Derrick. Maybe he had trailed after the happy couple for one too many evenings. Kit sipped her drink. When it was gone to ice cubes, she left the table for the bathroom.

The bathroom was dimly lit with an overhead light covered in an ancient-looking plastic ball. The stall doors were crooked and the floor was chipped paint over cement. Water ran only cold, and Kit looked around for some kind of heating vent because the room was freezing. She checked herself out in the small circle of a mirror over the sink. Her mascara had blurred, and the crisp look she'd aimed for had been replaced by something that was a cross between too little sleep and two black eyes. This, with the aggressive bra and tight sweater, made her look slightly trampy, which made her laugh because that was far from what she was feeling. She cursed her cheap make-up and vowed to save more efficiently to buy the fancier department store make-up the first chance she got, and then she wet her fingers to fix her eyes.

The band had taken a break while she was in the bathroom. The crush at the end of the bar blocked an easy exit, and she hesitated in the narrow, chilly corridor. The drummer leaned against the opposite wall, smoking. He silently offered over his pack. His eyes crinkled in a way that made him look smart.

She pulled out a cigarette.

"Bad habit," he noted. "You ought to quit."

She laughed and blew the smoke straight up in a neat, tight stream. "OK, doctor."

"I'm serious," he continued. "Me, it's all I've got left, but you've got no excuse." He pointed to her chest. "Sure, it's all pretty on the outside, but what's happening on the inside?"

Kit considered her companion. Tight black jeans on legs with no meat, but arms built up from the drumming, she supposed. Why were these rocker types all so skinny? Didn't they eat? And the hair, sure it was long, but it was straggly and gave the impression of hiding a face. How old was this guy?

"I see you're using the smoke to blow off the steam."

She smiled in spite of herself. "How much do you charge an hour for that psychological bullshit?"

He laughed, a throaty, phlegmy kind of noise that was half cough. "When we were in Amsterdam the groupies were a lot more agreeable."

She squinted in disbelief.

"Yeah, I'm not pulling your leg. We did two European tours with this band."

She leaned back against the wall and took another drag. "For real?"

"For real. We had a hit on the overseas charts."

She would have liked to tell him that she liked their music but she hadn't paid much attention.

"It's just that the lifestyle's so glamorous, I can't seem to give it up."

She snorted.

"But the nine-to-five shit is suicide."

Kit nodded without quite agreeing. She regarded the schedule of her job as a refuge, borders carved into an otherwise chaotic circus. She thought of her mother, rolling out of bed at uneven hours, her day dictated by her soap operas, the weather, her mood, all that freedom blurring one day into the next, with no discernible accomplishment or change. Maybe it would be different if music ordered your life. But here he was, on a Friday night, in some crummy bar in a town whose better days were fifty years ago.

"Can you make a living doing this?" She gestured with her cigarette.

"Depends on what you call a living, sweetheart."

Kit wasn't about to let discussion of economic details be dismissed, she who spent so much time worrying about them. "Rent," she listed. "Heat, electricity, gas, car insurance, phone, food, clothing."

"Ah," he answered, "we've got a ballbuster here."

Kit was instantly, unaccountably furious. As the fury threatened toward wet eyes, she took a deep breath to spare herself that embarrassment.

The drummer moved quickly to her side of the small hallway. "Hey," said. "I meant it as a compliment."

He pulled her into the crook of his arm, like a grandfather, Kit thought, except she had never known any of her grandfathers. He smelled like smoke and beer. "Here's the part where I coo like a pigeon," he said. "And you feel better."

She laughed, wiped her eyes with the back of her hand, careful not to resmudge her mascara.

"Besides," he continued, "we all need our balls busted once in a while. Most people don't have the courage in the first place, or they run out of energy for it."

Angela chose this moment to find her. "Kit?" she said, in a way that meant what the hell, I leave you for two minutes and you're in the hallway with a drummer.

"This is Angela."

The drummer straightened. "Tony," he answered.

Angela smiled wanly, and turned to Kit. "Kit, you were gone for so long I thought something happened. Matt wants to go find something to eat."

"She's coming," answered Tony, "aren't you Kit?"

Kit stamped out her cigarette. "Sure I am, Tony."

"And you'll be back next week. We can talk more about Amsterdam."

Kit laughed. "Sure." But she didn't look at him when she walked away because she thought she had liked him a little too much, and an impoverished drummer could only be a step down for her. But she reached her hand back as she walked away, and wiggled her fingers in the direction where he stood.

On the way home, the car seemed colder because Angela wasn't in the passenger seat, but it might have been that the heat chose not to cooperate. Kit hoped, for the sake of the budget, that the heat would stay cranky and not quit altogether.

When she pulled up in the drive, the lights in the living room were on. Kit feared it was her mother since Larry had been keeping such early hours. Ruby didn't care much for the late-night talk shows, and the TV movies were long over by now. If her mother was still up, she most likely had received another telephone call from Kit's dad threatening not to send the alimony check, or one of her so-called friends had kindly shared a gossipy tidbit about the replacement, as Larry called their father's second wife. Larry had long rid the house of liquor after he and Kit had come home one too many times to find their mother sobbing on the couch, drunk on whatever bottle she had come across. Ruby wasn't picky, but neither was she desperate enough to drive out to get herself something if it wasn't already available, which made Kit conclude that alcohol wasn't one of her mother's demons. Self-pity and lack of will were probably closer to the bull's-eye, Kit had reasoned, followed by an inability to judge people's character, and trailed by the caboose of sheer laziness.

Kit slammed the car door. As the echo waved through the quiet neighborhood, she hugged herself against the cold and looked at the stars, sharp in the late fall air. Thanksgiving was coming up, and Kit would like nothing better than to spend it in a lounge chair, with a frozen drink, at a hot beach in the sun, not that she'd ever been to a tropical island, but it gave her a good feeling to think about the possibility. She opened the side door, let herself into the lit kitchen. No one but her turned out any lights in this house, she cursed, because no one but her paid any of the bills.

She could hear the low-volume laughter of the TV on in the living room, but no harkening voice called out. Kit had only managed one sea breeze throughout the evening, but her day had begun almost eighteen hours earlier and she was tired. She ran a glass of water from the tap and peered around the corner. One glass emptied, Kit filled another, this time less quietly. Still no one called out to her. She stepped into the living room.

The Tonight Show was still on, and Larry had fallen asleep on the couch, fists curled under his chin, stocking feet hung off to the side. The heat was turned down for the night, but Larry was wearing one of his silk dress shirts, flashy and thin, more appropriate for June than November. His skin looked blue and cold. She nudged the bottom of his feet with her knee, but he barely stirred. She set down her glass of water on the coffee table, went to the hall closet, and returned with a blanket, which she spread over him and tucked as best she could around him and into the cushions.

Even though Kit was almost two years older than her brother, she never remembered a time without him. When their father had left, when their mother had spent long weeks locked in her bedroom, when their grandmother had died so quickly at the end of her senior year, she had never been alone. Even when Trey had caused all that trouble at school, it was Larry she'd called to come pick her up and bring her home, Larry who had driven her back and forth so she could take her final exams without having to go back to dorms and explain herself to her neighbors, and Larry who had helped her move out. None of that had been too much for him.

She picked up her water and turned off the TV, the

house suddenly so still she could hear the lights flickering from the cheap overheads in the kitchen. She hated those overheads, installed years ago as a bargain, long purplish bulbs that gave unflattering and dimmed light. Even Larry preferred working near the light over the stove, corralling all his chopping and arranging into one tiny cone of illumination.

Curious about why Larry was wearing his nice shirt to watch TV and crash on the couch, Kit sensed a mystery and lingered over her brother. He hadn't been going out much since his new horse job began. He didn't talk much about it, which was another mystery. He hadn't yet complained about a stickler boss, or an annoying co-worker. And Larry had never been drawn to cats or dogs, never mind horses.

Kit thought she saw him shiver. He was going to freeze out here, with just one blanket and that ridiculous shirt.

He turned onto his side and opened his eyes. "Whoa, Kit." He felt for the blanket, squinted at her. "You turning into Florence Nightingale?"

"Hardly. Must have been mom."

"Not really her thing, though, blankets, comfort."

"Maybe she caught a sentimental vibe." Kit yawned. "I thought you were her, though, when I drove up and all the lights were on, like the house was a Christmas tree or something."

Larry waved his hands, fingers splayed, on either side of his suddenly grinning face. "Did I tell you about the time I auditioned for *A Thousand Clowns*?"

Kit laughed out loud, although Larry had imitated their mother like this many times.

Larry smiled half-heartedly. "There's nothing left in the house for her to drink."

"Yeah, well. You can never be too sure."

"Lucky you, sis, it's just me." He wrapped the blanket tightly around him. "I've been freezing all day."

Kit sat, put her heels on the coffee table and crossed her feet. "Why are you wearing that shirt?"

He looked guilty, but shrugged.

"You go out?"

Larry yawned. "Here comes the inquisition."

"I do not ask too many questions!"

He reached out and grabbed her ankle. "Come on, Kit. You invented the question mark."

She laughed. Somehow when Larry said it, it didn't seem so hard to take. "I saw this great coat at Filene's, almost a perfect knock-off of the one I loved in *Vogue*, lambskin, fleece lining, beautiful buttons, wide stitching."

Larry perked up. "How was it dyed?"

"A nice soft tan, perfect for me."

"You should have grabbed it."

She kicked at him, caught him on the knee. "Do you have any idea how overdue the bills are? I cannot carry this place myself, you know, even if every penny went to the house. If Dad stopped his checks to Mom, we'd be out on the street. We may soon be anyway."

He shifted on the couch. "I buy a lot of the food."

"You eat a lot of the food," she snapped.

"I'm not making a fortune."

"Do you think I am? Do I go around town in out-of-season fancy silk shirts?"

Larry laughed. "You want to borrow my shirt? I don't think grays flatter you, though. And, it would be too big."

"Come on, I'm serious. I need money." But the anger seeped out of her. The lights flickered in the kitchen, and the tan curtains onto which Kit had meticulously sewn a two-inch black border several years ago looked drab, not smart at all. "Larry, don't you worry about things?"

"I'm worried about Linda."

This took her by surprise. His connection with Linda Appleton had felt off since the beginning. She wondered if he knew about the Appleton visit to the law firm, but she wasn't about to pump her brother for information that would benefit Jack Rioux. "Why?"

"Well, she was sick tonight, for one thing, and her skin was like paper when I got there."

Kit hesitated. "Like paper?"

"Yeah, you know, like paper."

"So what did you do?"

"I gave her some water and some soup, that's what I did. She was so dehydrated, and she had no idea." He shook his head.

Larry picked up the strangest information. As far as Kit knew, he had never even put on a Band-Aid and here he was dispensing medical advice. "You're not…"

Larry leaned his head back, closed his eyes. "Are you kidding me?"

"That's not what I meant," but she watched him carefully. Something about Larry had shifted lately, almost as if he'd brightened.

Larry opened his eyes with a start and sat up straight, blanket still wrapped around his broad shoulders. "This is what we'll do, we'll invite her and her mother here for Thanksgiving."

A thick gloom settled on Kit at the mere mention of the holiday. "No, Larry..."

"Why? I'll do the cooking."

"Please, I hardly know them."

"Kit, it's their first Thanksgiving since, you know."

Kit hated the holidays with a vengeance, but something about the expression on her brother's face made her hold her tongue. Sadness maybe, but it also looked like confusion or a struggle. More to the point, though, she figured that the Appletons would never come, that they would have somewhere else to go. Everyone always seemed to have somewhere to go. "OK," she relented. "If you do everything."

"Thanks, Kit." He stood up and flung the blanket across his shoulders. "I shall prepare a feast!"

We can't afford a feast, she thought, but her brother's gleeful mood stopped her from saying what she was thinking. She did, however, turn out every one of the lights before she went to bed.

Nine

Janelle Appleton's bedroom haunted Larry: the flowered patchwork quilt pulled tight over the empty bed, the solitary pink stuffed dog set against the pillow, the dusty piano trophies, the bedside lamp, a rose version of Linda's lemon yellow. When he thought of Linda and Mrs. Appleton sleeping on either side of that eerie emptiness, he understood why there was nothing in their cupboards but mousetraps.

It was these empty cupboards that led him to invite the two to Thanksgiving dinner. It never occurred to him that they might refuse, so clear was the picture he had formed of the meal, all of them sitting together around a table covered with food that he had labored to cook to perfection. He would convince Kit to do the decorating; once she accepted that there were guests, she might get carried away in the project, buy some flowers or place mats.

On the Wednesday before the holiday, the sky low with clouds, Larry arrived to work a little earlier than usual. Inside the barn, a dim light shone from the bulb hanging just outside the tack room. The door ajar, Larry found Billy half-asleep on a cot. A small heater purred and the room was warm and smelled faintly of sleep and Billy's sweat in the night, an acrid odor that mixed in an intense way with the fresh hay piled just a few feet away. Larry paused at the threshold, confused. Was this where Billy lived?

Billy turned his face toward him and smiled. He closed his eyes, and then patted the seat next to him on the cot, still messy with slept-in blankets. Larry's heart sped up as he sat down next to him on the thin mattress. As their arms touched, Larry scooped him up.

"Whoa there," Billy laughed quietly.

"Can't stop me now."

After a long while, Billy said, "Don't fall head over heels for the first guy you meet."

Larry tried to sort through how to answer this. "Mr. Rutherford?"

"You got it."

Larry grimaced.

"Come on, he's not so bad," Billy protested. "I got this great job out of it."

"It's all about the horses," Larry repeated what Billy had said to him. There are horses all over, he could have pointed out, but didn't because he knew how Billy felt about the crazy horse, Blue. Larry wondered if it was possible to be jealous of a horse. If he were to be jealous of anyone, it should probably be Mr. Rutherford.

"But now, the cot?" he asked Billy.

"I guess until it gets too cold in here," answered Billy lightly, and he stood. The horses needed to be let out of the barn.

Later in the morning Billy stood by the paddock to watch Blue. "Look," he called to Larry. "See how skittish he is." Blue ran solo along the far reaches of the pasture, back and forth at the edge of the far fence. Larry looked for signs of limping on the damaged front leg, but the horse galloped on uneven ground at some distance away, and he could discern nothing. Lady Cakes and Riding High huddled together fifty yards away.

"Looks like the others don't want to be near him today," said Larry.

Billy didn't take his eyes off Blue. "I'll be needed up at the house today, so you can clean up the stalls." He ran his fingers through his tousled hair. "Don't worry about Mr. Davis and that roof, but give yourself a full day's pay." He turned to Larry and smiled in a way that brought Larry right back to the barn cot twenty minutes ago. "We'll call it a holiday bonus."

Larry felt a childish glee in the shape his day was taking, and saw that he could easily be at the supermarket before one o'clock to begin his shopping. Then, he pictured Billy on his solo cot in the tack room. "I'm cooking tomorrow," he said suddenly. "Come on by."

Billy turned briefly to Larry and then back to Blue. "You having a crowd?"

Larry worried then quickly dismissed the thought that maybe Linda still thought she was his girlfriend. "No, just my mother, my sister, and some other…"

"Lost lambs?"

"Yeah," he laughed. "Lost lamb dinner. But I'm serving turkey."

When Billy disappeared into the big house, Larry pulled the wheelbarrow through the wide side door of the barn and positioned it just outside Lady Cakes' stall. Had Billy moved out of the big house? How long had he been there? He wanted to ask Billy all this, but was afraid to, maybe afraid of the answers.

He filled the wheelbarrow with load after load of the sodden hay. He recalled the familiar way Billy worked his way around Mr. Rutherford's kitchen, how he knew where to find the placemats for the dining room table, the familiarity with which he had stretched out on the large upstairs bed, covered in thick red material with the trimmings of gold brocade. The thought of Billy in that bed with Mr. Rutherford was so distasteful that he put it out of his mind as quickly as possible.

At noon, Larry parked the wheelbarrow back in its spot and stood at the barn door to survey the scene. Blue stood with the other horses, their heads turned toward Billy who, changed and cleaned up, was walking back to the paddock, apples in his hands.

On the edge of the property, Mr. Rutherford's green Mercedes crawled up the drive, home early, perhaps for the Thanksgiving holiday. Three well-dressed men, Mr. Rutherford and two companions, stepped out of the car and made their way quickly to the interior of the big house.

Billy fed an apple to Blue, then Lady Cakes, and finally Riding High, and their large, wet lips smothered his palm when they took their treat. He then wiped his hands on his pants and walked back up to the house.

Larry chose this time to leave. Barn cleaned, hay restocked, horses happy, Larry was more consumed by the question of how large a turkey he should buy and whether he had the cash to do the whole meal right than by his employer's idiosyncrasies.

When Larry came into the house with his first load of bags from the grocery store, Kit and their mother were in the kitchen, smoking. They flicked their cigarettes down the drain and turned to him, fake smiles stretched across their faces and telltale blue fog lingering along the ceiling.

He scowled.

"Do you need any help, sweetie?" asked his mom. "It looks like you bought a lot of stuff. We can't eat all that by ourselves," she continued, her voice swerving upwards in a trill. Ruby had hated the holidays since the divorce, but it was also fair to say that she had never liked them in the first place. Their demands were just too much work for her, a person for whom daily maintenance presented enough challenge.

Larry shifted the bags in his arms. "How can I prepare food in here when I've got the nicotine twins poisoning my kitchen?" He turned to his mother. "You promised me you wouldn't smoke in the house anymore."

"Aw, honey. Kit and I just thought that the kitchen would

be the best place."

At that, Kit turned and cranked open the windows over the sink. The temperature dropped immediately. She then opened the front and back doors, and lowered the thermostat.

"Kit!" shrieked Ruby. "What the heck! I'm freezing."

"I'm not paying to heat the yard, Mom." She took the bags from her brother.

Larry, pleased with his victory, became solicitous. "I'll put these away," he said to Kit. "I just have a few more bags in the car."

"A few more bags?" cried Ruby. "I can't cook all that."

Neither child mentioned that the last time Ruby had attempted to cook a holiday dinner, she had ended up in the hospital emergency room, her forearm burnt after she set the oven mitts ablaze. Larry took advantage of his sister's penitential mood and retreated to the car for the rest of the groceries. He took his time at the trunk, repacking a few wayward onions in order to give Kit enough time to deliver the news to Ruby that there were guests coming tomorrow. They had hoped to wait until the morning to tell her, but once Ruby was onto something, it was better just to spill the beans than to suffer her relentless pestering.

Larry returned and dropped the turkey with a thump on the counter. "Did you tell her?"

Kit laughed. "She's already calling them 'the in-laws.'"

"That's not funny!" He tore at the brown wrapping and string that had protected the bird, which he'd bought at the farm a few hours before, after he realized that all the birds in the grocery store were frozen and that he hadn't left enough time to defrost one. This fresh bird would be delicious, but it had used up an alarming percentage of his pay.

"What was I supposed to tell her?"

"That they were alone in that house and had nowhere else to go."

"OK, then. That's what I told her."

Wayward potatoes rolled out of a paper bag and across the counter. Larry had no time to fight his sister. "Have you thought about the table?"

"We have a tan cloth I can use—and oh, you should see this." Kit disappeared into the living room and returned holding a flowery centerpiece, all oranges and yellows and whites. "I took a small pumpkin, carved it all out and put carnations and water inside."

Larry looked up from washing the potatoes. "That's really classy, Kit."

"You like it?" She held it at eye level, turning it on her palm. "I bought some Halloween napkins on sale, orange to match the pumpkin."

"So you can set the table for six."

"Six? I thought you said five."

They were interrupted by their mother's voice headed toward the kitchen. "With no warning, I've got absolutely nothing to wear!"

The sight of Ruby in her bathrobe silenced the discussion. Kit placed her pumpkin gently on the counter.

"Come on, Mom," she answered. "I'm sure we can find something nice."

Ten

Sullen clouds, heavy with an incoming storm, kept the morning dark, and Larry overslept the appointed time to put the bird in the oven. Fortunately, as the designated chef, he alone knew what a disaster this might be for a meal planned for one o'clock in the afternoon.

Kit found him hunched over the counter, scribbling with a stubbed pencil onto a paper bag.

Larry did and redid the math—twenty to twenty-five minutes a pound, but that was for turkeys under eight pounds, it was more like fifteen to twenty minutes a pound for heavier turkeys, but only if they weren't stuffed—but could not land on a stable cooking time.

"What's going on?"

Larry looked up at his sister, her dark hair pulled back tight. This exaggerated the sharpness of her chin, her small upturned nose.

"Nothing. I'm just figuring out how long it will take to cook the turkey."

Kit retreated to the living room, and turned on the TV. "Mom," she called out. "You're gonna miss the parade!"

He could always get them drunk, Larry reasoned. Drunks never could tell how long they'd been waiting for anything. Too late for that now—he had purposely not bought any alcohol because of the unpredictable effects it had on his mother and now, on the holiday, the liquor stores were all closed. He swore. If it had only been the three of them, he would have gotten a small turkey breast, with plenty of leeway time for all sorts of mistakes. Linda hadn't acted all that thrilled in any case, and Mrs. Appleton had looked at him kind of funny. The memory of inviting Billy as well flickered through his mind, and the numbers on the paper made no sense. He threw the pencil down. He was just going to have to rely on the meat thermometer.

An hour before the guests were due to arrive, Kit pulled open the oven. "Larry, come here a second."

Larry, deep in concentration, contemplated his limited array of pots and pans.

"Larry!"

He had only two pots large and sturdy enough to boil the heavy vegetables, and he had purchased three different kinds of those, potatoes, turnips, and yams.

"Larry, this turkey looks hardly cooked!"

Then there were the pearl onions and green beans, as well as the extra stuffing to consider.

"I mean, it's not even brown on the outside. Should I turn up the oven and make it cook faster?"

And…the apple pie.

"Larry?"

"Everything's fine!" He snapped as he searched through the cabinets for a clean bowl.

"Larry, the turkey's raw."

He found an old bowl that his grandmother often filled with potato salad. Larry missed her suddenly with a ping of energy that did a slow burst in his chest. Just the memory of her sure efficiency in the kitchen was calming. "OK," he admitted to his sister. "I may have put the turkey in a little late."

"How late?" Kit opened the oven a crack to peek in.

"I'm not really sure. I've never cooked one this big."

"Can we do it in courses?"

"No! We can't serve it separate, Kit." He dumped the apples in the sink, ran water over them.

She crossed her arms and leaned against the counter. "How about an hors d'oeuvre?"

He found the peeler beneath a mountain of yam skins. "I don't have one."

"I can make one."

"What, what can you cook?" he demanded.

She opened the fridge. "Look, I can put cream cheese in celery. We even have olives."

Her careful, measured approach to cooking infuriated him. "As long as you do it far away from me, do it in the living room."

"You know," she said. "We might have to liquor them up."

"I thought of that."

She gathered her ingredients and headed toward the TV.

"We'll save that as a last resort."

An hour after the Appletons were due to arrive, Kit's plate of stuffed celery sticks lay neatly in the fridge covered in plastic wrap, the turkey skin had taken on shades of brown, and Ruby emerged from her bedroom so highly scented that her L'Air du Temps managed to cover even the odor of cooking turkey.

By two-thirty, Larry had assembled the pie, but with the turkey far from finished, he had no way to bake it. The pie required an oven set at 375 degrees, after a period of browning at 425, but the turkey needed to hold steady at 325 for another couple of hours. More troubling was the array of cooked vegetables and their varying warming demands; he worried that as the afternoon wore on, the vegetables would become colder and chewier while they waited for the turkey.

Larry also wondered where the guests could be, worried that he had mistaken Mrs. Appleton's thanks for the invitation as a yes and Linda's resistance for reticence. The thought of Billy coming to his house filled him with almost unbearable anticipation as well as panic. He just had to put it out of his head.

Larry walked into the living room where Kit and Ruby sat in front of the Chiefs and Lions game and clapped his hands. Flour puffed out from his sleeves. "I'm done," he exclaimed. "I even have time to clean up."

"Do you want me to check on the chicken while you're in the shower?" asked Ruby.

"For the last time, Ma, it's a turkey!" shouted Larry. "And," he added, "don't go near the kitchen."

When he was out of earshot, Ruby said, "Turkey, chicken, what's the difference. They're both birds and you eat them." She fiddled for cigarettes in the wide pocket of her peasant skirt; hemmed in little coins and flashy at one time, it now looked like an outfit more suited to a doll in native costume. "Do you think anyone will show up?"

Kit wanted to laugh, but Larry had worked too hard. "Who knows?"

"I haven't eaten a thing. Let's go grab a smoke."

"Mom!"

"I mean outside."

"We said we wouldn't."

Ruby leaned back, eyes on the TV. Neither was a fan, but football on TV was a habit left over from before the divorce, and no one thought to turn it off. "I miss your grandma."

It had been almost four years since Ruby's mother had died suddenly from what doctors had guessed was some kind of random blood clot that had lain in wait for years and then broke loose to block the vein to her heart. Without their grandmother, Kit couldn't imagine what her and Larry's childhood would have been like, what kind of devolving chaos might have eaten them up. Kit recalled the Thanksgiving dinners her grandmother had produced like magic from the kitchen, and then how she had filled in her mother's widening gaps of clarity until her own gaps began to form. "I miss her too," she answered.

They sat, staring at the screen.

Ruby sighed. "Let's have a smoke then, in her memory."

"You go have a smoke," snapped Kit.

Ruby stood up.

Kit scowled; the flowery top her mother wore was better suited to summer. "Put a coat on," she added. "It's cold out there."

"Kicked out of my own house by my children."

Kit recalled the English class she had taken her first semester. They had studied Shakespeare, and they'd read about a raving old man, homeless in a storm. The character had infuriated her in his refusal to see hard facts, but then gained her sympathy. "Just like King Lear."

"Who?"

"Someone who got pneumonia because he wouldn't put a coat on when he went outside for a smoke."

Ruby left for the yard.

After Ruby's mother died, the Lavoies were Thanksgiving waifs. They were invited once to the Minnizone's, but that clan was close to fifty people, too chaotic for her mother to handle. And now, with her soured relationship with Chris, Kit wouldn't go near that house on a holiday. One year they had eaten out, but that had been depressing, and very, very expensive. Another year, some recently widowed neighbor had asked—Kit's thoughts were interrupted by a knock, and then a pounding, on the kitchen door.

She glanced at the clock, already 2:38.

No Appletons were visible through the window at the back door, only what looked like a delivery boy. Kit opened the door. Not much older than she was, he had thick, light brown hair streaked with yellow that hung in waves over his handsome, small-boned face. The costly dress shirt he wore in a casual way, frayed at the collar, reminded her of prep boys she had met in college. Even his somewhat tattered ski jacket was like theirs, both extraordinarily expensive and worn down to the bone. Despite the large brown cardboard box he balanced in his arms, this was not a standard delivery boy. "Can I help you?" she asked.

"Just get the door," he answered. "I can handle the rest." He maneuvered the box sideways through the threshold and swung it up onto the counter. Bright purplish red bruises ran from the side of his neck into his shirt, and Kit thought that maybe he had been drinking.

But it was impossible not to let him in.

"You can wait on the glasses, we'll want to let this breathe a few moments." Out of the box came a dark green wine bottle by its neck, which Billy then palmed so Kit could see the label—an ink drawing of an imposing stone mansion on a light orange background with a pretty green border, and something written in French. The only word she recognized was "Château."

Taking a heavy metal opener from his pocket, he placed the bottle deftly between his thighs. "I'm not going to promise that this vintage will prove to be the finest match with turkey, but it will be delicious." The cork popped easily from the bottle. "I chose this particular Château because, frankly, it won't be missed, Mr. Rutherford not being a huge fan of the Bordeaux from the St. Julien region. And," he waved grandly at the box on the counter, "the supply was plentiful." The guest turned to Kit, perhaps noticed her for the first time, eyebrows raised. It was her turn to speak.

Who are you? was too rude a question for such a mannered person. Most likely he was the mystery third guest, but most of her brother's friends wouldn't even know how to open a bottle of wine, much less venture an opinion on whether it was the proper companion to the meal. Kit would have loved to have been able to return a sally regarding the pretty green bottle and its contents, but she too found wine territory so fraught with opportunities for humiliation that she hadn't even attempted to decipher the differences beyond white and red. Kit's nylons felt particularly itchy and her dress, almost a work dress, chosen in anticipation of the Appletons or nobody, now felt pedestrian. Nothing, she cursed, nothing she owned would ever be able to fray as gracefully as the shirt this person wore.

She held out her hand. "Kit Lavoie," she said, with the air of a hostess presiding over a vaster and more dignified gathering. "It's such a pleasure to meet you."

Kit knew she'd struck the right tone when he reciprocated. "William Potter," he replied and shook her hand firmly, "but I prefer Billy." He grinned then in such an open and sexual way that it struck her like a jolt.

Suddenly aware of her own sweat under the nylon dress in the hot kitchen, she was relieved to find Larry just behind her, until she turned and discovered he was still in his bathrobe, that crazy Chinese thing he'd bought in Boston.

"That's quite an outfit," said Billy.

Larry looked down at himself, almost as if to investigate what it was he had put on. "Yeah, it's real silk." He folded over the hem and held it out. "Feel it."

Billy reached over and fondled the material. "Well," he said. "This is turning out to be quite the little party."

"Knock it off," snapped Kit to Larry, but she felt her irritation include Billy. "Go put on some clothes."

"I was just choosing an outfit when I heard voices," protested Larry. "I wanted to see who was here."

"I can help with the choosing," said Billy.

"I don't think that would be such a great idea right now," answered Larry. "What happened to your neck?"

"Nothing to worry about," said Billy.

"How do you two know each other?" asked Kit, although she was now quite sure that this was the guy from the horse barn.

"I'm his boss," said Billy. He looked around. "Am I the only guest?"

Kit looked at Larry. "Yes, Larry. Is he the only guest?"

"No, the Appletons are coming. We're just running a little behind schedule."

Billy nodded. "How about some wine? Compliments of Mr. Rutherford."

"Sure," said Larry.

"We'll have a glass waiting for you," said Billy.

Kit went around to the cupboard in the living room to

retrieve some glasses with stems. Larry headed to his room before he circled back to his sister. "Kit," he whispered. "Kit, the wine could be a problem."

Kit turned to her brother. "The wine a problem?" she hissed under her breath. "You're not dressed and the turkey's not done!"

"Can we please at least eat the food, Kit? Promise me we'll eat the food."

"When will that happen? When will we eat the food?"

"Soon, Kit, soon."

"Larry," she cried out, then lowered her voice. "We'll eat the food when it's done."

"Thanks, Kit. That's all I want."

He retreated to his room just as Billy rounded the corner, waving the wine over his head as if he'd drink straight out of the bottle if a glass didn't appear soon. When her mother knocked at the broad living room window in her thin blouse, apparently locked out, Kit felt whatever normalcy the day had held to this point begin to slip away. She held up the glasses to Billy and placed them on the coffee table, in front of the still-flickering TV. "Let's use these," she said. "When you drink fine wine from a bottle, I find you lose too much dribbling down your chin."

He laughed.

Her mother banged at the window once more. Kit looked up, put her finger to her lips to shush her, and then held up her pointer to indicate she would rescue her in a minute. For God's sakes, she thought, the woman could just as easily walk around the house to the kitchen door as wait for me to open the back "Let me take your coat," she said to Billy, who appeared oblivious to the commotion. He put down the bottle, handed her the coat, and bent to remove his boots. Kit noticed that his bruises were more extensive than they'd first appeared to be; they seemed to run down his neck onto his chest.

After she'd safely stowed Billy's coat, Kit opened the rear door, which led into the living room.

"What took you so long?"

Her mom looked pinched and her skin was cold to the touch. "I told you to put on a coat."

Ruby caught sight of Billy pouring the wine. "Yoo-hoo," she called. "We have a guest!"

"Oh, I see the Appletons have arrived," said Billy. "Would you care for a glass of wine?"

"I don't think..." said Larry, who reappeared in a red silk shirt feathered in subtle gold lines.

"I'd love one," said Ruby.

"Billy," said Larry, "this is my mother."

"Charmed," said Billy, and handed her a full glass of red wine.

"Cheers," she replied, and without waiting for anyone else, she drank down a deep gulp. "Oh," she said when she'd swallowed, "this is something different!" She smiled demurely. "It's much stronger than I'm used to."

"It's much better than you're used to," said Larry.

When they all had their glasses filled, Billy raised his. "Here's to it!"

"Here's to what?" asked Ruby.

"To Thanksgiving," said Kit. "Here's to Thanksgiving and Larry's meal."

"To Larry's meal," echoed Billy.

The wine hit Kit hard; she hadn't eaten anything in preparation for Larry's feast and the wine was strong, stronger than any wine she'd ever had, a warm swirl of flavors in her mouth. "Wow," she said. "What is this?"

Billy held up the bottle and read, "Château Ducru-Beaucaillou, 1966."

Ruby held up her empty glass. "Hit me with some more of that boogaloo."

"No!" said Larry. "Wait for the food."

"Oh, Larry," said Billy. "Don't be such a spoilsport. It's a holiday and there's plenty more where this came from." He drained the bottle into Ruby's glass and went to the kitchen.

"Don't you drink another glass," whispered Larry.

Kit rolled her eyes. Why did he even bother?

He looked desperately at Kit. "Am I right?"

"Wait until the meal to have another glass," she said to her mother. "You haven't eaten and you'll get toasted and you know where that lands you."

"Where?" demanded Ruby. "Where does that land me?"

Billy's reentrance silenced the conversation. "Here's to seconds and the absent Appletons," he said.

By their third bottle, Kit lolled back on the couch and watched the football players swimming in front of her. For some reason, she thought of Mrs. Pierce, and wondered if she was cozy and warm in her dilapidated house or still wandering on the windswept marshes in her layers of rags, because that's what she had been wearing really, despite the jaunty green scarf, just layers and layers of rags. Stung suddenly by the thought that she should have added Mrs. Pierce to the guest list, she sat up. After all, Larry had enough food for an army, and no one in this house would even notice another stranger.

The doorbell had been ringing for a while when they noticed Linda Appleton banging on the back window.

Larry was startled to see her. He had forgotten she had been invited, forgotten also about the turkey roasting in the oven at 325 degrees since late morning as well as the collection of warming vegetables and the uncooked pie. He watched her a few seconds before comprehending that she was in some distress, asking for help. The shortened afternoon was almost dark, and the glare of the living room lights made her features difficult to discern; her untamed blond hair refracted light, maybe from the sunset or from the lamps inside. In any case, there she was, mouth open, yelling something, a name perhaps, and banging on the window.

Billy asked, "What's that?"

The doorbell pinged again.

"The Appletons are here!" cried Ruby.

Larry leapt up. "The turkey!"

"The turkey!" echoed Ruby.

They moved toward the kitchen as if to head off the crisis they could feel building somewhere beyond the edges of the fuzz of the alcohol.

Larry went first to the oven.

Billy was first to the door; Ruby and Kit hovered behind.

Mrs. Appleton, in her stiff brown wool coat and sensible shoes, seemed startled by the greeting party. Whatever annoyance she may have felt at being kept waiting was erased by the sight of the three faces, expressions conveying nothing less than that they'd been waiting only for her arrival for the party to start.

"Mrs. Appleton, I presume," began Billy. "We've been waiting so long to meet you."

Linda ran up behind her mother, a bit out of breath.

"Come in out of the cold," continued Billy.

"Who are you?" asked Linda, "The new butler?"

Kit winced. "This is Billy, Billy Potter. Come on in, Mrs. Appleton."

Ruby shadowed her daughter and leaned around her in a bobbing motion, a wide, static smile on her face. "Hello," she piped. "Hello."

"We need some help out here. We've got Uncle John, and what with the dark and your…" Mrs. Appleton hesitated for a beat, "uncertain driveway, we'll have a difficult time with the wheelchair ourselves."

Linda was more to the point. "Where's Larry?"

Larry, his face bright red from the heat of the oven, stood just behind with the turkey, brown and magnificent, on the roasting pan. "Look!" he said. "It's perfect. I can't believe this."

"Uncle John?" asked Kit, sure she hadn't set enough

places to accommodate all the guests.

"Put the turkey down, Larry," ordered Linda. "We need your help with the wheelchair." She glanced at Billy, suspicion on her face. "You, too."

Larry searched the kitchen, every inch littered with the detritus of his efforts.

"Just put it back in the oven," suggested Ruby.

"I'll take it," said Kit. Larry placed the pan in her hands, careful to wrap the dish towels at the sides so that she wouldn't burn her fingers. It weighed far more than she'd expected and after a second she needed to quickly find it a home. "Mom, help."

"Put it on the floor," said Ruby.

"No! I'll put it on the table. Just find something I can put underneath."

"Like what?"

Kit's forearms began to shake. "Like a cutting board, a trivet, some towels. Hurry!" she added as Ruby circled the kitchen like a dog chasing its tail.

Kit rested the end of the roasting pan at the edge of the stove, the weight lessened for the moment. Larry returned through the door carrying an ancient man wrapped in a brown plaid blanket. He wavered, unsteady.

"The couch," suggested Kit, who saw her brother was drunk. "Put him on the couch!"

Larry lurched toward the living room.

Mrs. Appleton and Linda, who carried a neatly folded wheelchair, followed. Billy held a smart brown fedora, with a small green feather in it. "Uncle John dropped his hat," he explained.

"Mom, where we gonna set him up?" asked Linda.

Mrs. Appleton looked toward Kit, who stood pinned against the stove with the turkey. "Well," Kit smiled. "Why don't we all sit in the living room while Larry gets the meal ready?"

Billy pulled another bottle from his carton and headed to the dining room. "Would anyone like some wine?"

Kit, alone under the bright overheads, surveyed the kitchen for evidence of a meal. Other than a cooked turkey and a raw apple pie, the rest of the covered pots and dishes were a mystery only to be solved by her brother, who had probably drunk a bottle of wine by himself over the past hour. The weepiness of drink threatened to overcome her and she shut her eyes tight. The minutes passed. Where was her brother? "Larry!" she called in a heightened whisper. "Larry!" she called a bit louder.

Clearly Larry, in the flush of the victory of the turkey, had forgotten the rest of the meal as well as the serving and the eating. She edged the pan onto the counter slowly as pots and spoons and peels and packaging shifted in response, until the pan was mostly on the counter.

In the living room, her brother was fussing over Uncle John. "Larry," she called as sweetly as possible, "I need you in the kitchen!"

"Honey," said Ruby, "go help your sister with the cooking."

“What about the pie?" prodded Kit when Larry appeared.

"In the oven, put it in the oven and close the door." He turned on all the burners, opened a few cabinet doors.

"What do you need?"

"A big plate for the turkey, bowls to put stuff in."

Kit searched the cabinets. She opened one and suddenly something smelled funny. A flash caught the corner of her eye. "Fire!"

A yellow burst leapt upward from one of the burners, toward the bottom of the cabinets over the stove. Larry reached into the flames.

"No!" shouted Kit.

He pulled a burning mass of dish towels into the sink and turned on the water. Larry stood over the running water, shoulders slumped. "I don't know what I was thinking. All the vegetables are cold and it will take a miracle to reheat them without burning the house down."

"Look, the turkey looks great. Did you make the gravy?"

He slumped further into the sink. "The gravy, I still gotta make the gravy. I am so tanked, Kit. I told you I didn't want alcohol."

"No one took a gun to your head!" She found the Gravy Master and handed it to him. "I can't make it. You're gonna have to."

"That's it!" He scrambled through the utensils on the counter. "If I make a ton of gravy, really really hot, people can pour it over their vegetables and no one will notice they're cold!"

Kit didn't have the heart to tell him that of his five diners, three were probably too drunk to eat, and one most likely had no taste buds left. She put her hand on his shoulder. "Billy's really nice, Larry. I like him."

"Oh my God," he answered, as he reached for the turkey bastings. "I know."

The turkey sat like a king in the center of the small dining table. Billy squeezed Uncle John next to Ruby. Mrs. Appleton sat at the opposite end, with Linda and Billy on one long side and Kit and Larry on the side closest to the kitchen.

Linda snatched up a mini pumpkin bursting with yellow and white mums just before it fell off the edge, pushed to the margins by the plate of yams. "Are we eating this?" she asked. "If not, it's in the way."

Larry, carrying a large carving knife and fork in hand, started to answer her, but he was distracted by her white and pasty skin and the wide black circles under her eyes. He was right to have invited her, he was sure of it.

Uncle John, wizened and cheerful, his legs wrapped in the brown plaid blanket, saluted with his full glass of Mr. Rutherford's Ducru-Beaucaillou. Ruby, whose own taste buds were gone from smoking and who sat within an elbow's reach to the wheelchair, arranged the meal on his plate, carefully cut his food into bite-size pieces and then watched him eat it.

He nodded enthusiastically and raised his glass to her again, maybe too much for the occasion, but he was unused to wine and hadn't eaten a bite since a small breakfast of runny eggs and white toast at the Easy Rest

Home almost ten hours before.

"Have some gravy, it's nice and hot," offered Larry. He pretended not to notice Mrs. Appleton, who began to cry, tears plopping into her plate of uneaten mashed potatoes. Billy assiduously refilled her empty glass, and offered small talk about the vast extent of Mr. Rutherford's wine cellar.

If Linda noticed her mother's distress, Larry couldn't tell. She ate her way through mountains of mashed potatoes and yams with gravy, but merely picked at her turkey and barely sipped her wine. Larry thought perhaps she wasn't used to the big flavor of expensive wine, since beer was her drink of choice.

The early dark turned to full night. What was outside disappeared, and what was inside reflected against the windows, like a mirror. Much to Larry's delight, he refilled the gravy containers two times, and the guests ate with vigor. Mrs. Appleton alone moved her food around her plate.

After dinner, the gray sky that had threatened all day at last delivered its snow, a light haze of quiet white. Forks and knives lay across gravy-covered plates, and it had been almost a half an hour since Billy retrieved another bottle of wine.

"Look at the snow," remarked Kit.

This set Mrs. Appleton's tears flowing again, but this time Billy drew her to his side in a broad sweep of his arm. Linda sat up in protest, but her mother turned her head into his sleeve, wetting the arm of his shirt.

Uncle John stared at the falling white until his eyes closed half in sleep, and his head nodded toward his chin.

Linda looked away from her mother and put her nose in the air. "What's that great smell?"

Larry started to his feet and dashed to the kitchen. Inside the oven, the apple pie bubbled over its browning crust. He grabbed the nearest dish towel to pull the plate out of the oven and returned to the table.

"The pièce de résistance!" cried Billy, and Kit smiled.

"What?" called out Uncle John. "It looks like a pie to me!" And since those were the sole words he'd voiced since he entered the house, this struck everyone as terribly funny and they laughed, even Mrs. Appleton.

Kit rose to get clean dishes, but Linda interrupted. "We'll just use these. It's much easier and we don't have to move." Kit glanced at Larry, who looked as if all he wanted in this world was for the pie to be eaten, and so she sat back down. They cleared a spot on the table and Larry divided the whole pie amongst the seven of them, no leftovers, using the same knife he'd used to carve the turkey, and served generous pieces on the used dinner plates.

Larry couldn't believe his luck—the apples were soft, the cinnamon balanced with the nutmeg, the juices sweet and tart, and the crust browned and firm. The warm forkfuls took the chill out of the icy landscape surrounding the small house. Even Mrs. Appleton didn't leave a bite.

"Well," said Billy after they'd leaned back into their chairs. "That was certainly quite a feast."

Kit looked around the table, at the empty plates and quiet faces. Larry's little party had gelled, he had pulled them in like circling atoms to be held a moment in his orbit until they scattered away again into the night. She took a deep breath and looked down at her lap, glad to rest a bit in her brother's field of gravity.

The flakes outside layered gently and persistently to cover first the brown grass and sidewalk, the windshields, the evergreen bushes overgrown in the front, and even the lips of the window sills. It then turned briefly to rain before it stopped and the temperature dropped again.

When it was time for the guests to leave, every exposed surface, each rut in the drive and bare twig, was covered by a thin layer of ice. Larry, Kit, Billy, and the Appletons stood at the open door and watched the wind blow the streetlight's orange glow in undulating patterns over the sheen, like broken moonlight over a stormy sea.

"It looks pretty slippery out there," said Larry.

Billy took the helm of Uncle John's wheelchair, which rolled easily over the ice at the slightest push of Billy's fingertips. His wobbly step and the ice were a perfect pairing of imbalance: using the pushing handles as a sort of walker, Billy whisked Uncle John to the Appleton's car in record pace. "Whoa," sang out Uncle John as they scooted along. "This is better than the fun house!"

"Don't let him roll downhill!" Kit called from the door.

Larry, stung almost sober by the fresh icy air, held out his elbows to Linda and Mrs. Appleton. Linda refused until her first step outside sent her reeling. She grabbed onto the ice-covered doorknob for balance, and dropped nearly to the ground in the split second before she clutched Larry's arm to stop her fall.

Mrs. Appleton took the offered arm. With Linda on one side and her mother on the other, the trio did a slip-slide to the car.

Billy, meanwhile, scraped furiously at the ice-glazed windows.

"All we need is a hole to see in the front and the back," said Linda when she got to the car. She tried to take the scraper from Billy, but he fended her off.

"A woman in your condition needs to rest," he said.

"You're in the same condition!" laughed Larry.

Mrs. Appleton, not one to let inebriation interrupt the social graces, called out charming phrases on her way to the car. "Thank you for a lovely evening!" and "I forgot to thank your mother!"

Kit pictured Ruby lay snoring on the couch in front of the TV. "She's cleaning up," she called out from the doorway. "I'll tell her you said good-bye."

Larry, everyone safely in the car, stepped away as Linda started it up. The engine resisted, then caught in a whir. Billy continued to dig out a small hole in the back passenger window so that Uncle John would have a view for the drive back. He stepped away when Linda backed slowly out, his arms spinning backward as he struggled to stay upright.

The three watched as the car fishtailed on the way down the drive, the back tires sliding right and left as the front went gamely forward. "Gee," said Larry as the car lurched slowly down the empty, snowy street, "I hope they make it home all right."

Billy clomped his heavy boots against the front step before he entered the house. "Come on," he said. "They got here all right, didn't they?"

Kit turned to face the unrecognizable kitchen, every surface littered with debris from the party. She was supposed to work tomorrow. Billy reached around her shoulders and pulled her in close. He smelled of sweat and booze and some strange other smell, something almost musty.

"Don't worry," he said. "I'm just as good at cleaning up a mess as I am at making one."

Eleven

Leftovers crowded the fridge; Kit pushed aside a number of bowls covered in tinfoil to reach the milk to put in her tea, and a plate of yams dripped onto the second shelf. She peeked in the carton Billy had brought—empty, they had drunk every bottle.

The storm of last night had passed, leaving blue skies and a gritty layer of light snow over ice. Kit thought how the wind would have blown in from the roiling ocean over the bare marshes, gathering force toward Mrs. Pierce's house. Did Mrs. Pierce eat a turkey dinner yesterday? Who would have come and picked her up and taken her somewhere to eat? Neither sounded plausible; she seemed to Kit a woman spun out of the orbit of human contact.

Kit considered. Maybe she could get rid of some of the leftovers, make a package of food and bring it to her. This side trip would make her late for work, but she could tell Jack that she'd been out doing more investigating. He only noticed what she did when something went wrong, in any case.

She put her teacup in the sink.

Larry's car still sat in the drive. Kit wondered who was caring for the horses this morning, perhaps Billy. In a flourish of hand gestures and smiles, he had invited the guests to come down and see his girls at the Rutherford Estate, a property not far from Mrs. Pierce's. Maybe wine spurred the invitation, but Linda had listened closely to his detailed descriptions of the horses, one of the few sparks of interest she had shown, that and when she'd dug into the apple pie. She'd devoured her piece as if she could easily have put down the whole pie. Kit had to admit that her brother had been right to invite the Appletons, not only right, but kind. The old expression, any port in a storm, came to her. Maybe she and Larry had provided a port to the beleaguered family. Billy, though, was different. Clearly his invitation wasn't issued out of charity.

Still in her pajamas, Kit made her way to her ice-covered car, keys in hand. The car door frozen shut, she used the scraper to knock off some stubborn ice along the seams before she was able to pull it open, start up the car and the blower. The car then running, she returned inside; while she dressed, the ice would be melted enough to scrape off the windshield.

To spare losing dishes, Kit put most of the food in makeshift containers of tinfoil and layered them into the carton that had stored Mr. Rutherford's wine. On the drive to Mrs. Pierce's, the sunlight bounced between the over-bright snow and the blue sky, and the random yellow mailbox or red shutter stood out sharply. A crust of sand

and ice covered the roads, forcing a slow speed. The conditions provided a ready excuse for Jack; she could tell him the roads were too bad to get to work on time.

Yet, as she approached the house, passing by the bare brown marshes and the leafless trees, she felt foolish. After all, wasn't Mrs. Pierce wealthy? She was probably vacationing this very moment somewhere warm, or had had a gourmet restaurant dinner on silver platters the day before. But as Kit maneuvered up the twisty drive, her optimism fell. This home, despite its size and location, had the forgotten and depressed air of poverty; the overgrown bushes, the sad state of the windows and doors, the slant of the house even, spoke insistently of weariness.

There were no footprints in the snow. Kit carefully took her package from the back seat. The front door, laced in vines, clearly hadn't been opened in a very long time, and the front windows were too overgrown with bushes to allow any view in. Based on the reception she had received the last time she was here, Kit scarcely worried about whom she was supposed to be or what she was doing here. Since she knew that once she rounded the house the gusts would pick up, she headed toward the leeward side of the property. She called out, "Mrs. Pierce! Mrs. Pierce!" but her voice was quickly sucked up by the vacant yard and the snow.

Tucked behind a stand of evergreens run amok, Kit found the side door. No dead tendrils gripped this sill, and a small but distinct area was free of branches. This must be the door Mrs. Pierce used. She peered into the dirtied four-paned window frosted with ice and thought she saw some kind of light in the distance, but it was hard to tell because the windows hadn't been cleaned or cleared in so long that her perspective was shaky. Balancing the carton of food on her hip, she knocked on the door with her gloved hand and waited. She knocked a second time, and then, without a thought, she reached for the doorknob, which she found was loose in its socket. The door gave easily in its jamb and swung a little open. Breaking and entering, Kit remembered, this would be breaking and entering, no matter what her intent. Before the door was fully open, she called again, "Mrs. Pierce!"

What struck her, though, was that no draft of warm air shot out through the open crack. The house must be cold, or this could be a remote entranceway, more like a mudroom of sorts. This emboldened Kit, and she called out once more and took a step in. "Mrs. Pierce!"

"Who are you?"

Gone was the shy gypsy of the marsh, sheathed in green scarves. The woman in front of Kit was tall, had once been taller than Kit, with sharp blue eyes focused in aggression, and she held a full-size pitchfork, prongs forward, just inches from Kit's chest.

Kit's legs nearly gave out in fear, and the carton of food veered dangerously toward the ground before she gathered herself enough to catch it.

"Mrs. Pierce!"

Mrs. Pierce registered her own name, and the prongs dropped somewhat, but then lifted. A patrician voice of rounded vowels and confident intonation rang out. "Explain yourself, or I shall be forced to take drastic measures!"

The voice was so at odds with the failing surroundings and Mrs. Pierce's disheveled appearance that Kit almost wanted to laugh, or look around for the audience with whom to share the dramatic joke. But the snarl of gray hair, the odd assortment of oversized sweaters, and the fierce look on her face that contorted her features to a single tightened mask of hostility were anything but funny. "Mrs. Pierce," Kit said, "it's Kit Lavoie."

The pitchfork quavered slightly, and Mrs. Pierce squinted. "Kit Lavoie?"

Her voice hesitated, and Kit grasped that Mrs. Pierce's once formidable ability to control any situation was compromised by age and circumstance, and that what was left of her refused to admit to memory loss or any other sign of decay. Kit, still fearful of the pitchfork, took the advantage and lied.

"Sure, Kit Lavoie. I was by last week and you asked about groceries, and now I've come with some groceries, for Thanksgiving. Here." She held out the box, way too big for the woman to handle alone, never mind along with the pitchfork. Kit consoled herself with the fact that she meant no harm, but had merely come with a present. "Let me put them in the kitchen for you."

"You aren't the regular girl. She knocks."

Mrs. Pierce's face and hands were red and raw, as if her skin was too much in the cold, and Kit couldn't help but shiver as the wind gusted in the doorway. "Mrs. Pierce, I'm sorry to startle you. I can just put the box down and leave." Kit bent down slowly, keeping Mrs. Pierce in her view at all times. She held her breath as she dropped down enough for the pitchfork to be at face level, and then backed away. Mrs. Pierce's eyes, blue and hard, burned into Kit's face. Kit wanted to turn away but was afraid that if she turned her back to the pitchfork, Mrs. Pierce would be more apt to use it.

Kit back- stepped to the door and then fled to her car. Sweaty with fear and the knowledge of having pushed an old woman into an ugly corner, she made her way down the unkempt, icy drive as quickly as she could, before Mrs. Pierce called the police and Kit would be in real trouble, newspaper trouble as her grandmother called it. I only wanted to help, she said to herself, but this mantra wasn't doing its work because of a nagging undercurrent of suspicion and doubt as to her true motives for the visit. She was struck, not the first time in the last couple of years, as to how little of herself she understood.

Kit's flagging car heat chose that moment to sputter, and by the time she got to work, she was shaking from chills and craving a cigarette. She didn't, however, allow herself that luxury.

Any opportunity for further visits to the Pierce property was curtailed because waiting to be typed on Kit's desk when she returned to Rioux & Rioux were Jack's draft papers for the civil suit against Vivian Faye Pierce, for the wrongful death of Janelle Whitmore Appleton on behalf of Linda Whitmore Appleton and Louise Anne Whitmore Appleton, with counts for the pain and suffering of Janelle Whitmore Appleton, Linda Whitmore Appleton, and Louise Anne Whitmore Appleton, and with the attendant counts of loss of companionship, contribution to household income et al, based on the charge of negligence and asking for one million dollars, a fantastic figure that Kit knew Jack had pulled out of a hat in his office. Once the papers were served and filed in court and Mrs. Pierce became the defendant in a lawsuit brought by Rioux & Rioux, Jack could be in serious trouble if he or any of his employees contacted Mrs. Pierce. He could be reprimanded by the Board of Bar Overseers or lose his license to practice law in Massachusetts. Kit's excursion this morning already tilted on some kind of legally ethical borderline that made her very uncomfortable, and would send Jack into a tirade if he found out. All the better, thought Kit, for she had no desire to ever visit the crazy, pitchfork-wielding old bat again.

Kit poured herself a large mug of hot coffee and spent her morning preparing the papers. She didn't expect Jack soon. He had taken part of the day to visit prisoners in jail. Or so he said; perhaps he was home in his pajamas watching TV. He never mentioned family; there were no photos of people neatly lined up on his desk, and no familiar voice called him at any regular interval. Either he was alone in the world or one of those people who carved separate compartments of their lives.

What discussions passed between Jack and the private

investigator regarding the assets of the Pierce estate, or what discussions took place between Jack and the Appletons, who hadn't returned to the office since their first visit, also remained a secret to Kit. The pace at which the suit proceeded seemed accelerated to her, but then again, since Kit had been working at Rioux & Rioux, Jack had never filed a suit that asked for so much money. Most of his cases had been small car accidents, and those defendants were well shielded by predictable yet thorough insurance company attorneys. His other batch of cases consisted of various indigent criminals who had been charged with serious crimes. Jack was their appointed lawyer and paid for by the state, so Kit's task was to keep a careful table of hours in order to submit regular invoices to the Commonwealth of Massachusetts based on hours worked. Even though her work was a merely secretarial and not professional, Kit still accounted carefully for her own time because, as Jack frequently reminded her, every penny goes toward a dollar.

Kit knew enough about the system to understand that, although the state paid for an attorney for you if you were charged with a crime and couldn't afford your own representation, you were on your own if you were sued by someone in civil court, where the penalty was financial and not incarceration. There were some organizations that offered legal services to the poor, usually for evictions and divorces. Perhaps Mrs. Pierce could find one of those. After the two visits Kit had taken to her home, despite her will to believe otherwise, her conclusion was that Mrs.

Pierce was completely out of money or completely out of her mind, or perhaps both. It was possible that the private investigator Jack hired to look into Mrs. Pierce's finances had come up with assets, another bank account, property elsewhere, enough to justify Jack's request for a million dollars in damages. On the other hand, Kit couldn't imagine Jack keeping that kind of news to himself. Mrs. Pierce's house may have once been grand, and it sat on a large and beautiful piece of land, but it was far from any city, and Kit doubted it was worth anything close to a million.

Jack was gambling. If he won, did that mean that Mrs. Pierce would lose her house and have no place to live?

She typed the court papers with growing reluctance, her usual efficiency bogged down with misspellings, skipped sentences, and the occasional wave of lightheaded nausea. If she didn't type these papers, it wasn't as if the lawsuit wouldn't go forward. She would be fired and someone else would type the papers. There was no sense in that. Even a loss of a week of pay would be dangerous.

I'm just following orders anyway, Kit reasoned. She remembered Jack's angry dismissal when she had told him how little money Mrs. Pierce held in the local bank and then just hinted that maybe it wasn't fair to sue. She had to conclude that he must know something she didn't.

The papers were completed before lunch. Kit placed them on Jack's desk and then pulled the number for the process server, guessing that Jack would want the charges served to Mrs. Pierce and delivered to the courthouse as quickly as possible.

At close to lunchtime, Kit decided to take a walk.

Most of the morning ice had melted under the noon sun, and dirt and salt had turned what remained on the sidewalks into harmless pockets of water and slush. Although the courts were open, most business was postponed and no new business started on the day after Thanksgiving. The streets were empty of lawyers in suits scurrying from car to court, as well as the usual clusters of anxious families gathered outside the criminal courts. Only a man in a tattered coat pushing a shopping cart of tin cans rattled along on the street across from her.

Despite her feeling this morning that she'd never be hungry again, Kit was starving. She had skipped breakfast and hadn't packed a lunch. I ate enough yesterday to last for days, she told herself, reluctant to spend any money. She pictured the unpaid bills sitting in the kitchen drawer and lost her appetite again in the swirl of panic that ran through her stomach. At the end of every month, there was always something due that she'd had to hold over from the month before as she juggled a shifting hierarchy of obligations and their consequences.

The mortgage always came first because the bank was remorseless in its application of late fees and deadlines. And without a house, they were nowhere. Next in importance came her car expenses, insurance, maintenance and gas, because if Kit couldn't get to work, the shaky Lavoie family financial structure would quickly collapse. After transportation came seasonal trade-offs. Electricity was critical in the winter, but it took ages before the electric company could shut you off, whereas the phone company could pull the plug no questions asked after three months. Another winter necessity was heat, and the oil company had no obligation to deliver any oil for the furnace unless she had the cash to pay for it. Plus Christmas was not too far away, and she needed money to buy presents. Unless Larry came up with some money, they would soon be into their third month with the phone bill, and Kit was sure the heating oil was low in the tank as well.

She stepped out of the shade of a drooping wet awning into a corner of sun, and pulled her hair back off her face with her gloved palms. There was no way Larry had any money for her. He must have spent everything he had on yesterday's dinner, a lot of which sat in their fridge. She stepped to cross the quiet street. Well, at least they wouldn't starve for a week or two. She thought of Tony, the drummer from the club, who had mocked her concern with income, and her anger flashed. What did he know, she cursed, with no one to support and nothing to lose? The stash of cash she'd hidden in the boot in the back of her closet was growing too slowly to finance any changes to her situation, and her present income and status were just a treadmill of crisis management, with no hope to jump off the present wheel and onto a more generous one. Where did people like Mr. Rutherford or Mrs. Pierce get all their money?

On her return from her lunch break, Kit passed Mr. Levinson's quiet office. No light was visible from under the door. He had probably taken the day off. Since the Appletons had retained Jack and they were about to sue Mrs. Pierce, she could no longer ask Mr. Levinson for advice about the specific facts of the case. But if she asked him a question in a hypothetical way, giving no names and preceding each question with a "what if," he could tell her what would happen to Mrs. Pierce if she lost the case or was unable to defend herself, which is what Kit could see unrolling in front of her as quickly as Uncle John's wheelchair had slid over the ice toward the car that would take him back to his nursing home. Kit knew as well as anyone that, for those with no financial protection, there was no mercy. Perhaps Mrs. Pierce was closer to pushing cans in a grocery cart than she was to keeping her house.

Twelve

When Larry entered the barn on Monday morning, Billy turned to him in the half-light by Blue's stall and put his fingers to his lips. Billy's bruises were now a translucent yellow-green shade, and could be mistaken for shadows or reflected light at a brief glance.

Billy had not gone home after Thanksgiving dinner. Larry had run his fingers gently over the stark purple blotches running down the side of his neck and onto his chest. "What would you do," Billy had whispered in his bed, "if you were in my place? He used to be a sound animal, before the accident. Just because he can't perform like he used to doesn't mean he isn't worth something."

Larry lingered near the small tack room that housed the cot and held his greeting as Billy baby-talked the horse. Blue snorted, moved quickly through the hay in his stall, and then delivered a sharp back kick to the wall. Billy retreated out of the way of the hooves; Lady Cakes and Riding High whinnied and circled uneasily as the tension zapped from horse to horse to horse.

"Take the others out," Billy ordered.

Larry approached Lady Cakes, the sweet-tempered brown mare, and she was more than willing to be led out of the barn. The docile Riding High followed.

Even after a few more kicks, followed by silence, Larry knew better than to go back into the barn. Blue scared him to the pit of his stomach in a way he couldn't control. Blue had never warmed to Larry, but then Mr. Davis had frequently said that Blue didn't warm to anybody, including Billy, and the sooner Billy knew that the better. Another kick came from the barn as Larry pondered where Mr. Davis went in the cold weather. Neither Billy nor Mr. Rutherford had ever discussed length of employment, but winter was a slow season for any outdoor work. Larry wanted to work at least enough to pay some money to Kit. In any case, as he didn't love horses or Mr. Rutherford, this barn job could never be more than a temporary solution to his employment problem.

Larry heard a commotion, and Billy and Blue hurried out of the barn. As Blue passed by, he turned his long, beautiful neck back and bared his large, solid teeth to grab a bite from Larry's arm. Billy pulled the horse forward before any harm was done, but Larry leapt back in terror. Blue started to trot, and then gathered his legs as if to canter toward the marshes, but Billy managed to pull him in before he ran off and hurt himself. When the horse was finally released into the large paddock area, Larry watched Billy watch Blue as the horse raced first over the brown grass, then back toward the fence as if he would jump it, and finally veer toward breakfast.

Larry turned away to tend to his chores. And with the ground frozen, what remained was the barn roofing, a tough job in the growing cold.

Larry had never nursed a fear of heights, but the roof was steep, and a fall from the two-story peak would land him on frozen ground. More to prevent himself from worrying than to really prevent this from happening, as he pulled the old shingles off, he nailed down a series of two-by-fours to act as braces in case he slid. The barn two-thirds roofed with new shingles, the days proved increasingly too cold or windy to work comfortably. Today he considered borderline, but he wanted to finish the job before true winter set in.

He questioned this decision, however, when the tar went from gooey to nearly impossible to stir between the time he mixed it in the garage to when he lugged it up to the roof in a plastic bucket. His fingers also lost their dexterity in the chill, which made him more liable to hammer himself.

After a bit, though, he worked up a rhythm, and absorbed himself in the smell of the tar and in the instant gratification that covering the roof paper with brand new shingles brought. As he made his way up, the angle steepened, and his movements grew more careful. At the end of one row just a few feet from the roofline, as he reached over to scoop more tar from the bucket, a particularly strong gust rattled the empty branches above him and his thoughts turned to Billy. The memory of how warm Billy's body had felt on that cot in the cold barn came over him in a flush of heat and arousal—his foot slipped on the frictionless roof paper. As he slid rapidly down, clutching the tar brush in one hand, a freezing panic spiked through him; this feeling accelerated as his boots ripped through the first safety brace he'd nailed down, and then the second. As he headed toward the third and last two-by-four between him and a twenty-foot fall, another part of Larry surfaced through the swirling chaos of raw fear. He reached out and grabbed the two-by-four that dangled by one nail just above him.

Then the third rail held.

He breathed again, heavily, his heart pumping so fast it pushed against his chest. Yes, he thought, I'm not going to fall. He hung for a few more seconds on the edge of the roof, strangely exhilarated. Then he worked his way back up the roof by way of the dangling two-by-fours, nailing the wooden stoppers in more firmly as he went.

At the peak, he swung his legs over ridgeline, bit back another second's panic in a quick gust of wind, and took in the view. The bare oak overhead clung to a few withered leaves, and in the distance the browned marshes reflected sparkling patches of water. The barn looked small, the horses diminutive in their toy-size paddock. And there was the tiny but potent figure of Billy. Just the sight of him gathering hay for his charges' evening meal made Larry feel unaccountably happy, like whooping and punching his fists in the air on the inside. He watched him for a bit before he went back to his work, sure-footed now, and competent.

When he was finished laying the shingles, he went back

down to the barn and waited for Billy back in a warm spot where the barn blocked the wind, and the sun had just shifted around the corner and onto his face; the heat of it was nice, and he closed his eyes.

Billy startled him, though, on the lee side, wired and upset. "Good thing Davis left for the Keys, 'cause this horse is good for shit and he always had it in for Blue, had it in for him from the get-go."

Larry had never heard Billy talk about the horses in that way, using such harsh words. He switched to the easier topic. "Davis is gone to the Keys?"

"Yeah. He likes to fish."

"Will he be gone for a while?"

"The winter. Nothing for him to do here."

Odd lifestyles seemed to grow around money as even old Mr. Davis was living the high life, but this thought only nudged Larry back into worry about his own employment future.

Billy absently probed the bruises on his neck with his fingertips. "Don't tell Rutherford about Blue, OK?"

Larry laughed. "Yeah, sure, I mean, it's not like I have a lot of private time with the guy."

"Blue's just going through a rough patch."

Going through a rough patch? Blue had been crazy as a loon since the day Larry started here, and even on their first meeting, Billy had spent a long time discussing Blue's problems as if he were his psychiatrist. One leg was clearly lame, and Larry knew enough about horses, especially ones kept for polo, that a lame foreleg was never a good thing.

Couple the injury with a psychotic personality—Larry was half an inch from losing a piece of his arm just earlier today, and Billy was covered in bruises—and anyone but Billy could see that the horse was doomed. Billy had closed his eyes to the sun, and Larry did the same. They rested there a few minutes, but Larry's money troubles wouldn't let him alone.

He tried to think of a way to tell Billy that he really needed a bigger paycheck. "There's this coat, sheered lamb's wool on the inside and soft, worked leather on the outside."

"Look, man, I don't have money."

A thick, acid feeling fell from Larry's throat down through his stomach. Why would Billy think he would want money from him? Why was it so hard to say what he meant? He reached over and pulled on Billy's arm. "I'm not telling Rutherford shit. I…" Larry searched for words. "The coat's something my sister wants and I owe her a lot of money."

Billy nodded. "With Davis gone, Mr. Rutherford. will probably keep you through the season."

Larry calculated. If he saved his money, he might have enough to think about a better job in the spring, get some training somewhere maybe, some kind of trade.

"But if you need some extra cash, Mr. Rutherford may invite you to some of his parties." He flipped his shoulder against the barn, as if rolling onto his side while in bed, and leaned his head against the boards like they were a pillow.

Larry's mind drifted to the beautiful interiors of the Rutherford home.

Larry opened his eyes. Billy's face was close enough to kiss, and he wanted to kiss him but he wasn't feeling that brave.

Billy clutched his arms to his chest in a chilly gust. "Mr. Rutherford likes having pretty boys at his parties, to cheer up the old folk. They survived the eighties…" he paused "...so they're just happy to be here."

Larry didn't want to think about how it might have been navigating the eighties, with friends dying of AIDS left and right. He wanted to pull Billy in under his coat, put his arms around him and warm him up. Or he wished he'd kissed Billy when he'd had the chance. "I'll think about it," he said after some length of time had passed, and headed away from the barn, back up the drive.

But what was there really to think about? Kit needed money so he needed money. Mr. Rutherford scared him a little, a little like Blue scared him—just a tight, uncomfortable feeling and the dread of something worse about to happen. He shook this off. He would just have to trust Billy's judgment.

Thirteen

The gray clouds and weakened December sun mirrored Kit's early morning mood, making her reluctant to turn on the overhead lights. Once she did, the bills on the kitchen counter flashed in urgent, red-inked-capital-letter announcements. She scooped them up—some bore the marks of Thanksgiving gravy or smelled faintly of food—and stuffed them indiscriminately into a drawer.

Back in her room, she reached into the back of her closet and pulled out a pair of winter boots. With rounded toes and blue rubber soles, they were purchased more for warmth than fashion, and she wore them only when the weather was unavoidably cold and wet. In the meantime, they housed her extra cash, with the understanding that whatever went into the boot could not be retrieved for household bills. Kit had put the first ten dollars in after she left school, abandoned her scholarship, and took the job at Rioux & Rioux. At that time, still shedding Trey, coming back home from the Boston College dorms had been both an enormous relief and a miserable letdown. That first cashed paycheck, after three weeks of work, had sat limp and unsatisfying in her hands. Somehow, the act of putting ten dollars into her boot made her feel less small. Was she saving for a new pair of boots? College classes? To move away? She hadn't yet figured that out. Now, almost two years later and the phone bill three months overdue, maybe it would be all right to take a few dollars out for bills.

She smoothed a bill with a slash of red marker and counted out three hundred and eighty dollars. Soft, thick, and foreign smelling, the money was suddenly too much to squander away. Maybe the savings wouldn't pay for a semester at Boston College, but it could pay for a business class at Salem State. If the phone was cut off, perhaps her mother would be motivated to earn some money, or Larry would finally understand the seriousness of their financial troubles. No, she would not pay the phone bill. She would let the phone company pull the plug. After all, she had access to a phone at work. And, with her world considerably shrunken since her ignominious departure from school, who called her at home who couldn't find her at work anyway?

She tucked the money back into the boot and vowed to lower the heat even further to forestall a visit from the oil delivery truck.

Mrs. Appleton appeared at Rioux & Rioux sometime before eleven, sporting another plaid wool skirt and her practical wool winter coat. Looking less tired than she had on her previous visit, she smiled warmly at Kit, and once again praised the merits of her brother's cooking. As she took the woman's worn coat and hung it in the closet, Kit was struck again by her manners, which resembled Billy's in their fluidity and wry confidence. Jack hadn't told Kit that a visit was scheduled, but something about her manner implied an appointment. Kit stalled by getting the woman a cup of coffee. When she returned, Jack was still nowhere to be seen, and Mrs. Appleton was settled comfortably in the chair in front of Kit's desk, staring into space.

In the silence that followed, Mrs. Appleton shifted her cracked leather handbag, and Kit struggled for an easy conversation starter. She might ask after Linda, but anything to do with her brother and Linda was an area into which Kit was sure neither she nor Mrs. Appleton wanted to venture. A question regarding the Pierce case was not professional and just seemed nosy. At the same time, the woman had spent hours at her house for dinner, accompanied by her daughter and her uncle, and the quiet seemed to reflect a lack of something on her part. "Attorney Rioux must be held up in court," she began.

"No bother, our appointment's not until eleven thirty. You just go ahead with your work."

Since her work for the remainder of that morning was a few investigatory phone calls that involved her assuming other identities, Kit scrambled to her afternoon project, which involved November's billable hours to the Commonwealth of Massachusetts for the work done by Rioux & Rioux for the indigent criminals of the state. She pulled out the forms, and the slam of the file cabinet echoed unhappily in the quiet.

"How are the piano lessons going?" she blurted.

Mrs. Appleton nodded. "They're going well enough. Linda was never interested, but, her sister…" Her fingers crept under the handbag and rested there. "Janelle played beautifully."

Pain and suffering, Kit thought, there's a reason they have a legal category for it. What state of mind was Mrs. Pierce in when she had gotten into her car to drive, in the dark night, in the rain? She thought to ask Mrs. Appleton whether she'd taught Janelle to play, but then of course she had, and although the question might induce Mrs. Appleton to speak further, Kit didn't have the stomach to ask it.

Still, the subject seemed to unloose something in Mrs. Appleton. She shifted in her chair in a heavy way and looked at the ceiling. "When I was a child, my grandparents took me to New York, to Carnegie Hall, where there were lights and music and perfume and the rustling of formal dresses. You can't imagine what kind of impression that made on me. To this day, when I smell a certain type of floral scent, I am taken immediately back." She toyed with the hem on her skirt, turning it over to examine the stitching. "I played for Harry Ellis Dickson." She looked at Kit to see if she had grasped the implications of that name. "Do you know who he is?"

Kit thought desperately, came up with nothing, but guessed anyway. "Doesn't he work for the ba…" she caught herself before she let loose with the word "band," which somehow sounded unrefined. "…orchestra in

Boston?" She hazarded Boston, figuring that, even in her financial and musical prime, Mrs. Appleton probably wasn't going to New York for piano lessons.

"Yes, of course, the orchestra in Boston," she answered, irritated.

Kit was reminded of a phrase her grandmother had used and, until this moment, Kit had never clearly grasped the meaning of, pearls to swine, her grandmother would say, that's like throwing pearls to swine. It was a statement loaded with assumptions, cruel on both ends. Mrs. Appleton's fingers had reappeared from under her bag and were now playing with the handle. Kit pondered the frustration of having the best part of yourself invisible and incommunicable to those around you.

Mrs. Appleton looked up and caught Kit staring. Her tone softened. "Do you know how many youngsters your age don't even realize that there is an orchestra in Boston?"

"People don't go to Boston, much. No one really, except my brother. He goes in a lot, mostly to Chinatown."

Mrs. Appleton nodded, and the sun shone in the window at that moment and caught gray hair in its rays, dulling the surrounding brown. I'm definitely dyeing my hair when I see one strand of gray, Kit thought. No doubt.

"Have you ever even been to New York, Kit?"

Kit was taken off guard by the question, by its implications. Heretofore, she had imagined that she and Mrs. Appleton were in the same club, and now she saw that she was on the outside. She wanted to retort that they had been to Florida once when the family was young and her father had had some kind of meeting, but she suspected that a vacation to Miami was not what Mrs. Appleton meant.

"Don't you want to see the world?"

Before Kit could answer, the door opened and Linda stormed in.

"Mom," she said, as if Kit were not right there, "I had to park, like, fifty miles away." Her face pasty and plump, she turned sideward to close the door behind her. Her tight blue sweater shifted and Kit noticed how her belly rose over her unbuttoned jeans in a ring of soft flab that circled her waist. In that brief glimpse, Kit thought she saw also how Mrs. Appleton followed her eyes to Linda's stomach.

Jack came in quickly behind her, hurrying from court for their eleven-thirty appointment. He entered the office with a cold bluster, smelling faintly of smoke from waiting with the other attorneys for their cases to be called, and aftershave. His eyes narrowed at the sight of the Appletons, and Kit was sure that if he had been alone and not carrying his briefcase, his palms would have sought each other in an anticipatory rub.

Kit wondered if Linda was gaining weight and losing her looks. She sneaked another glance, and Linda didn't look pregnant at all, just another girl who'd drunk too many beers on the weekends, barely fitting into her clothes. Kit was sure that if Linda was expecting, Jack had no idea, and that the Appletons would never tell him. Neither would she. Kit took her boss's coat with an unfamiliar feeling of satisfaction and calm, of which, of course, Jack took no note, busy as he was ushering his most lucrative clients into his office.

It was another twenty minutes before Kit asked herself whether it could be Larry's. Unlikely—although with Larry one never knew exactly. Kit was sure, though, that he didn't know; Larry couldn't keep a secret.

Anger intruded. The Appletons were hopeless, that was clear. Linda had had a thousand useless jobs, and Mrs. Appleton taught piano, an object lesson in penury as far as Kit was concerned, Harry Ellis whoever or not.

And then she remembered Mrs. Pierce. Mrs. Pierce was sitting on a piece of property worth enough to rescue them all. The voices coming from Jack's office were indistinct, a low murmuring quiet punctuated by Jack's enthusiasm. But she could guess the conversation as if she were sitting next to Linda, in her own used Harvard chair: how much money could they expect from Mrs. Pierce, and how soon would they have it.

When the meeting adjourned and the Appletons made their way out, Linda smiled as she shut the door behind her mother, a startling, toothy burst of light so unlike anything Kit had ever seen on that girl's face that for a second, she was unrecognizable

Fourteen

Billy paced while he and Larry waited for the vet. Larry kept silent, for he knew that the few words of consolation that occurred to him, "it's only a horse," were best kept to himself.

Blue had not easily left his stall for over a week and then, after mornings spent coaxing him out, he often refused to return to the barn at night. On one evening that was predicted to be unseasonably warm, Larry suggested leaving Blue out to save the trouble. Billy, after rubbing his hands over his eyes in a way that mimicked his sister's exasperation, had patiently explained that most evenings in the winter were too cold to let the horses out on their own. Plus, a horse used to sleeping in a barn all its coddled life would spook at being left alone outside for the evening. As Billy spoke, most of what he said was engulfed in his modulated, soothing tone, and Larry had the sensation of being shushed like a child.

Blue kicked at his stall and whinnied. Cloistered in the barn all morning, he was restless. This horse doesn't need a vet, sighed Larry. He needs a shrink.

The vet, Dr. Thompson, had worked farms in the area for decades and, as the barns had given way to housing tracts, he had moved easily from cows and sheep to a specialty in horses. This north shore of Boston area, with its pristine beaches and pockets of exclusive wealth, was home to enough horse people to garner a good living. Known for his understated manner, Arthur Thompson had a calm way with even the worst animals and an accurate diagnostic record. His reputation was such that even those traveling through for a show or polo matches often made an appointment with him to check on a horse that seemed, for reasons unclear, under the weather.

When the doctor at last stepped out of the barn, Billy moved to take the door from him and latch it. The older man nodded his thanks and slowly worked the buttons of his worn corduroy jacket. Years of delivering calves and foals in cold weather had stiffened his large hands. "Well," he pronounced after a moment or two. "This one's spooked beyond saving."

Billy swore, turned quickly and kicked at the frozen ground. He paced a brief circle. "What are you gonna tell him?"

All eyes turned briefly to the great house before the conversation resumed.

"I'm going to tell him what I tell you. This horse is no good for games. Even if his leg holds out, he's too unpredictable."

Billy looked out toward the paddock. "He could hurt himself."

"He could hurt someone else." Dr. Thompson laid his arthritic hand, perpetually bent and graced with fine white hairs, on Billy's shoulder, although he knew full well that it was Rutherford's horse. "I'm sorry, son. You've done all you can. More than most could." He moved slowly toward his old Dodge truck, parked askance on the frozen ground some dozen yards ahead. "I could use someone like you," he grunted. "I don't get around like I used to."

He glanced Larry's way, but didn't address him. Larry wasn't surprised at being left out. These horse people instinctively knew their own.

What would happen to Blue if he could no longer play polo for Mr. Rutherford? Larry was afraid to ask. It also occurred to him, though, that if Blue weren't in Mr. Rutherford's stable, maybe Billy would leave this job. Maybe they both could leave.

They were, in any case, more and more inside the big house as the date for the holiday gala approached. On their hands and knees, they scrubbed down all the floors with water and vinegar. They beat the large oriental rugs with brooms, far enough from the paddock so as to not disturb the horses. They pushed heavy tables against walls and rearranged sofas. When the rented tables and chairs arrived, Billy and Larry set them up, and when the decorators made their appearance, the duo helped to hang the yards and yards of holly, mistletoe, and ribbon.

For Larry, the scene created inside the downstairs rooms of the mansion was like something he had seen in a movie.

No mantelpiece nor table nor window was left undraped, and most of the lightbulbs in the house were replaced with ones tinted a warm peach tone. A section of living room was cleared away for the live band, and caterers brought their own freezer trucks and parked them outside to handle all of the food. Instructed as to dish and silverware alignment and where to place the linen napkins at the food stations, Larry watched as the endless details grew toward an effect that surpassed its parts.

Larry would have liked to think the unpaid household bills motivated him to bring up Billy's previous invitation to help with the entertainment. It was true that the bills weighed somewhat on Larry's conscience. Their debts were the kind anyone with a regular paycheck could manage, and he knew his sister wasn't extravagant. When she bought something expensive, it was usually planned for and budgeted over months, and, besides, she shouldn't have to support him as well as their mother.

But, it was when, when the rooms were decorated, the candles placed, the food and drink ready to be laid out, and the band's sound system set up all in the early dark of a December afternoon, the dying light of the setting sun was so shimmering and beautiful as it caught a tray of cut glass tumblers placed near a window that Larry became quite desperate to see how the evening would unfold.

He found Billy the first place he looked, down by the barn, in the midst of his nightly ritual of coaxing Blue back into his stall. When he got to where Billy leaned over the fence, Larry playfully grabbed his hips from behind.

Billy, though, was focused on his horse and pushed him away. "What's got into you?"

Larry ignored the rebuff. "I want to go to the party. I'm short of cash."

Billy remained on the bottom rung of the fence, his back to Larry, watching Blue disappear in the darkness of the twilight.

He pushed away a jealous irritation at the horse. "Billy?" Larry repeated.

Billy shifted on the fence. "OK," he said. "I'll talk to Mr. Rutherford."

Fifteen

At noon Ruby picked up the phone in the kitchen to dial a friend who sometimes met her for coffee in the afternoons. The phone, however, was unresponsive. She pushed at the buttons on the cradle. Nothing. The line in her bedroom was also silent. She peered outside into the December sun and discerned no wind or storm. Maybe a squirrel had eaten through a wire. She had heard of this happening, although at this time of year, there weren't many squirrels about.

When the phone still didn't work by afternoon, Ruby wondered in earnest. She decided to put on her coat and head down to the end of the driveway to see if any neighbors were outside, perhaps to ask about their phones.

Silent and still and chilly, the cold air burned her lungs. Meeting someone would be unlikely, as the houses on their street were not clustered together and close to the road like those near the center of town.

Close to sunset, light fled the sky in rapid pace. Ruby stopped halfway down the drive. The wires hummed, and as the noise grew louder, she felt a flash of nauseous agitation pass through her, as if she would be sick to her stomach, right there on the pavement. She stopped and bent over. The nausea stayed for a few more minutes and Ruby started to panic. This feeling she knew well—these overwhelming and uncontrollable surges of emotion had been a frequent visitor since childhood. On the first day of first grade, she had been sick. Before her audition for *A Thousand Clowns*--summer stock on the Cape—she'd retched so hard she'd almost lost her voice. The night before her wedding she spent in the bathroom. With the pregnancy and birth of Kit, and then Larry, the illness and nausea had become so persistent that her mother had come to live with them and had stayed until her death, three years ago.

Ruby stood up. A cigarette would help, and she forced herself to walk steadily to the house, a distance she covered more easily as she got closer to the door.

Back inside, the kitchen clock 4:13. Time to turn on a few lights, she supposed, but she got distracted by an investigation of the kitchen cabinets. Thankfully, they'd eaten the last of the Thanksgiving leftovers, Kit had insisted they finish them, and Larry was again making fresh meals. He should be home any time now with groceries. She retreated to the living room, pulled a blanket over her shoulders, and curled into the couch to wait.

Kit drove up the darkened drive and fiddled with her keys to let herself in. She flicked on the kitchen lights, and everything in the room was haloed in neon blue for a brief second until her eyes adjusted. As she had every evening for the last week, she picked up the receiver and held it to her ear.

"It's dead."

"Mom!" Startled, she nearly dropped the phone.

"It hasn't worked most of the day."

"Oh, really?" Kit had anticipated the moment when her mother and Larry would ask why she, Kit, the bill payer and the one designated to maneuver around financial catastrophes, had let this happen. She pushed at the buttons on the cradle to buy time, but her mother was unaccountably lucid.

"You're not surprised by this."

Feigning ignorance or error galled her, but admitting she had let the phone go was also hard. "Well, the bills have been piling up."

Ruby stepped into the kitchen. She had wrapped a blanket around herself, and the color reflected in an unflattering way on her pale skin. "You don't lose track of much, Kit," she said.

Hearing her own name triggered an angry burst, but the sight of her mother draped like a refugee tempered her response. Kit had taken many rides on the roller coaster of expecting-her-mother-to-be-like-other-mothers and then rediscovering her mother wouldn't or couldn't handle basic tasks. The time after her grandmother's death had been particularly unnerving, and Kit had learned that by far the easiest and most efficient path was to handle things herself. She turned away and pulled open the drawer of bills. "Do you even know the last time the phone bill got paid?" She picked up the pile. "Or the mortgage? Or the electric bill? Or how much oil is left in the tank?" She waved the envelopes in her mother's direction.

"There's no need to take this out on me."

"But it is your problem too."

Ruby folded herself into the blanket. "I get alimony from your father."

"It's not enough."

"It used to be enough." Ruby's voice thinned into a high register.

Kit looked anywhere rather than at her mother. "You used to get child support."

"What are you saying?"

The hysterical tone in Ruby's voice ignited fury in Kit. "That you have to bring in some more money!"

"I haven't worked since before your brother was born. I was an actress," she added, defensively.

Kit pressed her hair to her forehead in exasperation. Her mother would be useless in a modern office, with the complex phone systems and the advent of computers. This was a woman who couldn't be trusted with the mail. "Doesn't your friend Gloria run the Feenbits Nursing Home?"

"Oh, no," began Ruby.

"You could work there, as some kind of aide or something. It wouldn't be much, but it would be something."

"Oh, no, Kit, don't make me," Ruby began, but stopped

midsentence as Larry made his way through the kitchen door, arms empty of groceries. Ruby ran to her son and threw her blanketed self against him.

"Don't let her do it," she wailed. "Don't let her do this to me!"

He struggled to shut the door.

"I'm your mother. I do the best that I can. It wasn't my fault your father ran off and abandoned us!"

To Larry, his mother's wrapped blanket brought to mind a straightjacket, and the comparison at that moment seemed apt. He looked to his sister for a clue, but Kit, still in her coat, leaned against the counter, arms crossed and with an expression that did not encourage sibling commiseration. Feeling flung into an uncomfortable corner, he tried to make eye contact with Kit, to get back on her team, the winning team. The signs did not look good. She stared at the ceiling, lips rolled inward, and her knee shook from tapping her toe on the linoleum.

He addressed the sniveling bundle pressed against him. "Could you let me in the house, please?"

"Are you mad at me too?"

Larry struggled with irritation. "I'm not angry, I just don't want to let in all the cold." He wiggled around her, trying not to step on the fuzzy blue slippers that took up twice as much room as her feet.

"Since when have you been worried about the oil bill?" snarled Kit.

Larry opened his mouth to defend himself, but his words were lost in the mad dash of his thoughts as he tried to reconstruct, as quickly and as innocently as he could, what exactly had happened to all the cash he'd received from his almost seven weeks at the Rutherford estate. He grabbed at his wallet and fished out forty dollars. "I'll have more," he promised. "I just..."

Kit didn't bail him out by finishing his sentence. She was so angry that she closed her eyes as he spoke. He couldn't really blame her. Although he knew he had spent far too much money on Thanksgiving dinner, he couldn't even explain what had possessed him to buy so much food.

Ruby took advantage of the lull to push her own case. "Tell her that I haven't had a decent part since before you were born!" She whirled toward Larry in her blanket.

Larry spoke over his mother's head. "You want her to get a job?"

"Oh, and do you have any more money?"

"We don't need a phone!" insisted Ruby.

"A phone?"

"Kit let the phone go."

Kit stood straight and took a step toward them. "I didn't let the phone go!" She turned to her mother. "You let the phone go!" She pointed at Larry. "And you, you let the phone go!"

Larry couldn't argue with that.

Kit picked her bag up off the counter.

He panicked, though, at being left alone with his mother. "Wait, Kit, where are you going?"

"You figure it out." She slammed out of the house, and mother and son were quiet with each other as they listened to Kit's car start and then pull out of the driveway.

By a mile down the street, Kit knew that all she wanted was to put on her pajamas and curl up in front of the TV with a warm plate of food. But the thought of spending the night with her mother and brother infuriated her.

Figuring she had two dollars and change in her purse, she headed toward Angela's. At the Minnizone house, the kitchen light was already out and the unsteady blue flicker of the TV bounced from the living room windows. Kit had eaten thousands of dinners in this house, and so she knew that once the kitchen was dark, the dishes sat in the drying rack and the family sat arranged around the TV. Kit guessed that Matt had already logged a few hours in the same familiar position, perhaps even taking her place.

She knocked at the side door, as loudly as she could to be heard over the TV yet not so much as to convey any sense of urgency or desperation. When Chris answered, she was startled to see him. "What," he asked. "Did you forget I live here too?"

She moved by him into the kitchen. "No, just surprised to see you up off the couch."

"Don't worry," he said, closing the door behind her. "I just came in here to finish off my after-dinner six pack." He lingered a second longer than he had to. He had clearly just showered, maybe just home from work and on his way out with what's her name. It occurred to Kit that plumbing might not be glamorous, but it most likely paid the bills. People with their own trucks and tools probably never had their phones turned off.

She couldn't help it. She sighed, a deep inhale and exhale that she immediately regretted and moved to cover by an overzealous greeting of Mrs. M.

"Honey," cooed Mrs. M, "you just missed Angie. They just left for the Green Street. She must have thought you'd meet them there."

They, considered Kit. Angela and Matt were already a "they."

"Not a problem. I wasn't sure I could make it." She flicked a glance at Chris, who knew she was lying. She hated that about him. "You know, working-girl hours, and all that." Canned laughter came from the living room, and Lizzie Minnizone and an accompanying preadolescent squeal whipped around the corner and into the kitchen.

"Ten minutes 'til bath time," called out Mrs. M.

Kit felt suddenly that what she really wanted to do was eat some Minnizone leftovers and sit on the couch and watch bad TV, and that if she confessed this, Mrs. M. would go straight to the refrigerator and pull out something for the oven, and Chris wouldn't say a word. But to stay would be admitting something, exactly what, she couldn't articulate, but it sat like a stone inside her.

"But you know me," Kit continued, "still burning that candle at both ends."

"Is that what they call it nowadays?" said Chris.

Mrs. M. gave her a hug. "That's my girl. You have yourself a good time while you're young."

Kit inwardly cursed as she made her way down the steps.

What began as an impulse to escape her mother and brother was becoming more complicated. Since bands played at Green Street Thursdays as well as the weekends, now she would need money for the cover. And, although the cover usually wasn't too steep, she didn't have enough money for the cover and a beer and something to eat. Back at the car, she turned on the car heater and crawled into the back seat. Sometimes coins from her bag or her pocket or a careless passenger landed there. A few quarters more along with whatever peanuts or pretzels she might find at the bar would give her enough leeway to spend a few hours at Green Street. She found a dime on the floor underneath the passenger seat, and a penny between the cushions in the back. However, when she opened her wallet to deposit the coins, she discovered five dollars tucked into the change compartment. With her thrill at finding the cash came an unhappy realization that now she really was on her way to meet Angie and Matt. Still she hesitated. No one knew what she had in her wallet. If she hadn't found enough money, she would have come up with another more presentable alibi to cover her tracks, her mother was sick, she needed enough sleep to handle work. Now that she had enough cash to go out, she could still use the same excuses.

The image of her mother wrapped in a blanket in her fuzzy blue slippers stopped her. She headed the car to Salem.

The night grew colder still, and Kit hurried toward the bar, where the thump of the music pulsed from an open doorway. Conscious of still wearing her work clothes, without even having run a brush through her hair since noon, she pressed her shoulders back and fluffed her hair with her fingertips. Once inside the bar, she met an onslaught of smoke and heat and noise and bodies. The ticket taker, a large man wearing a jean jacket bearing the insignia of a local band, had left his post to investigate angry voices that had risen above the din, so she was able to sneak by him without paying the cover. That trouble avoided, Kit walked on toward the bar to see what kind of snacks might be left on the counter, but nothing lay on the bar but beer bottles and mugs in various states of emptiness. Cigarette smoke swirled around her. Although she'd barely smoked since Thanksgiving, she wouldn't last long in here without a cigarette.

As Green Street never bothered with dim or mood lighting, Kit could see every face in the crowd, but Angela didn't appear. She barely remembered Matt, and doubted she could pick him out from all the other wide-shouldered boys in short hair, jeans, and a flannel shirt. She wondered if the kitchen was open; no one was eating. As she scanned the crowd once more, she looked toward the band and recognized the drummer. Thin, black jeans, his dark hair pulled back in a ponytail, it was definitely the same drummer she'd met the last time she was here. He gazed above the crowd with great concentration as he moved the sticks easily from drum to drum and his leg tapped a steady beat, pinning the guitars and the voices to the ground. What was his name again? Tony? Hadn't he insulted her and then patched it up in a masterful performance? Conscious suddenly that she was staring at him, Kit turned to the bar. If she was here, she might as well grab something to drink.

With nowhere to put her coat, she quickly became overheated, yet to carry it and her bag over her arm with a drink in the other hand was awkward, so she unbuttoned the jacket and pushed it back over her shoulders. She ordered a beer on tap because it was cheapest and scavenged the last handful of mini pretzels from a wooden bowl. Bits of salt hit her tongue and then melted in a satisfying way along with a swig of cold beer.

Through the spaces between the scattered dancers, Kit peered at the tables lining the wall, where Angela, who had always disliked standing, preferred to park and watch. Kit had never minded not having a table. There was energy in the mobility and the sense of possibility that accompanied having to move from place to place as the crowd shifted.

Between the beer and a cigarette accepted from a man with gray sideburns, Kit's hunger thinned away. Buffeted by the crowd, the bluesy music so loud that it precluded any attempt at conversation, she almost forgot why she had come and merely enjoyed the suspension of time and worry, feeling only the pulse of the music. She may have stopped looking for guys at places like this, but she still knew how to stand comfortably by herself at the edge of the crowd at the bar, watching the dancers.

The drummer drew her attention. She remembered his putting his arm around her shoulders in the hallway. The gesture had been nice, but so self-assured, like it was nothing to him to comfort strange women. She looked around at the girls in their tight jeans and expectant, made-up faces. He would know how to play them to his advantage in a way that the younger, more awkward guys wouldn't. And this room was full of guys who fell into that latter category. Kit wished she didn't find them, all the guys like Matt, all the guys who said little and weren't bothered by the lack of conversation, so tiresome.

She ordered another beer and by the end of the set needed to use the bathroom. The guitar signed off, and taped intermission music filled the buzz left by the still instruments. Kit was a little wobbly; no more beers she told herself. She wondered why Angela would come here at all with just Matt. They'd found what most everyone else here was looking for, and so unless they were meeting other friends, Angela was probably kicking back naked in some hotel room on Route 1 and using Kit as a cover for her parents. This thought and the sight of her own overheated face in the bathroom mirror did not cheer her.

In the narrow corridor from the bathrooms a brief wave of nausea told her she should probably just go home. But she couldn't just let this night defeat her, so when she passed the cigarette machine, she put in her quarters to buy a pack. I'll only smoke when I'm out, she told herself, not in the car and not at work. The quarters slipped into the slot, and she pulled the knob in front of her choice, but nothing happened. She pounded the side of the machine with her fist, and repeatedly pulled on the coin return to retrieve her quarters. The machine didn't respond. "Hey," she shouted. "Give me back my money!" She kicked at the bottom, just underneath where the packs were dispensed. "Hey!" she shouted again. "Give me my cigarettes!"

"You should give those up." It was Tony, the drummer, standing at her side as if summoned. His voice cut through her beer fuzz and fatigue and snapped her senses to. How had she forgotten about his voice? It was so precise and calm and awake and hard to hide from.

"I was, but I got hungry."

"Hungry for cigarettes?"

She laughed. "No, food."

"You don't look like you need to lose weight."

"You don't remember me, do you?" she asked. If he didn't remember her, she expected him to lie, but she figured she would be able to tell.

"Sure I do."

Kit's eyes flicked away from his scrutiny, and then she came back to meet his gaze, feeling she wanted to make it worthwhile for him to continue to lie.

"You're the working girl."

Well, she conceded, maybe he did remember her a little. It hadn't been a month since she was last here, and she'd recalled him as well as his name. But she was used to holding onto facts longer than those around her.

"Most people call me Kit."

"I didn't figure you for coming back, that's the thing."

She nodded; he had her right. "I wasn't planning to," she admitted. "This is kind of an accident."

Tony laughed, and Kit felt a flash of being caught and reeled in. She took a step back, but her heel hit a speaker. Imbalance mixed quickly with nausea and just as she felt herself fall, she landed securely instead, supported at the elbows by Tony.

"Too much to drink?" But there was no judgment in his tone.

She shook her head. "I'm not drunk, OK? It's just hot, and I missed dinner, and maybe lunch. But it's my own fault." She pulled away from him and then wished she hadn't.

He held out his hand. "Look," he said. "Just sit down." He pulled out a chair and set it a few feet from the stage. "I know one of the guys in the kitchen and he can fix you a sandwich."

Not so far in the past Kit knew she would have jumped into this game, but now the implied expectations of his comment just sent her into a crazy retreat. "Look, I'm sorry. It's been a long day. I'll catch you later."

He held his hands palms up. "You won't owe me a thing."

Famous last words, she thought, but he looked nice enough, as if he really might leave her alone once she was done eating. She sat, a little chagrined by her own hard edge. This being taken care of was not her style, but she would like a sandwich, so she might as well be nice about it. He disappeared into the kitchen and when he returned, he pulled aside a small table and set it up by her chair, like a waiter keeping his distance.

He turned from her and curled over a drum to adjust one

of the metal pieces that hooked the instrument to its stand.

She watched his fingers as they gently twisted the fly bolt, and then gave the instrument a slight pull to check the tension.

"Do things come loose?" she asked.

"Not usually, unless we're rushed with the setup, which we were."

"Running late?" she prompted.

"Dave's sister borrowed the van to move some stuff and she had a flat and…" He stopped. "You don't want to hear all this shit." The guitar player called him, and he left to confer with the rest of the band.

The next set started. She was close to the stage, but the speaker was set a few feet further out, so she wasn't deafened by the sound. After a few minutes, a hefty guy in kitchen whites delivered her a sandwich and a ginger ale. She bit into a thick roast beef and mayonnaise sandwich, and it was warm and instantly rewarding. The ginger ale was cold and swooped all the flavors away in an efficient gulp.

When the food was gone, she sat and listened to the music, especially the drums. Sitting alone so close to the stage, she began to feel self-conscious, like a child waiting for its parent to finish up work. Whatever attraction Tony might have had for her seemed to disappear with the arrival of her orphan act. Acutely embarrassed, Kit was worn enough finally to be ready to go home. She reached for her bag and her coat to leave, but, not wanting to seem ungrateful, she sat back down in her chair and waited for the end of the set.

When the set ended, only a few words passed among the musicians before they moved to break up the equipment. Kit put her coat back on. "Thanks, Tony," she called out.

The guitarist glanced at her and then returned to his instrument. "Hey," Tony called over the guitarist's head, "Can you give me a ride home?"

His manner was so business-like that she held up her car keys and nodded. After all, he had mentioned something about a flat tire, and at least she could pay him back for the sandwich.

It took the band a half an hour to break down and load up. When the last of the wires had been rolled and put away, he took her arm and they left through the back door, after the equipment.

Once outside, he didn't let go of her arm, and instinctively they hunched toward each other against the cold. It felt comfortable. As she unlocked her car, she warned him, "Don't count on the heat."

"I never do."

That's not what I meant, she almost said, but stopped herself because it was fun to be with someone who returned her words right back at her.

He directed her through the streets to his apartment, a three-decker not far from the bar. After she pulled to the curb and put the car in park, he leaned across the seat and pulled her towards him in an easy motion. Once their cheeks and lips touched, he was so warm that any hope at a decision disappeared. She turned off the engine. As they made their way to his apartment, she barely noticed the flights of rickety wooden steps and, once inside, the spare underheated apartment, the unmade futon, or the clutter of clothes and sheet music.

She notices his bulk—how his shoulders and chest cover her completely, how if he took his weight off his arms and just lay on top of her, she would smother. His legs feel heavy as they nudge hers apart. NO *is what she is thinking, but another part of her answers, what will happen if I try and stop this now? "Why are you so tense?" he whispers, "Are you frigid or something?" She doesn't want to be frigid or cold; she wants to be hot, smoking hot. Her "no" feels so small and insignificant, pointless even; it will be over soon enough anyway.*

Then, something like panic catches—she is with Trey. The heavy weight of him presses her down, squeezes the air out of her, inch by vertical inch. She tries to speak, to protest, but no words form. Her face buried by his neck, she can't see, and she can't move her arms to push up against him. In another second, she is sure she will suffocate…

Kit woke with a start in the quarter light of winter morning. Her eyes blinked open, she emitted a slight gasp, and her shoulders twisted a tiny bit off the pillow. The hot body next to her acknowledged her movement with a murmur, and snuggled into her back. She froze and gripped herself tightly until her mind took back the reins—it's only a dream. He's gone and you won't let him back. You-will-never-let-him-back, she said to herself.

Yet two years after she had managed to rid herself of his actual presence, Trey still haunted. The sheets were warm, as was the body behind her, but her nakedness had become unbearable.

She reached away to feel for her clothes. In the pre-sunrise gloom, she barely made out the legs of a chair, and she shifted through various hard objects within inches of the futon on the floor. They were all cold, and the floor was particularly freezing. She couldn't believe she had actually fallen asleep in such a dump, and it wasn't as if she could blame it on the alcohol she had drunk or chock it up to habit; penury had kept her sober and, for all her bravado, last night was the first time she had ever gone home with a virtual stranger. Vaguely frightened and concerned about being late for work, she figured being up and dressed and out as quickly as possible was the best plan available.

A hand on her leg pulled her back. "Where you goin'?"

"Work," she said, tense and irritated at not being able to simply leave.

"Call in sick." He wrapped himself over her shoulders.

She started away, hesitated, and then leaned back into the warm body. She sighed. There was something very relaxing about this Tony person. His voice was so calm. She closed her eyes. Her heartbeat began to slow. This was all much better if she couldn't see her murky surroundings. "I won't get paid if I don't show up."

"Is that a problem?"

She almost laughed. "Do you have a trust fund?"

"What do you think?"

"Then it's a problem."

He let her go and Kit was slapped by unexpected disappointment. Well, she huffed to herself, he was easy to shake. He moved over to the other side of the futon and picked through a pile of clothes. He turned to her. "Am I getting up for nothing?" He pulled a dirty looking green sweatshirt out, and sniffed at it.

"What do you mean?"

"If you're not going to work, I'm not making you breakfast." He pulled the sweatshirt on, and returned to searching his pile.

Kit smiled, despite her disgust at the collection of unfolded clothes and personal possessions that emerged in the growing dawn.

"Thatta girl," he said. He plucked up a pair of ragged jeans.

The apartment was freezing, but at least the water was hot in his minute plastic shower stall. Kit let the warm streams run over her, and she worked to push Trey from her mind. She picked at her clothes; aside from their smoky odor, they were not so dirty from yesterday's wearing because it was winter and she sweated far less in the winter. And, after the shower, at least her skin felt clean.

Tony's kitchen space was the size of a dining room table, but he had managed eggs and toast and coffee by the time Kit finished her ablutions. The apartment was still freezing, though, and she grabbed her coat.

"You don't have heat?"

"It's controlled by the people downstairs, so it takes a while to rise in the morning." He put a plate in front of her. "I'm not usually up at this hour."

Kit sloshed an egg onto a piece of toast, folded the toast in half and chomped. The coffee was hot and warmed her going down.

"You like to eat," he commented.

Tony seated himself across from her, in a wooden chair that shook as he reached for his coffee. Dark hair hung around his hollow cheeks, where his years sat. His face was not plump and smooth like the guys closer to her age, but there were more shadows, as if he had more to say. She tried not to stare.

"What?" he asked.

There was no plate in front of him. "You're not eating?" she asked.

"Too early."

"This was nice of you," she said.

"It was nice of you to stay," he answered, unexpectedly gentle.

She looked down at her food, but she had eaten it all. Something about him demanded her honesty, so she nodded, unsure of what to say and unwilling to make something up. "I gotta go to work."

He caught her at the door. They kissed and Kit was in danger of heading back to the sloppy futon.

"Now you can find me, but I can't find you," he said as she edged her way out of his arms, toward the hall.

Kit glanced in at the ripped sheet hanging in front of a tall window. The only time she had lived away from her home was her two-semester stint in a dormitory. There, the constant noise and eyes on her had been an adjustment, but one that would have been easier if she and Trey weren't so often the object of gossip. This memory brought a sudden rush of shame, and in a flash she wondered if her judgment in men wasn't somehow fundamentally flawed, if she was doomed to bad choices and bad luck. This Tony was sure to bring her nowhere good. How could he?

"You can't call me because I don't have a phone," Tony continued.

"You don't?" This was worse than she thought. What kind of person doesn't have a phone?

"It's not a legal apartment so the phone company won't authorize one." He held on to the ends of her fingers as she backed away. "You're not gonna kiss and flee on me, are you?" But he smiled, as if he had never considered she would. What made him so secure?

She told him her phone number.

"Thanks."

"Aren't you gonna write it down?"

He shook his head. "I don't need to. I'm good with numbers."

Her boots clicked noisily down the wooden steps toward her car. He didn't know her last name. He didn't know she had no phone either, and she wasn't sure if you got your same number back when you got your phone turned on again. Tony had been really nice, special even, but she didn't know what to do with all that. Kit started her car and drove to work. It was easier this way, safer that he didn't know how to find her.

Sixteen

Kit let herself in to the darkened office. She hung up her coat and warmed her hands over the heating grate, sniffing at the underarms of her blouse to check for odor. No sweat, just a faint scent of use, nothing that keeping her sweater on throughout the day couldn't mask.

She sat down, and noticed her boots. Scratches incurred on the Pierce marsh remained, and the heels had worn rounded and discolored. Wasn't there some story she'd had to read in high school where the heroine had to blacken her old boots so no one would know how far the family had sunk? Maybe she should invest in some shoe polish as well. Or, she laughed to herself, Tony probably already owned some. She could borrow his.

A sharp buzz reminded her she was at work, and she answered the phone.

Angela whispered, "What did you tell my mom?"

"I didn't tell her anything," said Kit, trying not to let her annoyance appear in the tone of her voice, "because I didn't know anything."

"You were my cover, and then you show up at the

house!"

"Ange, next time I'm your cover, you should let me know." This came out softer than she had planned but, once spoken, Kit understood she had no anger left from last night.

"I tried, but there's something wrong with your phone." There was a pause. "It's Matt." Angela exhaled loudly. "All he wants is to do it."

"That's a problem?"

"You don't know, Kit. He spends all this money on motel rooms and all I'm worried about is that my parents will find out."

Kit considered whether anyone in the Lavoie house noticed when she hadn't come home last night.

"Once we're engaged, it should get better, I guess."

"What should get better?"

"Oh, you know. Stuff."

Isn't this supposed to be the fun part, Kit wanted to ask, the part where you fall in love and can't get enough of each other? Or maybe Angela was just talking about her parents.

"I just told your mom that I thought we were meeting at the house, before we went to Green Street."

"Did she buy it?"

Chris certainly hadn't, but Mrs. M. might have. "Yeah, I think so."

"So we'll just pretend that we were there."

"I was there."

Angela's voice rose. "You went to the Green Street by yourself?"

I thought you would be there, Kit wanted to remind her, but Angela was too caught up in her own cover story to remember that Kit wasn't in on it too. "It was fine. That same band was there, the one that played that time I met Matt."

"That time that skanky drummer was all over you?"

Kit paused. Skanky implied personal filth or underhandedness, not the person who had made her breakfast and pried her defunct phone number out of her. "What was wrong with him?"

"Come on, Kit. He was old for one thing, and weird for another."

"Weird?"

"Look, Matt's got some nice cousins, with real jobs and all."

The other line rang. "I gotta get this other line," said Kit.

"I gotta go to class now, but I'll introduce you," assured Angela.

Jack was on the other line. "Good morning!" he hailed like the announcer on a radio show. "Good morning to you!"

Oh great, Kit thought, an exuberant mood. They could be fun, but they also made her nervous, made her feel too much under a spotlight since she was frequently the sole audience for his one-man shows.

"Ho, ho, ho," she heard. The door opened and in walked Jack; she heard him both on the phone and in person.

"You heard me, now you see me! Do you wonder how?"

Kit stood up. "You got one of those phones!"

He sidled up on her desk, in full best-friend mode. "Look, I'll call us." He pressed on the key pad, and the office phone rang. Kit picked up, said, "Hello, Rioux & Rioux."

Jack hung up on her, and then burst out laughing.

"Let me try," said Kit. He handed her the phone and she dialed the office. Jack picked up the phone and in a high pitched voice said, "Hello, Rioux & Rioux?"

Kit hung up on him. He glared at her and for a moment her heart stopped but then Jack laughed, so Kit knew it was OK and she laughed too.

"No more lines at the pay phone. I'll be able to call anyone, anytime." He put the phone into his briefcase, and the tone in the little room dampened immediately.

Kit adjusted seamlessly. "So, it was just you at the Appleton hearing?" she asked him.

That Jack hadn't heard a word from either Mrs. Pierce or her lawyers hadn't daunted him at all. He had asked the court, and then was granted a hearing in order to secure her assets in case of victory, to procure an attachment on her known property, the house on Argilla Road.

"Just me," he answered.

"Success?" she asked.

"Of course," he answered before he disappeared into his office.

This meant that until the matter between the Appletons and Mrs. Pierce was resolved, Mrs. Pierce would be unable to sell her property. Notice of this legal binder was filed at the Registry of Deeds for all to see, and delivered, again by a process agent, to the Pierce address. So, in a way, Jack now controlled her house.

Kit guessed that since Jack had not moved to attach any other property or accounts, including the small bank account that Kit had found, no other large assets had yet been unearthed.

Kit doubted Mrs. Pierce had any knowledge of any of what had happened over the last couple of months: no notice of the summons and notice telling her that a suit had been filed against her, no notice that her property was attached in order to secure judgment in case of her loss. Each time papers were served, the process server had duly filled out the back of the form stating that he had left the papers at Mrs. Pierce's "last and usual abode." This because none of his three attempts at knocking at her door to deliver it in person were successful—Mrs. Pierce may have been wandering in the marshes when the process server arrived or hiding somewhere in the back of the house, ready with her pitchfork.

Kit guessed the papers were probably still wedged somewhere near the front door, which she clearly hadn't used in years. Eventually they would be snowed or rained on or blow away. And, if she saw the papers, they would read like legal nonsense even to the most informed person. How could someone like Mrs. Pierce make any sense of the accusations and deadlines? Most people who receive such a package hire a lawyer without bothering to decipher its contents.

Jack poked his head back out. "I'd like some coffee when

you get a chance," he said.

Kit sighed. Jack hadn't paid his firm's share of the coffee fund.

She knocked on the outside of his door even though it was open. "Um, Jack, you're overdue on the coffee fund."

Jack was bent over an open bottom drawer. "And?" he said without looking up.

"Ten dollars," said Kit. "Or no coffee."

Rioux & Rioux was chronically late with its coffee dues. Although no one ever said anything to Kit, she knew they all kept track.

Jack reached into his wallet, pulled out a five, and threw it on the desk. "That's all I have," he said. "Can you spot me the rest?"

He had asked her to do this before, and she had never been repaid. "No," she said firmly. "I can't." Still she took the bill, put it in an envelope labeled "Firm Coffee," and put the money in her top drawer, next to her emergency cigarettes.

The crinkly, unopened packet beckoned. She raised to her nose for a slight sniff, then quickly flung it down, and slammed the drawer shut. Perhaps she could weasel some more money out of Jack over the next couple of days so she could comfortably go back to the lunchroom for coffee when she felt the familiar craving.

An errand promised for Mr. Levinson spelled a shorter lunch hour. This was fine with Kit since her adventures of the previous evening had left her without a lunch or the funds to buy one. Sometimes people left extra snacks in the kitchen downstairs, especially during this festive time of year, but she was embarrassed to help herself if Jack hadn't paid up his coffee debt. Kit considered paying the five in the ruse that she had thought Rioux & Rioux was only one month behind and not two, a tactic she'd employed once or twice before, but in the end she didn't, whether because she had lost the heart for the deception or because Mrs. Bergen, with her preternatural intuition, was impossible to fool, she wasn't sure. What she was sure she would never do is take the five and buy herself lunch. Kit had never had any interest in money she regarded as belonging to other people.

The errand for Mr. Levinson took her to the section of Salem of old narrow streets, to a shop with cloudy sienna windows covered in chipped painted lettering. Shadows from the close buildings left the entranceway in gloom, but a cheerful bell hung over the door announced Kit's arrival. Two steps inside the dimly lit store, Feingold's Stationery, she stopped, overwhelmed by the number of items for sale. Shelves lined the high walls and proceeded from the entrance back in uneven lines, almost like a library. Colored paper of all kinds, as well as envelopes, invitations, and personal stationery crowded for space. One section held valentines, pink cupids and red hearts surrounded by thin gold ribbons. Another featured invitations—for birthdays, baby showers, weddings, and luncheons. Yet another section included a glass case stocked with hundreds of different pens and inks.

Near the back, on the only bit of free wall, hung neatly

framed diplomas, some with gold seals and colored ribbons, lined up in crooked rows. She peered more closely, but the ornate Latin inscriptions were impossible to decipher.

A portly man in a misshapen maroon cardigan appeared at her side. Although graying, he bounced slightly on his toes; this gave him the appearance of a much younger man. "In the market for some credentials?" he asked her.

His somewhat disheveled appearance seemed a natural outgrowth of his surroundings. A more precise man would have been out of place here. "What are these?" Kit asked.

He waved his hand. "Merely a side business. See here. I've got the colors of all the local schools. Here's one for Harvard, crimson and white, and here's one for Tufts, blue and brown." He sped through his descriptions as if there were hundreds more lined up and ready to go.

"What are they supposed to be?"

"Why diplomas, of course."

"Isn't that illegal?"

He chuckled. "It's America! Here you can buy everything." He turned serious. "Why would it be illegal? I don't sell transcripts, and anyone can call a school for an accurate record."

"I guess you're right." She remembered her errand. "Are you Mr. Feingold? I'm here to pick up an order for Attorney Levinson."

He clapped his hands together. "Of course, why didn't you say you were a friend? I could give you a special deal. Maybe buy one as a gift. It's that time of year."

Kit smiled to think of Jack opening a present of a fake Harvard diploma. He would joke about it, but she was sure it would end up on his wall, right above the Harvard chair. No, there was no sense in encouraging him.

"Not today, thank you."

"I didn't know Aaron had someone working with him now."

Kit, sensitive to Mr. Levinson's predilection for discretion, wasn't sure how to respond. "I just help out from time to time."

"We go back a long time, we two, through the good times and the bad." He paused here, and Kit held her breath in wait for the story that clearly sat at the tip of his voluble tongue, but Mr. Feingold closed his mouth and patted her arm. "Just wait here, and I'll get the papers."

When Kit returned to his office, Attorney Levinson was on the phone. He nodded at her and motioned for her to sit down. She'd run quite a few errands for him over the last couple of weeks, and she hoped that his invitation meant that he was going to pay her. Not that she was worried, he always paid her, generously and in cash. But it was his company, too, that she enjoyed, his orderly office and his comfortable chair.

The phone conversation continued. He stood against the window, the creases on his pants precise, his jacket hung neatly on a hook, sporting the tan and gray sleeveless cardigan he often pulled out on cold days when he wasn't expecting clients. Even the strands of his few gray hairs were in order. She wondered if his house was as neat, or whether his wife was inclined to squalor.

Kit settled into the chair, tired from the night before and feeling a little self-conscious about her own clothes, which she had now worn for two days in a row. She stared at the row of pictures Mr. Levinson had lined up across his credenza. There were new pictures of the two boys next to the sweet-looking girl with dark eyes and straight hair who stared right at the camera, her mouth in a wide, open grin seldom seen in posed pictures. As she sat, she noticed something. There were a series of pictures of the boys, aging from babies to now-handsome men who looked about Kit's age, but the little girl's picture didn't have any older companions. A sudden uncomfortable feeling rested then in Kit's body, making her legs heavy and her skin hot, and she turned quickly from the photos to catch Mr. Levinson staring at her. It was all so quick, he turned away before she was sure she hadn't imagined his sharp glance, but she was left uneasy.

She heard him hang up. "Your friend Mr. Feingold's a funny guy," she said as soon as the phone hit the cradle.

Mr. Levinson laughed. "What did he try to sell you?"

"Phony diplomas," she answered.

He held up his hands, stop. "I don't need to know about that."

I didn't buy one, she wanted to protest, but didn't because she knew that he would never entertain the idea that she would consider it. "Everyone needs to earn a living," she said instead.

"You're right, Kit."

And Kit felt a sense of satisfaction at having pointed out something that he hadn't duly considered, a sort of righting of a wrong.

He handed her an envelope. "For all your help."

"Thanks," she said, awkward. "It's never much to do and I don't mind at all."

"No," he corrected her. "Value your time and effort."

She nodded, unsure of how to reply and so stood to go. "Mr. Levinson," she asked as she reached the door, "what happens if a person gets served with a complaint but they never know it so they don't get a lawyer and they miss all the hearings and the court rules against them, attaches their property, and then tries to take their house?"

"Well, given your broad set of facts, it would be hard to say exactly."

She should have known better than to expect an easy answer, but that was why she'd learned so much from him—he saw the curves in the straightest of lines.

"We really don't have the time to fully discuss all the implications right now because each situation varies. But," and here he frowned somewhat, "what I think you're asking me is a question that goes to the root of the fundamental fairness of the system. Yes, there are judicial remedies, called relief from judgment, that can be invoked in very specific circumstances, within, of course, strict time limits."

"Relief from judgment? It sounds like something from out of the Bible." Kit had the double pleasure then of making him laugh.

Mr. Levinson continued. "Different facts can invoke these protections, excusable negligence, fraud, an incompetent defendant. It's in the Mass General Laws. Rule 55 or Rule 60 is a good place to start."

She nodded. Mr. Levinson knew she couldn't ask particular questions if they would reveal the details of a specific case, and he of all people would never encourage her to reveal any detail, no matter how random, of an ongoing case.

He saw her hesitation. "Sometimes, Kit, you have to remind yourself that whether something is fair is something every good lawyer, every person, should always consider."

Jack would never have said that. If questioned, he would probably point out that real estate law is a lot more about money than criminal law, and so has different rules. But Kit felt the rightness of Mr. Levinson's words, and was grateful for their underlying decency.

"Thank you," she said. "As usual," she added. When she shut the door behind her, the bright eyes and smile of the girl in the picture stayed with her. She shook off the shivers the image brought. Stop it, she chastised, before you turn into Mrs. Bergen.

Back at her desk, she wrote the laws Mr. Levinson mentioned down on a piece of paper and stored it in her top drawer. Then she put the envelope of money in her purse to count later, out from under the watchful eyes of Jack Rioux who, she had to admit, if he caught her in one of her weaker moments, could easily weasel it out of her for the coffee fund.

Seventeen

Larry chose to wear one of his Chinese silks to Mr. Rutherford's party. After rejecting a blue hued one as too sedate and another with a black background as not festive enough, he chose a red rising phoenix with bright yellow eyes over a swirl of fiery colors. The sleeves billowed, but he tucked in the waist because he liked the crisp effect of the belt pulling in the fabric. Larry preferred to think of his wardrobe choice as the alternate route of color and innovation, but it was also true he didn't own a suit.

Toward seven o'clock on the designated evening, snow began to fall. Larry drove the slick roads carefully. As he made his way down Argilla, thick, wet flakes clung to the desiccated grasses, causing the marsh to loom white in the distance.

He parked in the back by the barn so as to not take spots from the real guests. Although he had spent the better part of the last several days setting up for the party, this knowledge didn't detract from his enjoyment as he walked through the front door. Peach glow from the lamps reflected and sparked in the gold and silver ribbons, which wound their way through the miles of holly. I am transported, he told himself, a line he remembered from an old movie, one of hundreds he'd seen with either his mother or his sister from the dull comfort of their couch. I am transported.

Part of the large foyer had been converted into a coat check. Three long coat racks were cordoned off by red rope and guarded by an ancient gray-suited man with a sprig of holly in his lapel. He took Larry's parka solemnly in his gnarled hands and walked at a hobbled pace toward the rack. Unsure of whether waiting for the man to hang the coat would be considered rude, as if he weren't trustworthy, or to turn away before the deed was done would the rude thing, he hesitated. Impatient, he could barely watch as the end of the hanger went first into one arm, then into the second and, after two or three passes at the rack, was finally properly hung.

The early guests comprised mostly older women sporting wrap garments constructed of elaborate fabric and custom buttons, purchased during their sojourns east, when they were living out of country with husbands transferred by large corporations or some branch of the foreign service.

Spying neither Mr. Rutherford nor Billy, Larry walked up to the bow-tied bartender set up for duty along the broad wall of the sitting room. Something about the men in black suits and the low notes on the bass coming from the jazz band in the sunroom reminded him of Frank Sinatra in *Ocean's 11* and so he ordered what Frank had ordered, a scotch and ginger ale. He sipped as it he ambled through the rooms, admiring his handiwork, as the party slowly filled with guests.

Larry's opportunity to be helpful appeared a good way through his first scotch, when he spotted an older woman in a pink satin jacket with butterfly buttons in trouble, as she attempted to balance her appetizer plate, martini glass, and pink silk purse in her two trembling hands. "Oh my," she exclaimed as Larry set her up at a small side table, much to the amusement of her companions. One, tucked into a peacock feather–patterned kimono, pointed to his chest.

"I do like this," she said. "Such a lively pattern. Such details, it must be Chinese." She tilted her head, her gray hair piled high and held in place with small chopsticks. "Some of those old patterns are so lovely, but the workmanship hasn't been the same since the war. And you know, of course, things being what they are, Stelton and I were never able to make it back there."

"It's tragic," agreed the lady in pink. "I'll never go back to Saigon in this lifetime. And, you know," she looked up at Larry over a forkful of blue cheese, "if I do get back there, it will never be the same. How could it be?"

Although unsure of the exact source of her nostalgia, Larry shook his head in commiseration. "The old tailors would be gone," he offered.

The ladies laughed at this witty remark, "Mr. Rutherford always has such charming young men at his parties!" Before long, Larry moved on to waltzing the women around the dance floor. For this talent, he silently thanked his middle-school teacher, Miss Switzer, for forcing the whole class of reluctant eighth graders to learn to waltz, samba, and cha-cha. He had loved those lessons, learned them so quickly and well that he'd become an instant hit with the girls, as well as Miss Switzer. When not so much his prowess as his enthusiasm on the dance floor had ignited a sense of betrayal among the boy classmates, Larry had backed down, feigned clumsiness, aped boredom. The whole incident he recalled now in great shame. He'd had to squirt milk through a straw up his nose the following lunch to regain the trust of his companions. Had it been worth it?

When the older ladies grew rosy with exertion, Larry left them to recover on plush couches with promises to visit later. "Go," they chased him away. "Go play with someone your own age."

The party grew, couples arriving, men in black suits and women in expensive evening wear. He spotted one woman's hair that was swooped up in a roll, her dress fit tight like a clasp. Everyone, it seemed to Larry, moved securely through the rooms, drinks in hand, smiles on their faces. Who was he supposed to be?

When he eventually spied Billy, he nearly raced across the room to him, but pulled up when he saw Mr. Rutherford appear at his side and slide his hand across the back of Billy's neck, resting there in a possessive clasp.

Larry turned away quickly, his breath short, his face heated. What kind of life was Billy living? Did he really sleep in the freezing barn, with nowhere else to go, and desperately need money? Well, I need the money too, he thought, but what is it I'm supposed to be doing?

He returned to the bartender for another scotch and ginger ale, which he drank quickly.

Someone tapped him lightly on the shoulder—Billy, whose features blurred by drinking floated spectrally over his sharp, dark tuxedo. "Hey," he whispered, "have you tried the brie canapés? You must try the brie canapés."

"Come off it," said Larry, unaccountably close to tears.

"Shh, shh," said Billy. "They're really tasty."

"The act is not necessary," he repeated. "For me," he added, in case Billy's chatter was somehow a part of Mr. Rutherford's job description.

Billy pulled at the wrists of his dress shirt, held his arms out in front to check sleeve length, and then brushed his hand along Larry's arm. "Come on, it's a party."

Larry stepped back a few steps in protest as the ladies in pink and peacock paused by them on their way to an early exit. Larry made introductions all around, and the women and their encouraging coos cheered him.

"That was quite a bevy of geisha girls you infiltrated. Did you know the one in pink's deceased husband was very high up in the state department?" said Billy.

Larry laughed. "She mentioned something about her time in Vietnam."

"Serious connections, my boy, that lady has some serious connections."

Larry watched as they trailed toward the exit. What does that mean, exactly, he wanted to ask. And how is that helpful to me? He drank the last of his scotch and ginger ale, the ice long melted, and placed the glass on a tray.

Billy ran his hand quickly through Larry's hair, as though adjusting a wry cowlick, letting his thumb linger on his cheek. "Larry," he whispered. "Don't be silly. Come on, just play geisha girl, you're half-dressed the part anyway."

Larry understood then that his loud shirt marked him as much as the bowties on the bartenders. The other male guests were uniformly in sharp suits or some kind of tuxedo. The bright yellows and reds that had seemed so glad just a few short hours before now seemed to him more like clown colors, something worn by a person you don't take seriously.

Across the room, Mr. Rutherford was looking around. Billy followed Larry's gaze. "Check out the library," he called back as he hastened away.

The library was darker than the rest of the house, and books on shelves lined the four walls, tempering the voices of the dozen or so men, all older than he, seated or standing in clumps. A fire gently crackled in the fireplace. Larry walked in a few feet, and, unsure of what to do next, found himself reading the book titles. One had a pretty green binding with gold letters, and he plucked it out.

"Do you enjoy French literature?"

A man with a fuzz of red-blond hair stood close to his elbow. Larry thought of Kit and wished she were here. She would know what to say to smart people. Maybe she could even hook one for good and end their money troubles forever. She was pretty enough, and smart too, at least she used to be when they measured those things, back in school.

Larry held up the closed book and grinned. The man plucked the book from Larry's hand, checked the inside front page, and called out to someone across the room. "Look at this translation, Van! It's older than the original." He laughed, his companion laughed, and Larry laughed too.

Soon three or four people were gathered around the book Larry had chosen.

"This must have been done simultaneously, when they refused to print it in London."

The red-haired man switched to another language, and the others answered. Larry guessed French. "Bonjour," he recalled from school, but that meant good morning, and by now it was close to midnight.

He felt a tug at his arm; a hand attached to a velvet jacket pulled at his sleeve. "Come down here," a voice said kindly, "where the air's not so hot."

On the embroidered yellow couch that Billy had pointed out to him on their first evening sat a much older man with short white hair like a brush, wearing a pale yellow silk shirt under a maroon jacket. He patted the cushion next to him.

Larry sat.

"And how do you know Charlie?" His tone was smooth and calming.

"Charlie?"

"Our host."

"Mr. Rutherford?

The man smiled.

"Through Billy."

"Ah, Billy. Oh," he said, "forgive me." He held out his hand. "I'm Jerry Sorgen."

Jerry looked right at him, as if taking him in, every bit of him, as if ready to see what else Larry might say, and Larry relaxed and felt right then that he could actually be friends with this person. He shook the man's hand. "I really like your jacket," he offered.

"You said you're a friend of Billy's?"

"Yes," said Larry. "We're together," he blurted.

Jerry patted his arm. "I'm glad to hear it," he said.

Larry, though, barely heard the words, through the panic that surged through him. As true as the statement was to him, he hadn't yet told Billy, nor anyone else. Why confide in a man he'd just met because he seemed nice and wore a great jacket? Larry had no idea.

The conversation in French continued behind them.

"What is it about that language," remarked Jerry, "that turns some people into peacocks?"

"I wonder what he'd think of all this," said Larry as he nodded toward the picture of Rutherford's stern ancestor in the yellow cravat who hung, as if in disapproval, over the fireplace.

"That one?"

"Yeah, the shoe baron."

Jerry put down his wine glass and laughed hard. "The shoe baron?"

Larry liked this man like he'd liked the lady with

chopsticks in her hair. "He made the family money in shoes." Jerry listened to the story he clearly didn't believe. Larry tried to remember what Billy had told him, but as he spoke he grasped that whether the anecdote was true or not was not the point, it was that Mr. Rutherford felt the need to construct a story about himself at all that was interesting to Jerry.

"Charlie always did manicure his image. What else did he tell you?"

"Something about the Mayflower."

Jerry shook his head. "Charlie's a brilliant financier. It's funny that's not enough for him."

The image of Mr. Rutherford's arm across the back of Billy's neck came back to Larry, but its impact was blunted as Larry began to build his own case—just because a rich man wants something, doesn't mean he gets to have it

It was past two by the time Larry returned to the coat room, and the old coat-check man in the gray suit was nowhere to be seen. Dozens of coats still hung quietly on the long metal rod, but Larry had no trouble spotting his parka, its fake fur hood rakishly unfit for the trim hanger. He stepped behind the rope to grab his coat and there, hanging on the next hanger was the exact coat Kit had picked out from her *Vogue* magazine. He paused. Music played on in the distance from the center of the house, but the kitchen was quiet, as were the hall and the front entrance. He touched the soft leather, the even softer sheared lambs' wool. When he gave one of the intricate buttons an exploratory twist, the coat slipped off the hanger. He bent down to pick it up and, on an impulse, scooped it over his arm and trotted quickly out of the house.

Halfway across the front lawn, he swore. He hadn't checked the size. What if it was the wrong size? But, somehow he knew it wasn't, that it would be just perfect. As he threw the coat in the back seat of his car, he remembered that he had left his own coat back in the house. Feeling suddenly trapped in a bad TV episode, he knew that to leave his own coat next to the missing coat was like leaving a calling card. He only owned one coat; someone would be sure to recognize it. And if not, who knew what kind of evidence he might have left in its pockets to trace it back to him?

He trotted back across the lawn, feeling the dull cold on his skin, yet breathing so fast that the temperature didn't register as pain or cold, just a kind of ache. To go back in the front door would be a give-away if the man in the gray suit had returned to his coat-check spot, so he made his way around the back of the house in the dark, to where he knew some French doors opened onto a back garden. After three days with the decorators and the caterers, he knew this house, at least the downstairs, very well. His scotches and ginger ales caught up with him now, and he stumbled, tripping once and landing fully on his palms, cutting one on the frozen ground, he thought, but it was hard to tell in the moonless dark.

Luck held, though, as he found the outside doors that led to an unused summer porch. He opened the porch window, crawled into a little used servant's bathroom, slipped into the darkened hallway, and back into the central section of the house without attracting notice. Larry then made his way to the front hall, where, sure enough, the older man in the gray suit sat on his stool by the emptying coatrack.

"Long night," commented Larry, but the man barely shrugged. "Mine's the olive green one," he said, as if he needed to distinguish his cheap nylon parka from the sea of dark wool overcoats. When the man turned his back, Larry glanced at his hands. Both his palms were bleeding. He made sure to take the coat with his fingertips because he'd seen enough detective shows to know that almost anything gives away a thief—and blood even more so.

Eighteen

The next afternoon, the coat sat in a ball of fur and skin on his bedroom floor.

Larry picked it up gingerly. Other than a whiff of cigarette smoke, it was perfect for Kit. Size six, it looked hardly worn, with no traces of perfume around the neck and the only items in the pockets a few unused tissues and a half a theatre ticket stub—"My Own Pr" it read, playing at the "American T."

Even though lined in sheepskin, the coat was surprisingly light and carefully trimmed. Particularly nice were the buttons, the leather covers worked into a neat cross-hatch pattern; big, not bulky, they fit precisely into their assigned slits, which were sewn closely all around with thick tan thread. He put one arm through the sleeve, but the back of it barely covered his wide shoulders and he was afraid to bring his arms close toward his body for fear of pulling something irreparable.

A bigger problem than cigarette smoke, which Larry supposed could be explained away by it being left at a friend's house, was the lack of price tags. He would have to find some kind of replacement. Using the black silk label "PK" sewn in minute stitches under the collar on the inside, he would have to find the *Vogue* magazine in her room and search out the coat from its pages to see where it was sold. Then he could go to the store and steal some price tags to match, all in time for Christmas. The intervening week would give him time as well to air out some of the smoke from the lamb's wool lining.

After he heard Kit leave with their mother, he went to her room. Although Larry was rarely in Kit's bedroom, she kept it so neat that he had high hopes of finding the magazine. It wasn't on her dresser where he had last seen it, when Kit had shown him the picture, but he doubted she had thrown it out. *Vogue* was an expensive magazine, and she always bought September's because that issue featured all the new fall and winter fashions. Sure enough, on the small painted table by her bed lay a tidy pile of magazines. He picked up the shiny pages, distracted at once by the glamorous photos of stark models draped over old cars and burnt out buildings.

He found the coat, and then checked the back section to see where it could be bought locally, a trick Kit had taught him. The store was in Boston, as he had suspected it would be, but the price churned his stomach. The coat easily cost more money than he made in two months. Kit would kill him if she thought he had bought it, thinking of all the unpaid bills. Too late to return the coat to the Rutherford house, a little theft turned to grand larceny.

Larry reviewed his actions of last night. Had anyone

looking out the window during a dull moment at the party seen a figure skulking along the dark edges of the house? Or deduced that he was still at the house when the coat was stolen, in the later hours of the party, him a hired hand and not a real guest? For he hadn't been a real guest. Real guests didn't steal the other guests' personal items.

Then he remembered—hadn't Kit seen a knock-off version of her treasured coat at the mall? He could simply pretend the coat he had stolen was a knock-off version he had purchased at what he hoped would be a much more reasonable price. He could go to the mall, steal the label, and steal the price tags. This wouldn't be too much of a problem. Linda could come with him and pretend to be looking for a coat to avoid suspicion. She wouldn't ask too many questions, she never did, and he could offer her something in return.

Energized by this new plan to make the coat legal, he raced to the kitchen to dial her number. Except the line was dead, and he remembered. They no longer had a phone.

His mother entered the kicthen, along with a blast of chilly air. "Does the phone work again?" she asked, hope in her voice. She wore somber-colored pants that contrasted with her bright orange winter parka and Florida-themed macramé bag boasting a sunset on one side and a flamingo on the other.

"Nope," said Kit, coming in behind her. "The forty bucks you gave me wasn't enough, plus they're charging a turn-on fee of five extra dollars. But," she added, "Mom's got good news." She turned to Ruby. "Tell him, mom. Tell

Larry what you just did."

Ruby intoned without emotion. "I got a job at the nursing home."

"That, with Larry's paycheck, will give us a cushion," she said to her mother in a tone that suggested that this phrase had recently been much repeated. "Isn't that good news?" she prompted her brother.

Larry just had to marvel; there was no end to his sister's ability to make things happen. He couldn't imagine how Kit had gotten their mother out of the house, dressed almost like a regular working person, and through an interview to land a job. "Wow."

"Wow is right," said Ruby. "Now, if you'll excuse me, I have to recover."

When she had gone, Larry looked at Kit for an explanation. She shrugged. "It had to happen," she said. "I didn't have a choice. Now…"

"I get paid tomorrow," interrupted Larry. "I might get a, er Christmas bonus too. I promise, you can have all of it, or close to all of it."

"Well, we've just had one Christmas miracle so I'm not counting on two. But give me what you can."

Larry showered and dressed in clean clothes. He wondered whose coat it was he had stolen; he hoped it was someone rich, who could just go out and buy a new one no matter what it cost. How did some people have so much more money than others? This struck Larry as grossly unfair, but he also knew it was still stealing when you stole from a wealthy person.

He arrived at the Appletons. Focus, he told himself, you can't get caught for this.

Linda answered the door looking somber. "Sure," she replied when he asked her to take a drive to the mall with him. Larry hadn't even had to launch into his story of needing her to try on coats for his sister.

The mall was claustrophobic with holiday shoppers. As they maneuvered the crowded aisles, he tried to interest her in a linen sale, but she idly turned over the different madras prints in holiday colors. They turned as if by accident toward the coat department, and the knock-off coats, being the latest style, were prominently displayed at the front of the section, near where the wide aisle accommodated dozens of passing shoppers per minute. In no time at all, Larry had taken out his nail scissors and snipped the price tags off one of the remaining coats. He carried three more toward the dressing rooms.

"Come on," he urged Linda. "Try these on."

"They're coats. I don't need the dressing room for coats."

"The dressing room has that great three-way mirror, so you can see from every angle."

"I don't need a coat."

"If you don't like it, Kit might. Try them on so I can see."

"You know Kit would never like something I would," said Linda. "She's so…" she faltered. "You know." She tilted her head to the side.

She's not so bad, thought Larry as he coaxed her into the

dressing room, she'll land on her feet. He handed her a coat, while he sat in a small alcove just outside the changing areas. Bending over in case there were security cameras, he sneaked the scissors from his pocket, and snipped at the resistant stitches that held the manufacturer's label in place, just below the collar. He'd managed to loosen one corner and start down an edge when Linda emerged.

"It's kind of puffy," she said.

Larry looked up. She was right. This coat, the knock-off version, was not as finely made, and the lamb's wool puffed out in an odd way along the front. Or maybe it was that Linda, who had gained a few pounds, did not carry the coat well. "Try a bigger version," he coaxed.

"Do I have to?"

"Yes."

He had just gotten the tag ripped off, hardly even tearing the material underneath, when Linda returned, coatless this time, and plunked herself down next to him.

"I really hate shopping," she said, "especially with all these crowds."

"I know," said Larry. "Thanks for coming."

"I had to get out of the house."

He nodded.

"It was really nice of you to remember, to make up this story about needing a coat."

He fiddled with the tag, and put it in his jean pocket.

She began to cry. Not sobbing, not crazy Linda-like, but the tears just seeped out of her eyes and quickly wet her face. "I'm sorry, but we were dreading this day, the anniversary, kind of…" She couldn't continue.

He nearly dropped the scissors. How could he have been so stupid? He wrapped his arms around her shoulders and pulled her in.

"My mother," she began. "You know she thinks you're my boyfriend."

Larry hesitated. He could no longer keep this up. "You know that I'm…"

"Duh," she interrupted, more like the Linda he was used to. She put her head on his shoulder. "I told her you were just a nice guy."

He was so relieved, he probably would have slept with her again just to thank her, but, fortunately, this seemed no longer necessary.

Larry feared that Mrs. Appleton would have to be dragged out of her bedroom with unwashed hair and in a dirty bathrobe, but that was not the case. She was clean and dressed and seated at the kitchen table when he and Linda arrived with the bags of groceries. The Sunday paper sat in front of her, but it was unread, and her cup of tea was full and no longer steamy.

"How about some chicken pot pie?" asked Larry by way of a greeting.

Mrs. Appleton nodded and smiled slightly. "You must stop feeding us."

"Maybe he will when we can start feeding ourselves," said Linda.

Larry gently moved some dirty dishes off the counter

and into the sink.

"And the place is filthy," Linda continued. "Who can cook in dirt? Larry?"

Larry looked nervously in her direction.

"Can you cook in dirt?"

"Um…"

"Well?"

"It makes it a little harder," he conceded. He had never cooked in dirt because his sister would never allow it, but Linda had lost her sister.

"OK, then," repeated Mrs. Appleton. "That's settled. No more cooking in dirt."

"I mean it, Mom," said Linda.

Her mother patted her daughter on her hand. "I know, honey. I know you mean it."

Larry rinsed the chicken under cold water. The image of the water—always on the move—cheered him, and he told himself that sometimes you just have to wait for a thaw for things to change.

Nineteen

The accretion of wet snow layering on the windowpanes had plunged Rioux & Rioux into an early gloom, when a young man with the severely short hair and stiff demeanor of someone in law enforcement stepped abruptly into the office. After a quick glance around the office, he scowled.

Kit waited.

"Attorney Rioux requested service," he announced.

"It's practically Christmas Eve," she replied. "I don't think so."

He shrugged, and then looked side to side, as if he expected to be overheard. "That's what I thought," he lowered his voice, "but our office got the call, and they sent me here."

The Pierce case, Kit realized. The date by which Mrs. Pierce or her attorneys should have responded to the legal documents sent to them by the Appletons was today or yesterday, Kit would have to check the file. Technically, the date for filing an answer to the complaint was twenty-one days after the complaint was delivered.

Still, lawyers usually gave each other the courtesy of at

least thirty days to respond. Even though Jack had anticipated this event and had her prepare a motion for summary judgment of the case on the basis of nonresponse when she had prepared the other papers, almost a month ago, he wouldn't have someone get legal papers a few days before Christmas. Would he?

Her face must have given away more than she meant to.

"Maybe you better ask the boss," the man suggested.

She buzzed her intercom. "Jack, did you request a process server for today?"

His response was curt. "Pierce case, in the cabinet."

The process server watched as Kit walked over to pull the Pierce file. There, sure enough, was the completed request for a motion for summary judgment she had filled out earlier, with all the other paperwork completed by Jack. She handed it over, along with the check for his services.

The process server now had to deliver these papers to Mrs. Pierce. Judging from his age, he was probably new to the job, thus his office shuttled him all the crummy assignments. His eyes darted back to office that hid Jack, and he nodded. "Well," he said, "you and your boss have a very merry Christmas."

Kit felt her face heat up. The fact that she was only doing her job did nothing to protect her from a sense of overwhelming shame.

Twenty

At the Rutherford estate, the marsh turned winter brown and the air still. The song birds had all gone south, leaving only the seagulls and the quiet winter birds, sparrows and finches and the occasional red cardinal.

By Monday, the catering trucks were long gone, and Mr. Rutherford retreated to his world of financial services. It fell to Billy and Larry to finish cleaning out the big house, a task they could spread out over several days. Furniture returned to its spot with museum precision, spilled wine was cleaned up off the floor, cushions sent to the cleaner when necessary, and rugs re-laid. They left the decorative boughs up and repaired those that had come loose because Mr. Rutherford also hosted a New Year's Eve party, a more intimate affair, but festive, Billy assured Larry, nonetheless.

The picture of Mr. Rutherford's fingers in a possessive clasp around Billy's neck would not leave Larry alone. He wanted to flee, a familiar impulse that had led him to leave his previous positions. This, he insisted to himself, was different.

The first tangle was the stolen coat—if he quit now, his

departure would surely draw suspicion. The second was his sister. Kit couldn't carry him while he left one paycheck and waited for the next. And, third, well, that was the biggest tangle of all.

Larry switched the vacuum off, and the same stillness that had enveloped the grounds took over the house. The heavy cord flopped on the floor as he wound it back around the small machine. All that remained was to reset the couch, the one with the pretty Chinese silk pattern that had so caught his eye that day of his job interview with Billy. This couch, although small, was heavy and so rather than risk marking the wood floor, he went to search out Billy to help him replace it more carefully.

He found him, wearing a formal-style blue cotton button-down shirt that had seen better days, his hair tied back in a red bandanna, bent over a section of baseboard, scrubbing. His shoulder bones and the top knobs of his spine molded out of his shirt as he moved back and forth with his work.

"What are you doing? We already cleaned the spills."

"I just found some bits of something, canapé maybe, stuck to the baseboards."

"They must have been microscopic."

"Well," Billy admitted, "I can see how we missed them the first turn around." He arched his shoulders back in a stretch. "But the sun came out for a second and shone right on the mess."

Billy dipped his rag into the bucket of soapy water, squeezed it, and looked up at Larry. "By the way, I've got your bonus from Mr. Rutherford." Larry noticed how the blue shirt popped his blue eyes from what seemed to him as an improbably white, an almost unhealthy, pale face. His irises, though, were the color of the oceans as seen from outer space, beautiful, both alien and familiar.

"Do you know that painting's a fake? He's not even related to the guy."

Billy looked away. He put his rag into his bucket of dirty water, and then pulled it out and squeezed it tight. "Does it make any difference?"

"He's pretending to be something he's not. I mean, he says he's one kind of person, when really he's another kind."

"Isn't that something you're very familiar with?" Billy asked quietly.

Larry looked out the window. This one had a view all the way to the ocean, a narrow, bright blue sliver of light beyond the dead winter marsh. "I need some help with a couch," he said at last.

Later that afternoon, as Larry pulled away from the grounds, the sky over the marsh in the east turned black-blue, and the shadows of the trees blended to dark. When he turned out of the drive to the main road, his direction shifted west, toward where the sun had just set and all along the road displayed a pinky lilac horizon, sliced by the stark black trunks of the leafless trees. The color took him by surprise. As it faded, he watched the night creep toward the sunset like a closing hatch.

Back at home, the coat aired out in a tree in the back

yard, and Larry went to work on it. By the time he had managed to gently tease off the old label, find the right matching thread to sew on the new label, and fuse the thin plastic string that held the tags onto the coat via the open buttonhole by holding the ends together over a thick candle flame, Larry was tempted to figure it would have taken far less effort to simply work enough to pay for the coat outright, until he remembered exactly what the new garment cost. Then he hung it more gently and, before he hid it under the bed, rolled it carefully. This he did because he had never trusted his mother. She was usually too distracted to snoop around his room, but if the urge ever took hold of her, he knew no scruple would keep her from a desire. For her to discover the coat before Christmas would never do. He wanted to surprise Kit completely.

Twenty-One

On Christmas Eve, Kit, in a better mood about the Lavoie's financial stability since her mother's job at the nursing home and Larry's steady employment, bought a small, discounted tree on the way home. She placed it on a green towel on a side table in the living room and arranged the base so the fuller part of the tree faced the couch and the spindly side, the window to the backyard. Their big colored holiday bulbs were too heavy for the diminutive branches, so Kit scavenged some tiny white lights she had purchased for Angela's birthday party several springs ago. These fit the mini tree perfectly.

Ruby watched these activities from the couch. Despite her status as a new employee, her mother had gotten both Christmas Eve and Christmas off. Ruby was reticent on the subject; this lack of acknowledgement of her luck, Kit concluded, was likely due to her mother's ignorance of the true rigors of the workplace, where seldom do those in the caring professions get holidays off.

Kit stood contemplating her next step when Billy arrived, unannounced and with, he claimed, one hundred twenty year old scotch from Mr. Rutherford's liquor cabinet. You don't have to bring pilfered luxury items every time your feet cross the doorstep, she wanted to tease him, but refrained because she didn't want to deflate the charming patter—almost that of a door-to-door peddler—that had accompanied each of his offerings from Thanksgiving on. Instead, she searched out the heaviest, most squat glassware she could find in which to serve the scotch, to please his as well as her own sense of appropriateness.

The project of the mini tree captured him completely. When they discovered most of the Lavoie decorations were too bulky for the slim branches, Billy had Kit find some wrapping ribbon. He showed her how to make shapely bows, and they hung those from the small, twisted wire hangers that usually carried the weight of colored balls and snowmen. Enough tinsel remained wrapped around last year's decorations to pull out for this year's limbs. Careful placement of the silvery strings gave the illusion of fuller branches, dancing with light. They then dimmed the living room bulbs, letting the tiny tree sparkle in the corner. Kit placed the few presents she had bought around the base, and they sat to admire their efforts.

Kit had bought Billy a present, and wondered when to give it to him. Would he be with them on Christmas morning? He seemed to have no family at all. She pulled out the small gift wrapped in red tissue paper and tied with green yarn and dropped it in his lap.

"I couldn't wait," she said.

"For me?" he asked. He looked surprised, and leaned

forward to place his glass on the table.

"It's Christmas Eve so you can open it."

He untied the gift and out fell a cerulean mohair cap. When Kit found it in a small shop in Salem, she had thought immediately of Billy's eyes.

He put the cap on his head, turned to her, and grinned.

"You can't wear it to the barn," she admonished, "and gum it up."

He took her hands between his and smiled at her. "Thank you."

"Well," she said, unnerved by his sincerity, "you're the best person my brother's ever brought home."

At that, Larry, back from his food shopping, hailed them from the kitchen. "Steak," he called out. "Steak and mushrooms and eggnog." Kit didn't give him the third degree about where he'd gotten the money for that kind of food. She left the boys alone and stayed by the tree, closed her eyes and leaned back on the couch in the quiet half-light of the white bulbs. As the smells of the cooking wafted in from the kitchen, for the first time in what felt like decades, she relaxed, and no worrisome thoughts came.

Christmas morning was gray, and Larry insisted they exchange presents as soon as his mother and sister were up. Kit had purchased a Hawaiian shirt for her brother and a collection of lavender bath products along with a new purple-swirled robe for her mother. If circumstances hadn't been so tight, she would have bought her brother a silk jacket she had seen in an upscale secondhand shop in Salem.

The lapels were brocade, as were the buttons, sewn into a rich burgundy material. But the jacket was a week's salary, and no amount of budgeting would have made that work by the holiday. She regretted her pragmatism, though, when Larry carried in his gift for her. When he first brought out the big package, roughly wrapped in yellow tissue paper, Kit thought it would be some kind of pillow because Larry had a weakness for home furnishings and accessories and because of the bulky shape of the gift. As presents go, a cushion could be useful, Kit reasoned, and Larry did have an eye for fabric.

Ruby perked up. "Oooh," she sing-songed, "what is that?"

"It's for Kit," answered Larry. "She deserves it."

Kit tore away at the fragile wrappings. At first glance it was a jacket, but then the whole length of the garment emerged. She stood, and the instant she put her arms through the sleeves, she knew that the coat was expensive. It just fit so well, around her shoulders, across her back, and through her arms. With a stab of panic, she worried that Larry had bought the *Vogue* coat and she twisted her arm to check the tags: Filene's. This wasn't the coat she had tried on before, but she couldn't believe what an amazing job the department store had done to secure such a decent knock-off. The fleece was so soft and the suede so pliable. She hugged herself into the coat and twirled around for good measure, sure that she had never worn such a wonderful article of clothing.

"Do you like it?" asked Larry.

"I'm never taking it off."

"So you like it?"

"She's never taking it off!" exclaimed Ruby. "Of course she likes it."

"Where did you find it?"

"Like the tag says," answered Larry.

"I can't believe it," said Kit. "It's just too nice." What she really couldn't believe was that something this nice would end up being worn by her. She hugged Larry. "Thank you," she said, "thank you." She was close to crying for some unaccountable reason so she searched for a distraction. "Where's Billy? I want to show him my coat." She turned to her brother. "Is he here?" She twirled around once more

"No," said Larry. "I mean, you can't show him your coat. He's gone to do the horses for the morning."

"That's all right," answered Kit. "Sooner or later, everyone will see my wonderful coat."

"That's right dear," said Ruby. "And you can tell them all that it was a gift from your fashionable brother."

An early afternoon call from the Minnizone house interrupted the quiet day. When Kit came to the phone, Angela squealed for a few seconds before she was able to speak.

"Guess what?"

A few weeks ago, a few months ago, Kit could have predicted her friend's news, but still she feigned surprise. "What?"

Angela squealed again, but Kit heard in her voice a true

excitement.

"Congratulations," she said, and meant it. Angela had always wanted to be married. Although she rarely pointed out guys in a crowd or nurtured crushes, Angela noticed what kind of snacks mothers on the next bench packed for their children when Kit hadn't even noticed that there was a family nearby, and had for years maintained a looping mental list of her favorite names. Maybe, Kit considered, it didn't matter so much who you married after all, as long as the couple made and kept the same promises. Maybe this Matt was good to his little cousins. Maybe he was as happy sitting in the Minnizone kitchen as she had been.

Kit accepted the invitation to join the Minnizone family in celebratory champagne with the anticipation that, at the very least, she could wear her new coat out into the cold for the first time. She dressed in light rayon clothes so that she would be chilly in Angela's house, which always had the thermostat down low, and then have an excuse to continue to wear the coat indoors.

Kit parked half on the frozen lawn, half on the street, the spot considered hers she had parked there so many times over the years. As Kit made her way up the stairs, the early sunset had already turned the sky a pinky orange, and somehow these colors caught hold of her, and she held her breath. Nothing would be the same. Just as high school graduation had barred the exit behind her, Angela's marriage would do the same. The darkening sky brought a fresh chill, and she wrapped her coat full around her.

Angela greeted her at the door, opening it before Kit had

time to knock or try the knob, and gave her a huge hug. Her excitement sent little waves of energy out from her body. With huge eyes and a heightened expression, she flitted across the kitchen to fetch Matt in a dance step Kit had never seen her do. Even Matt looked a little dazed, and Kit's fears about his future weight seemed grounded in reality because his face looked really too round over his V-necked sweater. Kit shook his hand awkwardly.

"Congratulations," she said. "Have you set a date?"

He rocked a bit back on his feet and put on a serious expression, like a mask of an adult reaction. This, too, Kit concluded, did not bode well for his future, as she envisioned this habit in twenty years when, by then, insecurity had hardened into pomposity.

But maybe she was just being difficult, as Angela had accused her of being on the last outing they'd shared, now almost a month back. Everyone else was so happy.

They stood in a circle in the kitchen, each holding wine glasses full of pink champagne Matt had brought. Even Mr. Minnizone got up off the couch and offered a somewhat reluctant raised glass. Perhaps he was thinking of the cost of the wedding, Kit thought, or maybe he was just being himself, a man rarely unmoored by the swirling family around him.

"A toast," said Mr. Minnizone, and the party around him hushed. A short but sturdy man who had worked all his life in the tanneries in Peabody, he wore what must have been a Christmas present, a red plaid flannel shirt. All eyes turned. "To the happy couple," he concluded.

Lizzie ran circles around the bright kitchen. “Can we wear pink, huh Ange? Can the flower girls wear pink?”

Kit took a celebratory sip. The champagne was lukewarm and sweet and sat too long in her mouth before she was able to swallow.

Angela caught Kit’s arm and pulled her to the side of the circle. “Matt insists that his sister be the maid of honor,” she whispered. “I’m really sorry but I have no choice, but you’ll be in the wedding won’t you, Kit? Won’t you be a bridesmaid?”

“We’ll most likely get married in the summer,” said Matt.

“Ooh, that’s so soon!” exclaimed Mrs. M. She took Angela’s arm. “We have so much to do, honey. Matt, honey, where are your parents? They should be here by now.”Kit accidentally stepped back into Chris, who hovered on the outskirts of talk. He fingered Kit’s sleeve. “Nice coat,” he said.

"Thanks," said Kit. She smiled at him.

"Really nice coat."

Defensive, Kit pulled her sleeve back. “Larry got it for me.”

Chris chose to skip any more comments on her wardrobe, a favorite topic in the past. He nodded.

Kit nodded back. “Where’s what’s-her-name?” she asked.

“She was too bossy.”

Kit laughed. “I thought you liked bossy girls.”

Chris looked at her. He had shaved off the beard, and he looked relaxed. “Well,” he began.

Mrs. M. stepped between them and squeezed Kit’s cheek.

"It'll be your turn next, honey," she said. Mrs. M. smiled, pleased at her own thoughtful words, but led Kit firmly away from her son.

Kit looked over her shoulder at Chris and gave him a shrugging glance, as if to say, what's up with this? But inside, she was irritated. Maybe she was no longer good enough for Chris, but more likely the message was simpler than that: this was Angela's time to shine, and Mrs. M. would make sure her daughter was the center of attention for at least as long as it took to get her down the aisle.

Back at home, Kit found her mother, Larry, and Billy squished onto the couch, lights dimmed save for those on the tree, watching an old Christmas movie. She plunked down next to them. Over the flickering blue of the TV, she watched as Billy, sporting his blue cap, nudged his thigh against Larry's, and Larry sank into his contact.

Kit leaned into her coat, which she had taken off and laid against the back of her chair. A lecture from a philosophy class she had taken came back to her. The professor had been an ancient Jesuit who had taught the introductory class for decades. Close your eyes, he had said. Think of the million stars you see in a black night sky. Is it a shock, a surprise, to see stars in the sky? No, of course not—a surprise is something you don't expect, like to be hit by a car while crossing the street. We know that there are stars in the sky. Yet what is that feeling you get when you look up into the dark at those varied twinkling miracles? Kit had sat in class and thought, took in the immensity of all that was beyond her. She stretched her thoughts to the end of black sky and twinkling light until she could go no further.

The old priest had continued. Although you know the stars are there, there is still a sense of something new and special each time you encounter them. That is revelation. You see something you have always seen, yet somehow you understand it in a different way.

Kit leaned against her coat, grateful for this lesson because it put this Christmas day in perspective for her. The coat had been a surprise. Angela's engagement had been neither. Her brother, like always, was a revelation.

Twenty-Two

Ruby put her earnings in cash on the kitchen counter every other week. Not a large amount, still Kit welcomed the thin margin it provided the household income, as well as her mother's effort.

On one dark and frigid evening in early January, Kit scooped up the money and noticed that the twenty-dollar bill on the top of the pile bore a slash of red marker. Like a cloud racing over the sun on a windy day, an uneasy shade passed through her mind. She tried to shake it off her suspicions, lots of twenty-dollar bills are damaged, but doubt gained a foothold.

Without taking off her coat, she went straight to her room and into her closet. Pulling out the pair of boots that doubled as a safe, she saw at first glance the stash was smaller. Suddenly overwarm, she tugged her coat off her shoulders and reached for the money. The diminished pile totaled eighty dollars. Her mother had stolen three hundred dollars from her in six weeks of work, or, as Kit now understood, six weeks of pretending to work.

She pressed her eyes into a squint, but tears were not

what came to her. Was it more unbelievable that her mother would steal money from Kit's closet, pretending that she had earned it working, or was it more unbelievable that Ruby would docilely take a job, albeit part-time, for the first time in over twenty years and just hand over the cash?

Kit had spent her life both holding her mother close and pushing her away. She'd taken her cue from her grandmother, who'd come to live with them permanently after her father left the house and quietly taken over the business of keeping them all together. She'd cooked; she'd paid the bills; she'd met with the teachers. When she had died, Kit and Larry had been old enough to divvy up their grandmother's jobs and carry onward.

So she knew her mother was never going to be a help. But this—this was deceit, and it sapped her spirit. How could she have been so stupid? Who saves money in a boot? She should have put the money in a bank, and that's what she would do first thing tomorrow with the remainder. She sat against her closet door, exhausted. It wasn't even that much money. How could it be? Jack Rioux was underpaying her because she was desperate for work and didn't have a degree or even secretarial training. She had nothing to argue for a higher salary.

Still in her coat, she sat on her bed. If she had any kind of degree, law firms in Boston would pay her higher wages for the same work she did for Jack. If she made more money, then she could actually pay for classes to get some kind of degree. She could even go to law school; Attorney Levinson had often told her she had a head for the law. At present, she was caught because she couldn't afford to get the degree she needed to get herself out of low-paying jobs.

An image of Tony's ramshackle apartment came to her. This house, her house, was much nicer, and she didn't want to lose it. If they ever lost it, they would spend the rest of their lives in apartments like Tony's. She shivered.

The fake diplomas on the wall of Feingold's Stationery came to her in a flash. She knew from her investigative work at Rioux & Rioux that only the rare person asked for facts or proof; most people believed whatever you told them and would be fooled by a nice diploma on the wall. But for those others, like herself maybe, she would need a transcript, grades and all, something she could attach to her resume to prove she went to college. How hard would it be, with White Out, a Xerox machine, and a course catalogue, to put together the right courses for whatever major she chose, to create a transcript for four years? She would need to go to Boston College to get a transcript and a current course catalogue. She would just use it for the first job, she reasoned, just to get herself on her feet, and make sure to get a real degree later.

Kit put the money in her pocketbook. Her grandmother had invariably asked her, when she complained that this or that person wasn't being fair, what are you going to do about it? She had guided Kit to focus her effort on fixing a problem and not to dwell so much on how the problem had landed in her lap. So Kit wouldn't waste her energy and confront her mother right now. She would let her find the empty boot while Kit figured out how to keep them in their home.

The next morning, Kit headed not to work but toward the highway. Her hands shook as they took the wheel. Her car shimmied in what were at times alarming skids on the cold, slick roads, and the tall banks of roadside snow gave her the sense of never being able to see around the corner ahead. When she at last parked the car, she was relieved to be rid of the driving.

Once on campus, a sharp wind came at her as she climbed the steps to the administration building, but her new coat kept her warm. She marched past the undergraduates, a lot of them sloppy and underdressed. By the end of her own first and only year, Kit had worn sweats and old jeans to class more often than not as fatigue and pressure had closed in. Despite the familiar hills and neat paths amidst the Gothic buildings of the campus, she felt like an alien among the students. This would have been her senior year, and she worried she would run into someone she knew. Of course she had prepared a story, rehearsed on the drive here, having to do with transfer credits and a great job awaiting her in June, but she hoped she wouldn't be tested.

The walk steadied her, but once inside the administration building, her agitation returned as her mind spun more and more quickly. She tried to calm herself. I am here for a transcript. And may I have a course book please? She rehearsed these requests in order to make them seem simple and innocent. In the wide hall, as she took off her gloves and unbuttoned her coat, memories of her last days here hit her broadside, in all their raw ugliness.

That last exam, she had shivered in her sweatshirt on a raw May day, crying on and off through most of it, as some thick-necked blond guy, huge and tall and unsmiling, glared at her each time she reached for more tissues. Boston College, a Catholic school with lots of opportunities to attend Mass and with courses taught by priests, had been a most uncompassionate place when she hadn't followed the rules.

And just after Trey's attack, after she, in her borrowed shirt, had been guided by the police past the line of undergraduates who had come out their rooms to gawk, there was that one girl who had stepped back and wrinkled her nose in disgust, as if Kit smelled.

This served not to drag her down after all. The humiliation merely renewed her sense of purpose. She climbed the stairs to the Registrar's Office. This place owes me, she vowed, and I'm going to use it any way I can.

Back at Rioux & Rioux, with the Xerox machine, an old typewriter normally kept in the closet, White Out, and the BC course catalogue, Kit spent the morning creating a college transcript. Careful to choose the correct number and distribution of classes to meet graduation requirements of 1996, she also couldn't help feeling a bit of excitement as she read through all the offerings she could take. One on Psychology of the Criminal Mind caught her attention, as did another on Women's Role in the Labor Movement. Careful to give herself good, but not exceptional grades, she also chose a major in the popular department of Psychology. She had taken Psych 1 in her freshmen year, and it had been interesting enough, and she had discovered then that a lot of people pick that major, those who wanted to be doctors, nurses, social workers, or teachers, so the choice stood a greater chance of being passed over briefly as an unremarkable detail. In no real rush to finish, as what would have been her last semester was just underway, Kit still wanted to be prepared to leave Rioux & Rioux as quickly as possible.

She was close to planning herself into law school when the Appletons appeared. Jack rushed out of his office and ushered them into his lair before they even had their coats off. Kit chose not to take this personally, convinced that he wanted to act as if he were earning his percentage of the judgment.

Kit put her doctored transcript in her bottom drawer to dry. The sight of the misplaced papers made her imagine where the process server had left the papers addressed to Mrs. Pierce; "the last and usual abode" was what was written on the form returned to Rioux & Rioux. Perhaps the wind had scattered them over the frozen marsh, or perhaps she read them slowly over cups of Italian coffee.

What Kit did know was that since Mrs. Pierce had failed to reply to the motion for summary judgment for failure to respond, and then failed again to respond to the issue of notice of default, Jack had requested the court to grant the

Appletons a damages assessment hearing. At that hearing, a somewhat lengthy procedure involving evidence and testimony, a judge would decide how much money Mrs. Appleton and Linda deserved for the death of Janelle. This request had just been granted and the hearing scheduled for a date two months hence. Now, time ticked by like some kind of perverse Advent toward the day that the court would take Mrs. Pierce's house to satisfy the default judgment. Jack was gleeful, and had wasted no time in calling the Appletons for an in-depth discussion of the pain their family had suffered due to the accident, in preparation for their day in court.

The meeting took an hour and a half. Kit was sure she heard crying interspersed with the low mumble of conversation. As badly as she felt for the Appletons, she couldn't help but wonder if Mrs. Pierce hadn't somehow already paid whatever debt she owed, in the beggar's life she led, in having lost a son to war.

When the meeting ended, Jack ushered the Appletons past Kit's desk and out the door. After he retreated to his office without a glance, she listened to the mother and daughter as they talked quietly while pulling on their scarves and hats.

Without a plan, Kit stood up and followed the Appletons into the hall. The space was dark and very cold. Kit shivered as soon as the door to the warm office shut behind her.

Mrs. Appleton turned and gave her a dismissive, irritated look, unlike anything Kit had ever seen on her. "What is it now?"

Kit almost turned back, but she pictured all the unanswered court papers piling up and then blowing over the desolate Pierce property. She addressed herself to Mrs. Appleton, which struck her because she had always thought that it was Linda behind the lawsuit, and she suddenly knew that she had been wrong.

"She doesn't have any money," Kit faltered. She glanced at Linda, who stared down at her boots. "She only has the house."

Mrs. Appleton's visage contorted. "Why shouldn't she lose her house," she cried, "when I have lost my daughter?"

She left quickly, her words hanging in the small space.

Kit and Linda stared at each other. Linda's expression was open and yielding, full of an odd sort of resignation and acceptance. Kit's eyes darted to her full belly, and then back at Linda's face. Linda patted Kit on the arm. "Don't worry," she said, and almost smiled. "It isn't Larry's." She followed her mother out.

Money wouldn't bring back Janelle Appleton, but Kit had never looked at the Appletons and felt that this case was about the money.

She hunched her shoulders in the chill and returned reluctantly to her desk.

Twenty-Three

Larry felt the eerie strangeness of the deep winter dawn as he drove to the Rutherford estate shortly after the New Year. To the east was only the precursor of sunrise, the sky a gray half-light, and in the west, a full moon dominated the sky as it set, draping its silvery glow along the snow-covered flatness of the marshes. As he stepped out of his car, quiet fell around him like a blanket. Absent was the ever-present whooshing wind, and the grounds sat in a distilled silence.

His boots hit the frozen ground with a hollow thud; the car door slam echoed into the sparse trees. He listened to the high-pitched wail of a lone gull and the engine of a car driving by in the distance on the main road, while he kicked around the yard without a sign of Billy. When pink crept up the horizon, Larry ventured in.

His footsteps into the barn echoed. Larry gave two of the horses their morning oats. "Hey Lady Cakes," he addressed his favorite, the sweet-tempered brown mare with a rounded behind. Her black mane lay loose across her face, and she shook her head at him and returned his greeting with a soft whinny.

Larry took off her night blankets and gave her a quick brush. Riding High nosed over her side of the stall to join the party. "Your turn next," Larry promised.

He avoided Blue, who had not settled down since Dr. Thompson had been to see him before the holidays. Although the vet had declared Blue useless and dangerous, the horse remained in the stable. Maybe Billy had made some bargain with Mr. Rutherford to keep the horse, but Larry found it hard to believe that such a pact would last. It cost a lot of money to keep and feed a horse, and Mr. Rutherford kept a stable to play polo, not out of sentimental reasons. His boss shared his stable of three horses with a partner in Hamilton, the next town over. Since a player needed six animals to play a match, if Blue was no good, Mr. Rutherford was short a pony and couldn't field his half of a team in the spring.

When Lady Cakes and Riding High were ready, he walked them outside. Pink faded to pale blue as the two horses ran the length of the paddock, their hoofbeats fading as they went.

The malcontent whinnied from the barn. Although he had grown comfortable with the basic chores around the horses and had learned some of their little tricks, Larry still would not go near Blue. That horse was like a criminal, an animal with no conscience, and unpredictable. He could wait in the barn all day.

Even as the sun rose, the wet of the marsh made the air heavy and raw. Larry didn't idle in the chilly weather as he waited for Billy; rather, he set at some of the chores. After he had chucked the two empty stalls, he strung a rope line between two trees, hung the saddle blankets over it, and beat them with the orphan end of a shovel until the dust had mostly cleared. The noise was partly sucked away into the woods, with the rest traveling more widely over the marshes toward the water in small booms. This probably didn't cheer Blue any—Larry could hear his whinnies and kicks from the barn—but, by now, Larry had gotten used to just about everything bothering the skittish horse.

The sun shone through the bare branches in shafts of chilly light and had risen almost over the roof of the great house before Billy finally made an appearance. Even from a distance Larry saw right away that something was wrong. He walked funny, in an odd, scalloping, indirect way, as if he were on the deck of a ship. His coat was unzipped, and his arms hung from his side in a gangly way.

"You're a mess," Larry told him when he approached.

"I'm tired."

Larry nodded. Billy had been tired a lot lately, spending, he suspected, more time than ever with Mr. Rutherford over the holiday season. Wildly jealous of Mr. Rutherford, yet also secure in Billy's affections, Larry was torn between letting the relationship run its course and dragging Billy away from the place kicking and screaming.

Billy tilted his chin up in a mocking way, and flashed a thin smile.

He acted like a prisoner, but of course, he wasn't. Not really. Larry reached for his hand. "You could come home with me, you know."

Billy watched the two horses running in the paddock, and then glanced to the marsh beyond.

"One big, happy family."

"Why not?" asked Larry.

"Kit would love that."

"She would."

Billy could say nothing. This was true.

Blue whinnied from the barn. "I'm coming," Billy called out, and headed toward the barn.

"No strings attached," Larry added.

Billy turned, his blue eyes level and steady. "You don't want strings?"

Larry's heart clutched in his chest. "That's not what I meant!"

"You've got to make up your mind."

"I have," began Larry, but he stopped as Billy suddenly leaned over and threw up.

Larry ran to him, and put his hand to his forehead. "I knew it. You've got a fever."

Billy shook him off. "It's OK." He trudged toward the barn.

"You're too sick."

Billy stopped at the barn door and leaned, palm against the door frame, his old jaunty self. He gave Larry another thin smile. "You gonna deal with Blue?"

As a rejoinder, Blue kicked the side of his stall. Billy disappeared into the barn.

Larry leaned against the side of barn to catch the morning sun on his face, which by now had risen high into the sky. Why couldn't Billy come home with him? If Billy contributed, Kit wouldn't object. He listened to Billy try to wheedle the horse. It wasn't going well. Something about Billy's voice lacked his usual endless calm. Blue, wired tight as usual, was sure to pick up on that.

Soft curses followed several kicks. Larry contemplated going in to help, but Blue knew his fear. Instead, he closed his eyes and let the red blotches of the sunlight play against the inside of his eyelids. Larry had declined the invitation to the New Year's Eve party; he now wished he had asked Billy to skip it too. What did Mr. Rutherford really want with Billy?

Larry stopped at that thought.

When questioned later, Larry was not sure how it happened. He remembered watching as Billy led Blue out of the barn, and the horse just spooked. Maybe it was the screech of an overhead seagull, it certainly wasn't anything louder, but in an instant Blue reared up on his hind legs, while the two front hooves, shod in metal, pawed the air inches away from, and then into, Billy's head. This sent Billy flying backwards and Blue, game foreleg still wrapped in bandages, couldn't hold his own weight in the landing. The horse stumbled, was thrown sideways in an awkward twist, and banged against the side of the barn, back left leg splayed out at an odd angle.

Breathing heavily, he made strange, whimpering noises. His eyes rolled back, the black coat wet with sweat, his great sides heaving in and out. Afraid of his teeth, Larry spoke quietly, soothingly to the horse, thinking of a baby, a crying baby who didn't know what was happening, and he continued to speak in this way while he kneeled down next to Billy, who was bleeding from the side of his head, not moving. "That's OK, Blue," he said, as he picked up Billy's wrist and found a pulse, and then double checked, head on chest, to make sure Billy was breathing. His breath was steady, but he was unconscious. Larry worried that Blue might move and injure Billy, but Blue's eyes were dazed, and the horse looked as if he might be in shock.

The blood gushing from Billy's wound came close to unnerving Larry, but he shoved that image down to clear his head. Larry had no choice but to leave them. Billy needed an ambulance or a doctor as soon as possible, and so he ran as quickly as he could toward the big house and a phone.

He began to call out before he had made it to the kitchen door when he saw that Mr. Rutherford's green Mercedes was still parked in the drive. Larry pulled open the side door, sped through the entranceway and into the broad, black-and-white–checked kitchen, dark now that the morning sun had passed its windows. He repeated his calls to Mr. Rutherford, help, call an ambulance.

Larry had barely made it to the dining room when Mr. Rutherford, his pale face red with anger or exertion and wearing a navy blue suit and yellow tie, met him.

"What's wrong?"

Even in the emergency of the moment, Larry had to admire how quickly Mr. Rutherford grasped the full situation based on his own halting words.

"It's Billy, Blue just spooked and kicked him in the head and he's out cold but breathing, and the horse too."

Mr. Rutherford gestured to Larry to follow as they raced through the dining room to the phone in the entranceway, which Mr. Rutherford handed to Larry without a word before he disappeared into the recesses of the house. Larry picked up the heavy black receiver of the old-fashioned phone and calmed himself down to dial the emergency number. As the police answered, he heard a door slam—Mr. Rutherford, perhaps, finally going down to the barn to check on Billy, or Blue, or both.

Larry was halfway back to the barn when he heard the gunshot. The sound of it nearly made him stumble--echoes rung around him like a bell in an empty room. In his confusion Larry thought, Billy's been murdered, until he came upon Mr. Rutherford, his light hair shining in the sun now streaming over the marshes and his neat figure bent over Blue. As Mr. Rutherford stood and replaced the gun neatly in his belt, a chill of dislike went through Larry, and he turned his eyes away as his boss he leaned over Billy.

Blue lay eyes open, staring at the sky. Larry noted the precise hole where the bullet entered, the masses of blood pooling quickly in fits and starts around his head, slowed by the cold and then sped up by the volume pouring in from behind as it ran over the frozen ground in little rivers toward Billy.

Larry grabbed the blankets off the line, rolled some of them to sop up the flowing red, and put one on Billy so he wouldn't lose any more body heat. By this time, the sirens were coming down Argilla Road, their piercing waves spiraling closer to the Rutherford estate. The increasing noise both heightened the tension and calmed Larry with the hope of rescue. Mr. Rutherford bent down again to take the pulse Larry knew had been there a few minutes before, but rather than insert himself into the situation, Larry ran toward the driveway to direct the ambulance to the barn.

He also stood back when the EMTs arrived and moved Billy quickly onto a stretcher and into the back of the ambulance. He and Mr. Rutherford watched as the doors closed on Billy, still covered in the horse blanket, and then Mr. Rutherford turned to him. Larry was suddenly full of fear for coming recriminations.

"Call the vet and deal with the horse," he said. He spun on his heels and jogged up to the house.

Larry stared at the ambulance, sirens on again, as it turned from the drive onto the road and headed off, and he felt a tug inside him in Billy's direction. The thinner branches rattled behind him. The wind had picked up and he shivered. A few minutes later, Mr. Rutherford's Mercedes sped down the drive. Larry thought, for the first time, of Lady Cakes and Riding High. He looked toward the paddock. The horses huddled together, their great bodies side by side, their noses touching, on the far side of the field. Larry went toward them, climbed the fence, and walked with his hands outstretched slightly, palms up. He knew that's what Billy would have done had the situation been reversed.

"Shh," he whispered to them as he stroked their heads and rubbed down their bellies, "everything will be OK." Because he believed it would be, because he could not contemplate an alternative.

Back in the Rutherford house, Larry went directly to the phone in the entranceway. He picked up the receiver to dial the operator to get Dr. Thompson's number, but his hands were shaking too much. So he made a call to Kit instead. He didn't care whether this would show up on Mr. Rutherford's records or not, or whether he'd get into some kind of trouble for it. He just dialed the number, and the moment she picked up the phone, he felt much better.

The cleanup turned out to be even more dreadful than Larry had anticipated. Although Dr. Thompson quickly contacted the correct removal people, who responded within hours, Blue weighed over a thousand pounds, and his disposal involved complex maneuverings of noisy and slow machinery, made even more difficult by the onset of rigor mortis. To make matters worse, Blue's corpse lay in front of the doorway to the barn, and Larry knew he could never lead the other horses back to the barn until every drop of blood had been cleaned, a process further prolonged by the frigid temperatures and the early nightfall, which dragged this section of the job on, later and later, into the dark

In the end, though, he was struck by the compassion of the men driving the trucks, and the great care with which they removed the body. When he could finally bring the horses back into their stalls, Larry had to use all his newfound horse wits to coach the reluctant and spooked animals back to the barn. At last, he forgot they were horses and spoke to them of their loss in human terms. This seemed to work the best, and his small victory was heightened with the knowledge that he had a great story to tell Billy when he finally got to the hospital, one to offset the devastation he knew Billy would feel once he learned that Blue had been shot and carried away.

Twenty-Four

The phone rang. The office fell away, and Kit heard only her brother's voice, clipped, somewhat unhinged and unfamiliar. Rushed and close to incoherent, Larry insisted she go to the hospital to watch out for Billy, who was in some danger, perhaps due to Mr. Rutherford; something about a crazy or dead horse kept her brother from going himself.

"I need to go," she told Jack. The current of emergency had its effect on her boss too. His eyes opened wide, and he nodded his assent.

Once outside, the cold was brutal. The river out of Salem, frozen in all directions, formed an icy white path to the harbor.

The old brick hospital was set on a hill, and a rough breeze whipped dead leaves around the parked cars. Once inside, Kit hesitated. She had assumed there was nothing terribly wrong with Billy or Larry would have come on his own, but once she stepped into the hushed, antiseptic-smelling building, her momentum slowed. What disaster, exactly, was she supposed to intercept?

A slow-moving woman in oversized glasses directed her toward Billy's room. After a ride on a cranky elevator shared with a cart of dirty of sheets, she arrived at his floor and then, once past the nursing station, his room. Here the smell that had greeted her at the door was intensified, antiseptic, sour.

At his door, she hesitated. It was closed, and she wondered if anyone else was in there with him, or if he was asleep. She knew nothing about his family, other than Billy's offhand remarks that the family wealth had been squandered by his father.

As she raised her hand to knock, the door opened, and out stepped a furious-looking man in a neat navy suit, his blond hair close to white and sharply parted on the side of his crisply groomed head.

As they shifted position, Kit toward Billy's room, the man toward the corridor, they circled each other, like prize-fighters in a ring.

Maybe this is Mr. Rutherford, she wondered.

He stepped by her, apparently judging her an unworthy opponent, until he brushed against her shoulder in passing. Then, all in a moment, he stopped short, picked up her coat sleeve between his thumb and forefingers, and stared at her. "Who are you?"

Kit had learned, from the times Trey had been overzealous and left her with bruises she didn't want to explain, the details shifting to match the needs of the listener, that the lie closest to the truth was nearly always the best.

"I am Kit Lavoie."

"Well, Miss… Lavoie, it's so kind of you to come."

She almost smiled. The assurance, the exaggerated manners, the pause between the "Miss" and the "Lavoie" that could only be interpreted as condescending made Mr. Rutherford appear like a stock actor in a bad movie. Kit regained her composure. "You haven't introduced yourself."

"I am both his employer and a close personal friend."

With a start, Kit understood that Mr. Rutherford was talking about Billy, not her brother. As a rival to Larry, he would have been comical had it not been for his money and his familiar way with power.

By now, their positions had been reversed; she stood by the door to Billy's room, and Mr. Rutherford stood in the corridor. One more second, she figured, and she would escape without giving away too much information, as to what she was doing here, for she intuited that any stray fact might implicate her brother.

He turned to go and Kit allowed herself to shift her shoulder away from him, but Mr. Rutherford halted. He looked back.

"Miss, ah, Lavoie, you can tell your brother that his bumbling concern is not welcome here."

Now Kit was furious. She stepped toward this horrible little man.

He continued to stare. "You're wearing a very nice coat, young lady."

Mr. Rutherford didn't wait for her response. He

continued on down the corridor, his shiny shoes clicking smartly on the linoleum.

What, she asked herself in a panic, had her brother done to get her this coat?

Kit escaped into the hospital room. Overwarm, she took off her coat and flung it across a chair.

The sight of Billy lying on the large metal bed refocused her attention.

He looked small. She sat down on a chair next to his bed. Eyes closed, his head was wrapped in a bright white bandage. Under the covers pulled up to his chin, she could make out his narrow frame. Absent his usual confident motion and quick chatter, Kit noticed that his body looked almost frail. She wondered if the doctors had had to cut his wonderful hair when they applied the bandages. He wasn't in intensive care, although he was hooked up to an IV and a machine that looped steady waves on a dark screen.

She watched Billy as he slept. He had charmed her, and charmed her mother as well as her brother. Since his arrival at Thanksgiving with his case of fancy wine, he had made things brighter for all of them. Mr. Rutherford had seemed pretty anxious to exert control over him, as if he were some kind of possession, but maybe that was the only way he knew how to protect his attachment, whatever that was exactly. She worried for Larry, for his affection for this odd, sweet individual was obvious and without restraint.

The whole business with the coat also worried her. Its beauty worried her, and she wondered how Larry had gotten hold of it—despite its tags, it didn't seem possible that an item of such precision and elegance just hung, affordable, on a rack in Filene's. Maybe she could get rid of it, but it seemed the damage had been done. With Mr. Rutherford it seemed Larry was in trouble, in over his depth.

Out the window, the short day was ending and the bare branches of the trees cut a jagged line into the reddish sky. She would stay only as long as it took to get some information about Billy and then go home. She didn't want to run into Mr. Rutherford again.

When Kit pulled in the driveway, every light in every room was on.

Before she had stepped into the house, Ruby scuttled across the kitchen, wrapped tight in a bed blanket.

Kit crossed her arms. "Now what, Mom?"

"I don't know," she stuttered. "It's so cold. Everywhere I go, I'm just so cold. It's just not right. Where's Larry?"

"I'm not sure. He called me to go check on Billy in the hospital."

Ruby gasped and clutched the blanket under her chin.

Kit peered into the living room. "Did you have to turn on all the lights?"

"What's wrong with our Billy?"

"Why do you have to turn on every bulb? Why can't you come home and turn on a modest living room lamp?"

Ruby looked around. "I didn't turn them all on, Kit."

Kit slammed her bag on the kitchen counter in disgust.

"Kit." Her mother's tone of voice was quiet, calm.

"Forget the lights." She sighed. "You need to be more like your brother."

Kit stopped short. In the flickering, ugly light of the kitchen, the only exposed piece of Ruby was the circle of her face in the unflattering brown blanket. Her mother looked pinched. The look reminded her of the ancient man who collected bottles and cans by the town wharf to redeem them, and of how her mother had collected her own bottles and cans and delivered them to him for years, befriended him really, when few others even noticed him searching through the trash barrels.

Who knew why any of us are here and what we're supposed to do with ourselves? Kit thought all at once. Plus, her mother was right—why was she going on about the lights? One worry isn't like another unless you let them pile up on you.

"Billy's just got a concussion, Mom. He should be fine. I'm not sure how it happened, but I think it had something to do with a horse."

Larry, armed with the room number courtesy of Kit, traversed the empty parking lot, skipped past the unguarded front entrance, and after a little wandering along faded linoleum corridors, found Billy on the window side of a double room. His head was covered in white gauze in a way that reminded Larry of a movie he had seen about World War I, in which one of the main characters spends most of his time wrapped in bandages and wearing a bathrobe at a hospital. He couldn't remember the name of it—he'd seen so many Saturday afternoon movies on TV, never choosing any particular one but watching whatever ran.

The second bed lay empty, so Larry pulled a heavy armchair from across the room close to where Billy slept, attached to a few machines. Not wanting to wake him, Larry sat silently and held Billy's hand. His fingers felt cool, but Larry was sure they curled responsively at his touch. When a nurse slipped into the darkened room, Larry started to unlace his fingers with Billy's, but then caught himself and stayed put, holding hands. The nurse, an older woman with short, graying hair, acknowledged him with a brief nod and switched on a small light above the headboard. She swiftly checked the IV lines, glanced at the chart, and switched off the light, leaving them in the half-dark of a hospital room at night.

When the door clicked shut, Larry breathed again. That hadn't been so hard; she had treated him like he belonged by the side of the bed. It had been a small thing, but it felt like firm footing. He couldn't wait to tell Billy all about it.

Twenty-Five

Kit arrived at work to find Jack in her chair, all the desk drawers open. His apparent searching stopped by whatever it was he held in his hands, he stood up, squinted at her in an appraising way, and said, "I could fire you for this."

Kit immediately pushed any thought of what he could be holding out of her mind so as to appear innocent, aggrieved even. Internally, she mounted an offensive charge: you can fire me anytime you want to; why are poking around my desk; try and find someone else who can do what I do for so little money.

"OK…" She moved, in an even, careful way she hoped would project a good balance between respectful and casualness, toward the coat closet. "What seems to be the problem?"

He followed her movements. "While looking for the Pierce file," he shook the paper, his face without affect, "I found this."

His unreadable face unnerved her. "All the Pierce papers are in the file cabinet."

He shook his head. "Come take a look."

She approached the desk. He motioned her closer so that

she had to bend over his shoulder to see what he held.

It was her forged transcript.

Suddenly too aware of Jack's musty-sweet aftershave and the scent of coffee on his breath, she took a step back.

"It pisses me off that you could be so stupid. Haven't you learned a thing? The legal profession is about keeping what you do legal, and this just doesn't fly."

In the flush of heat, Kit struggled with her thoughts. Hadn't Jack spent the last two years telling her that what flies is what you can get away with? Anything she knew about the actual law she had learned from Mr. Levinson. Jack had never taken the time to teach her anything. How was she supposed to know what was right and what wasn't? Kit shifted her focus. Maybe Jack wasn't really all riled up, though he was pretending to be. He had to have known she didn't have a degree when he had hired her, how could she have? She was too young. He was going to use to this as an excuse to lower her pay, she just knew it.

"Am I fired, then?"

He stood, leaned in on his toes, flared his nostrils. "You think I should fire you?"

Although she knew it was the wrong path, she continued because she could see no other way. "I'm just asking 'cause I want to know."

He smiled at her, and this was the most unnerving of all. "Modern European History," he read. "That's a solid if somewhat dull choice."

Kit noticed the weight in his belly, his thick arms, and how his dress shirt wrinkled awkwardly around his shoulders.

"Cognitive Development, a classic girl class."

She swiped at the paper. "That's mine."

He pulled it away. "No foreign language?"

She wanted more than anything to run out of the office and never come back.

He took another step toward her, his manner possessive. "Every sophisticated girl learns French, at least."

She tried to hold her ground, yet by now she was only a few feet from being backed against the wall. I could quit, she told herself, Jack Rioux wasn't the devil and she hadn't sold her soul to him, although she saw what he meant in a flash. A waitress job might pay more money, but by sitting in a law office she could pretend to herself and others any number of things.

"You should learn a few words, I'm sure a girl like you could make it work any way you want it to."

She tried to ignore his coffee breath, his sickly aftershave.

He moved toward her, just slightly, and she realized then that she could put this all to rest if she just walked into his arms. Then he might even give her a raise. She didn't mean a thing to him, he was just throwing his weight around, in the heat of the moment and because he thought he could get away with it. She worked this insight, the toehold it gave her.

She let him stand close to her, but gave him no encouragement. When she didn't answer, his manner settled.

He took a step back. "Classic courtroom rules—the

fewer facts you give them, the fewer places they can tear a hole in your story. Like I said, you should know that by now."

Kit tried to remain as calm as possible.

He placed the paper on her desk. "Another courtroom rule, never admit to anything they can't prove."

Unaccountably triumphant, he walked toward his office. "We're more alike than you think we are," he sallied as he slammed the door behind him.

She rubbed her hand over her face. He was voluble, but this bothered her more than his previous outbursts, most of which had missed their mark. She picked up the forged transcript from her desk, folded it in half, and hid it in her purse. She wanted nothing more to do with it because, now, she felt that the measure of the work she put into making the fake papers was really a measure of her own sense of unworthiness.

Kit sat back at her desk and, with shaking hands, closed each of the opened drawers. What was it, exactly, that she wanted so badly? To be rich? To be able to walk into a room and have people say, oh, there goes Kit Lavoie, isn't she something?

Maybe Jack was right, she was more like him than she realized, her striving, her willingness to bend rules when they suited her purposes. She shouldn't blame his lack of guidance for her own lack of conscience. Maybe she should just walk out of this office and never come back. But she knew she wouldn't, she couldn't. She needed the money, and now more than ever.

After Jack's outburst, and her exposure, something loosened in Kit, as if she had taken off a mask she hadn't known was there. Once it was gone, she felt freer to act. What bothered her also was that her falseness had influenced her brother, and that a coat had appeared that maybe she didn't really want or deserve. Then again, the truth, no matter how painful, can be bracing and bring its own energy.

She felt untethered, as if she had spent too much time watching other people live their lives, without really having acted in her own. And as Jack busied himself in the office a wall away from her desk, another doubt presented itself—Mrs. Pierce. Something just wasn't right about the whole case, and the deadline to do anything about it was drawing to a close.

When Jack left the office, Kit retrieved the file from the cabinet. While she wasn't forbidden from looking at the files, she didn't want to arouse suspicion in case Jack returned unexpectedly. Careful to keep the pages in order, she grabbed a newspaper to throw over the whole enterprise in a pinch, if the need arose.

Kit thought about the money. It had been several months since Mrs. Minnizone had revealed to her the amount in Mrs. Pierce's bank account. Had that number changed? If so, was Mrs. Pierce close to being bankrupt? If not, how was she living, eating, paying her taxes? She might have been able to get away without paying her income taxes for a few years, but if she missed any property tax payments, the town would waste no time pursuing her.

With this in mind, Kit called Town Hall and was

forwarded to an efficient, amiable woman who informed her that yes, said property on Argilla Road was up to date in its taxes as well as its municipal bills.

She considered calling Mrs. M. for an update, but held back. Kit had had such little contact with the Minnizones since Angela had found Matt, and she felt, too, that this was the direction her relationship with the whole family was headed. To call on a favor was like emptying a bucket that would be a long time in refilling. Instead, she turned back to the file, starting with the original deed to the property, with its attendant trusts and discharges.

Although her Xerox copy was fuzzy, she could make out the name of the law firm that handled the trust that had devolved at Mrs. Pierce's son's death: Payne, Floutt & Giroux of Boston. She wondered if this firm really had a Mr. Payne, a Mr. Floutt, and a Mr. Giroux, unlike Rioux &Rioux, which had only one Rioux. A quick glance at the endless sentences in the trust document told her she was in way over her head, so she flipped to the back page to see which attorney had signed off on them. It was a Thompson Fielder, Jr., and he had worked on these papers almost forty years ago.

On a whim, she retrieved the heavy Boston phone book from atop the file cabinet. Sure enough, there was a Payne, Floutt & Giroux on Devonshire Street in Boston, followed by a phone number. Her fingers raced to dial it, but she stopped herself. This was clearly an old and most likely prestigious Boston firm, and she might get only one chance to gather information. Unprepared is ill prepared, as Mr.

Levinson liked to say. On paper, she listed what she wanted to know, and then she thought about how to create a plausible ruse to tease the information out of whomever answered the phone, all while willing Jack to take a long lunch.

"Payne, Floutt & Giroux, how may I help you?"

The voice was bored, the sentence quickly uttered—receptionist. She did not have to tell this person much of anything. Kit thought of Winston Endicott, a preppie boy she'd known at college, and how he would sound in twenty years, how his voice would drip with exhaustion and imperiousness. "In which department is Attorney Thompson Fielder, Jr.?"

"Attorney Fielder is in Trusts and Estates."

"Attorney Fielder, please," she said.

"One moment."

"Attorney Thompson Fielder's office."

This second voice, a secretary perhaps, did made her nervous; at once elderly and cultured, it conveyed a politeness that was in reality a kind of vetting. Kit sat up straight in her chair before she answered.

"Hello," she paused for a beat as she decided quickly to use her own name. Most people, she found, never remember who you say you are, and your own name always flows more easily. "This is Katherine Lavoie calling on behalf of a client of Attorney Fielder, a Mrs. Vivian Pierce."

"In regard to?"

"In regard to some property."

"One moment please."

Kit waited, on edge. If Mrs. Pierce was a client of this firm, then it must mean that she had lots of money somewhere. That fact alone would be a huge amount of information—information that, because the files listed a professional valuation of the house but nothing else, she assumed Jack didn't have.

The phone clicked, and she heard some wheezy breathing followed by a charming, elderly voice. "Mrs. Pierce, it's been a while."

"This isn't Mrs. Pierce, sir. I'm helping her out. It's in regard to a piece of property."

"I'm not at liberty to discuss my client's properties, Miss ah, ah…"

Kit knew she should hang up. She had what she needed—a little hook to hang a plan onto, that Mrs. Pierce had some money somewhere, and that lawyers came with it. She knew, too, that this call, claiming to be on behalf of a client your firm was suing, violated all kinds of legal ethics. Curiosity, however, would not let her hang up. "Yes, of course," she answered. She took a wild leap. "But she is getting on in years, and is confused about the consequences of selling a foreign property."

"Of course. Why don't you set up an appointment with Mrs. Atkinson for Mrs. Pierce? I'll put you through."

"Thank you so much, Attorney Fielder, you've been most helpful."

He harrumphed, and Kit was afraid maybe she'd gone

too far. When Mrs. Atkinson got back on the line, Kit, swept into the moment, agreed to make an appointment for Mrs. Pierce.

When Jack returned, Mrs. Atkinson was apologizing for the third or fourth time for the many holes in Mr. Fielder's schedule, explaining that as he was getting on in years, his hours were commensurately diminished.

Jack stood in front of her desk and frowned at her.

"Hair appointment," she mouthed.

"On your own time," he barked. He lingered at the desk and stared at the newspaper, suspicious.

Her hands trembled as she hung up. He would murder her if he knew what she had done—unless, of course, she had found more money, and then he would most likely be thrilled.

By the time he disappeared into his office, she had started to sweat, and she felt as if her heart beat uncomfortably close to her throat. What had she done? Wrong to call an opposing party's lawyers, but also wrong to let a woman lose her house without a chance for a defense? Did she feel less sympathy for Mrs. Pierce now that it seemed she did have money? What would happen when she failed to keep the appointment Kit had set up for her? Was Kit obligated to tell Jack what she had found out? She replaced the file into the cabinet and had to laugh. How crazy would that be, the Appletons rich in the end? Maybe Larry should claim the baby.

Twenty-Six

Larry occupied the same spot in from of the TV every evening when Kit returned from work. As she sat down in the arm chair next to the couch, Kit watched her brother's profile while he stared at the screen, slumped in his seat, a blanket wrapped around his knees. The show was about a guy who had slept with his brother's fiancée.

"Where's Mom?"

"Out."

Kit frowned. "That doesn't worry you?"

"What harm can she do?"

If Larry noticed that his mother wasn't going to work, he hadn't mentioned it to Kit.

"How can you watch this?"

He laughed. "I'm thinking of sending my own sad story in, except I don't know how to phrase it."

Kit studied him. Since he'd lost his job a week earlier, he was banned from the Rutherford property, and banned from seeing Billy. That's all he would tell her. He'd shut down like a clam, a stance he'd perfected over the years, and an indication to Kit that she needed to leave him alone.

"Looks like I've got a job down at Periwinkle's," he said after a bit. "Aren't you happy?"

She mustered herself, "Sure I am. That's good news."

"I answered an ad for a dishwasher, but it looks like they might let me do veggie prep. You know, once they found out I had some, er, skills. In that area."

Kit nodded. What about Billy, she wanted to ask, but she was interrupted by their mother's entry into the living room.

Presumably because of the cold weather, Ruby wore one of Larry's old coats from early high school, a nylon parka with an oversized hood that jutted out several inches beyond her face, giving her an arctic explorer kind of look. "You wouldn't believe what I found out!"

She sat down on the couch and turned her enormous hood toward Larry. "I decided to visit Billy today."

"Mom, I can't hear you from under that thing."

She lifted the hood off. "I went to the hospital to visit Billy, and guess what? Lorna Hills from the Home was there…" At this she cast a guilty glance at Kit, but rallied. "And when I went to his room it was empty, but because of my work connection to Lorna, she could look it all up and tell me that he was discharged."

"That's great!" said Larry. He sat up and smiled.

"Yes, but where is he?" demanded Kit.

"Well, I don't know where he is," Ruby admitted. "I suspect he's at home."

"What home?" Kit persisted.

"He'd be at Mr. Rutherford's," muttered Larry.

“Well, there,” said Ruby. “He’s at Mr. Rutherford’s.”

“And that’s all right with you?” Kit asked Larry.

“You know I can’t go there.” He tucked the blanket back under his knees where it had gotten loose.

Kit stumbled. “Does Billy know why you can’t?”

Larry looked briefly out the large picture window into the darkness. “I told him.”

“Was he conscious when you told him this?”

"Kit,” said Ruby, her adventure bringing her newfound courage. “What a thing to say.”

“No, really, was he awake and listening when you told him this?”

“Look,” said Larry. “He knows.”

Ruby twirled the strings from her hood. “What exactly does he know, Larry?” Kit persisted.

Larry looked at Kit, and now his face was set and calm. “He knows everything he needs to, OK?”

Ruby hunched forward, with her legs tight together. She patted her son’s knee. “That’s right, honey. We know what you mean.”

Kit had no idea what he meant, and, she more than suspected, neither did Ruby. More than likely Larry would just refuse to consider that Billy was probably gone for good, sucked up into who knew what on that Rutherford estate.

This exchange left Kit restless. Perhaps Larry couldn’t do a thing about the outcome of his sad little story, as he put it.

Maybe Kit could.

Twenty-Seven

In winter, the sun slid over the old mansard roof of the law offices and hit the back steps of the communal kitchen at about eleven-thirty. Without wind, this was a fine place to smoke a cigarette even in the worst cold, and Kit went outside the minute Jack left the office for an early lunch. The unlit cigarette smelled good, inviting, and she was glad she didn't have matches or a lighter.

Going over her game plan, she began with an initial assessment of her position. As it stood, she was sure that if Jack were to come across another cheap secretary with some brains, she would be out of a job with no notice. In preparation, she had cleaned anything remotely personal out of her desk. Lip balm, extra mittens, telephone numbers, attempts at a resume, all these went into a shopping bag she could carry between car and desk without too much trouble. So she had little to lose in that department.

Looking forward, although Larry had his job at Periwinkle's Restaurant, it was clear she had to go back to school because the little education she had wasn't doing her much good. In the meantime, a waitress job would pay more than Rioux & Rioux. Either way, she wouldn't be working much longer for Jack.

Gathering her courage, Kit rolled the cigarette between her fingers. What she had in mind would probably break some rules, but she couldn't find a way out of it. She flung the cigarette to the ground and headed back into the building to find Mr. Levinson.

She knocked on his door and stepped in. The morning chill lingered, for Mr. Levinson's offices got the best of the afternoon sun, but little of the morning. On the phone, he stood by the window and motioned for her to sit.

The phone conversation continued. Kit looked at the pictures of his children—the grown boys and the lovely, smiling, dark-eyed little girl. What had happened to her? Something horrible, she was sure. What was it like for him to look at that picture each day?

In the silence, Kit realized that Mr. Levinson had gotten off the phone and was waiting for her to speak. Kit got quickly to her point.

"Mr. Levinson, about trusts."

"An involved topic."

"One question. If a lawyer is in charge of keeping the trust, wouldn't he be in charge of protecting it?"

"Define protecting."

"You know, from lawsuits and other people who want the money."

"Well, without a case in front of me, I won't give you a blanket yes, but you are on the right track, Kit. There is, in most cases, a fiduciary obligation."

"An obligation to protect the money?"

"Yes, in a manner of speaking."

"And a court would recognize this?"

"Yes."

It occurred to Kit that when she left Rioux & Rioux, she would be leaving him too.

"Kit?"

"Yes, Mr. Levinson."

"It's important to remember that no matter what the circumstances, one always has a choice."

"You mean that doing nothing is a choice as well."

"That's exactly what I mean." This is where Mr. Levinson would normally smile, a sort of good-bye-talk-to-you-later kind of smile, but he stayed serious. "You have a legal mind, Kit. You anticipate the problems."

Kit nodded, flustered at his attention. Maybe, she considered, Mr. Levinson would hire her if she left Jack. "Thank you," she added.

"You're welcome." He smiled now, his fingers poised over the phone to make another call.

Back in her own office, Kit looked at the clock. She would not do nothing, and she had enough time to execute her plan.

Courts are set up so that each side is defended by a trained person. Thus, the process moves more quickly and there's a better hope of a fair outcome. In this way, the system is almost more important than the individuals. That's one reason why lawyers are appointed to indigent criminals. Kit's plan was to bend the rules so that the rules would work better, so that both sides would be represented fairly.

The Pierce file was not in the cabinet, which meant that Jack had left it in his office, or was now storing it in there, as he did sometimes with important files--Jack stood to collect as his fee thirty-three percent of whatever the Appletons collected.

Her heartbeat quickened as she opened the door to his office. The window behind his desk offered a straight view of the front steps, a good look out.

She rummaged through the piles on his credenza, making sure to check out the window every few seconds. At his desk, she slid open the top drawer, but no file. She moved to the bottom drawer, which held a metal bar across the top for files to be hung on little clips.

There it rested. Before she pulled it out, she counted the files hung around it to make sure she could put the Pierce file back in the same place. Then, while still glancing out the window, she unclipped only those papers she wanted, papers that were public and had formally and legally been delivered to Mrs. Pierce. She replaced the file, slid the drawer back, and left his office.

Kit took the papers to the copy machine near the kitchen, made two copies of every page, and returned to her desk without incident.

Even though it was close to noon, she decided to risk returning the papers rather than have Jack discover them missing. She had lifted the metal tabs and clipped the papers back into the file when a quick check out the window revealed Jack approaching the front of the building.

Rioux & Rioux was on the second floor, so she knew she had a few minutes, but Kit felt the panic and fought to recall whether the file had hung second or fourth in the row. She placed it both ways before she remembered for sure that she'd had it right the first time.

Calm yourself, she whispered, careful to place Jack's chair back where she thought it had stood. I have time, I have time, she said to herself as she closed his office door, walked to her desk, and slipped the copies into her shopping bag.

When Jack walked in, she had time sheets in front of her, ready to enter into the computer. He scarcely glanced her way. "Connors file," he barked as he headed for his office. "Right away."

When he shut the door behind him, she noticed the sweat ringed around her forehead and dripping down the sides of her ribs. She glanced at the clock--she had to wait him out before the next step.

When Jack left for the day at four o'clock, Kit waited a few minutes and then left after him. Her errand was best done in daylight, and the late January sky still held a bit of sunshine. On the way to her car, she dropped one copy of the papers into the mailbox, addressed to Attorney Thompson Fielder, Jr., at Payne, Floutt & Giroux, no return address. Maybe the attorneys didn't really care about Mrs.

Pierce, but she was sure they would care about her money.

Her first stop was Argilla Road.

The Pierce drive was snowed in and close to impassable, so Kit left her car near the road and continued to the house on foot. Her feet were cold in the snow, and the wind bit at her face as soon as she hit the yard. She poked around by the front and side doors, but saw no sign of papers. And, after her last reception, she knew better than to try to knock.

On impulse, she left the house and headed down the path toward the marsh. As she turned the corner of the house, the sky opened up, a panorama of winter blues, purples, and hints of yellow, the marsh with glints of gold from the sun set, and the water gray.

Repeated boot tracks made a well-worn path through the snow. Kit caught sight of Mrs. Pierce almost at the water. Wrapped in her signature collection of layers of odd clothing, she held a pair of binoculars to her face. Kit approached one slow step at a time, and then, when she was close enough to be heard over the ever-present wind, she called out.

"Delivery!"

Mrs. Pierce turned, held a finger to her lips, and then motioned for her to come closer.

Her eyes were runny in the cold, and red rimmed, but the blue held a sparkling certainty that seemed to reflect lucidity and command and invitation.

"American bittern," Mrs. Pierce whispered.

Kit followed her gaze.

She handed Kit the binoculars. Kit shifted her envelope under her arm and took them.

"Just fasten your gaze over the water, just below that log."

Kit saw only the gray of the water, but Mrs. Pierce gently lifted up the binoculars, and Kit caught the brown of the marsh, then the black log, and then a long-beaked bird with brown and white stripes along its slender neck. "I see it!"

"Isn't it lovely!"

"It really is!"

"And far from home, I fear. It's a wonder it's survived the cold."

Kit took one more look. The bird blended almost perfectly into its surroundings. She returned the binoculars. "Thank you."

Mrs. Pierce nodded. "You've brought me more papers, I see."

"Yes."

"I'll put them with the rest."

"No," said Kit. "You've got to call the number, see…" she pointed to the oversized numbers she had written on the envelope in black ink.

Mrs. Pierce nodded.

"Call this number, and this person, see," she pointed to a name written in similar fashion.

"Will he be able to explain?"

Kit nodded and rolled the envelope slightly to fit it into the black leather case that had held her binoculars. "You won't forget?"

Mrs. Pierce patted her arm. "No dear." She raised her binoculars to her eyes and scanned the opposite bank.

Kit retreated up the path. What she had just done was most likely illegal, and she certainly wouldn't want to explain to Mr. Levinson the messy circumstances that had backed her into this corner, one litigant of a lawsuit interfering with another, but odds were that no one would find out. She wondered if the papers would end up in a pile like the others, or if Mrs. Pierce would remember to call the number. Kit didn't know if Mrs. Pierce deserved to lose her home or not; she just knew that her part in sneaking it past her wasn't right. In this she was sure Mr. Levinson would agree.

Back in her car, Kit hadn't far to drive to her next errand.

Clumps of snow sloughed off an overhanging tree onto her car as she drove slowly along, looking for some indication of address. One lump jammed the windshield wipers so the driver's side blade went only partway up. After she wiped the snow from her windshield, there it was on a mailbox, Rutherford, in gold letters.

She recalled the frightening blond man with his precise hair and neat suit, but, she reassured herself, a man like Mr. Rutherford would still be at work. She was here to just check on Billy, without anyone else seeing her. She started the car down the drive, a broad, well-kept path lined with large trees.

The drive sloped down toward a barn to the left before it curved formally in front of the large house. For a second she forgot why she came, the grounds were so beautiful, bathed in the peachy half-light of the winter sun, the house an enormous brick structure with sharp black windows, with the ocean in the distance. A green Mercedes was parked in front.

The house, though, was dark, with no sign of life. A gust of raw wind came over the marsh from the water and Kit shivered. This was a large place to be alone in. She ignored the ornate brass knocker, and pushed the doorbell. Inside, vast chimes echoed. No one answered, and it was almost too much just to stand there when the door opened, and there was Mr. Rutherford.

He was dressed in a blue suit, a nice one with faint lines and precise lapels, but he looked haggard and worn, much older than he had in the hospital. He narrowed his eyes at her.

"You," he said and nodded his head. "Well, give me the news and move along."

How had recognized her from one chance meeting in a dingy hallway? "What news?"

He stepped toward her and pulled the door closer to shut. "Is this some kind of game?"

It was as if she'd been dropped into the middle of a strange conversation. "I'm looking for Billy."

For a second his look softened into a question. "You don't know where he is?"

"Isn't he here?"

Mr. Rutherford regained his composure and laughed, a bitter, cold bark. "He's given us both the slip, then, hasn't he?" He began to shut the door.

Kit felt her game plan slipping away in a tide of anger. "Wait!"

"Our little interview is over."

"What have you done to Billy?"

Mr. Rutherford held the door open, and he smiled, charmless, chilly. He reached his hand out and patted the arm of Kit's coat. "Why don't you ask your brother if he feels he got the fair share?" He watched her face as he shut the door.

It was all her fault, her own greedy fault. If she hadn't desired the coat in the first place, something out of her reach and something she didn't need or deserve, it never would have occurred to her brother to get it for her, however he had managed it. Larry would never blame her for anything. He never had. She tore off the coat and left it on the front doorstep, ringing the doorbell before she raced to the car.

Before she turned the curve to the road, Kit glanced back at the house; its only light came from the hall from where Mr. Rutherford had just answered the door, and the windows in the darkened rooms gleamed black and impenetrable. Now he had his coat back, and from the looks of the house, maybe that was all he had to keep him company.

Twenty-Eight

Unsure of what to tell Larry, that dilemma was for the moment postponed when her mother met her at the kitchen door.

"Look, I made supper for us," Ruby announced. "Do you want Turkey Dinner or Hungry-Man Meatloaf?"

Ruby wore two oven mitts sewn to look like ducks, and between the orange bills she held two silver TV dinner trays.

"Larry agreed to eat this?"

"He was at that clamshell periwinkle place, so I cooked. They're running a Shirley Jones movie fest all weekend. Go sit. I'll bring you your dinner, and we won't miss Elmer Gantry."

TV dinners and Shirley Jones? Larry, who wouldn't eat jarred sauce and had put his hands over his ears when people broke into unexpected song, must have had a lobotomy since she saw him yesterday.

"Where is Larry now?"

"In the shower, I think," she answered haphazardly, basking in the pleasure of her own competence.

"OK, Ma. I'll take the Turkey Dinner."

"Excellent choice."

"I'll be a second, though." Kit poked her head in the living room. No Larry. She walked down the hall that connected the three bedrooms, but didn't hear the shower running in the bathroom.

Larry's door was closed, so she knocked.

"Yup," he said.

Larry had inherited their grandmother's large bed. He sat on the crumpled red plaid sheets, dressed in pajama bottoms and a bright yellow T-shirt.

Kit sat down next to him. "How's Periwinkle's?"

He nodded his head. "It's good. Only nicked myself a few times today."

"I returned the coat," she blurted.

He stiffened and she sensed the way his shoulders went up and the ease left his body. "I…" he faltered.

It came out in a burst. "I should have known what it was. Even if you had bought it, I should have made you take it back. You didn't need to do that for me."

She watched his body slump.

The next words were harder to say, but she made herself say them. "It wasn't a fair trade-off. You risked too much."

"Kit, stop it."

Kit and her mother settled into the couch. "Now, honey," said Ruby, "she doesn't do any singing in this one, so don't be disappointed."

Kit peeled back the tinfoil and started in on the cranberry

sauce. This reminded her of the Thanksgiving dinner Larry had made, when the Appletons had come and they had first met Billy. She wondered where he had gone. She feared they would never see him again, that her brother's optimism was based on hope, and that hope had no substance.

Twenty-Nine

Whether it was because the gray sky lengthened the night or because they merely needed the sleep, they awakened late. Larry made coffee, had insisted on grinding cinnamon into each cup, and was heating up the griddle for pancakes when they heard the pounding. Each turned to the back door, but no one was there.

The pounding sounded weirdly hollow. "It's the front door," Kit said. The three of them scurried to the living room. Someone, face obscured by a blue hat pulled down low, banged on the picture window. Kit's first ping of fear was that Mrs. Pierce had gotten loose and followed her home, but that couldn't be it, this person was much more vital.

Larry knew at once. "Billy!" he cried. The lock at the living room door stuck and, instantly impatient, he retreated out through the kitchen door.

Kit turned and looked out the broad living room window. She watched Billy's face as he waited for Larry. It was both bemused and heartbreaking, the kind of look you see on little kids when they hope something good will happen, but since they have no control over anything they open themselves to the fates: the look is both full of expectation and ready to flinch. That look vanished when Larry wrapped his arms around Billy, pulled him close, pushed off his hat that Kit recognized as her present to him, and kissed his ear, then the top of his bandaged head, then his cheek in random glee, Billy returning the embrace until he found Larry's lips, and their heads turned out of Kit's view, which was clouded by this point with the tears that dropped down her face.

She turned away, to see her mother standing a few feet behind her. Ruby stared at her son, with a look that Kit could only describe as beatific. She held out her arm toward Kit.

"Would you look at that," she said in a quiet voice. "They're in love."

Kit could only nod, overwhelmed by the understanding that, for the first time in as long as she could remember, some luck had come into the Lavoie family, something crazy and beautiful that touched them all. She smiled as the world cracked open in front of her, suddenly full of possibilities.

Acknowledgements

Heartfelt thanks to Dale Kerester and John Dalimonte for their expert legal advice; to thoughtful readers Kitty Babakian, Randy Blume, Edward DeAngelo, Amy Forman, Susan Golden, and Ilana Katz; to my indispensible coherts Margaret Eckman, Lana Owens, and Laura Smith; and to Russell, who anchors it all.

deahn.berrini@gmail.com

CPSIA information can be obtained at www.ICGtesting.com
Printed in the USA
LVOW101747191112

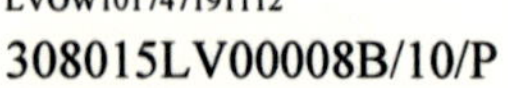